W9-BRG-641

THE DISAPPEARANCE BOY

BY THE SAME AUTHOR

Who Was That Man?
Ready to Catch Him Should He Fall
Mr Clive and Mr Page
Skin Lane

THE DISAPPEARANCE BOY

Neil Bartlett

BLOOMSBURY

NEW YORK · LONDON · NEW DELHI · SYDNEY

Published by Bloomsbury USA, New York
Bloomsbury is a trademark of Bloomsbury Publishing Plc

All papers used by Bloomsbury USA are natural, recyclable products made
from wood grown in well-managed forests. The manufacturing processes
conform to the environmental regulations of the country of origin.

LIBRARY OF CONGRESS CATALOGING-IN-PUBLICATION DATA HAS BEEN APPLIED FOR.

ISBN: 978-1-62040-725-7

First U.S. Edition 2014

1 3 5 7 9 10 8 6 4 2

Typeset by Hewer Text UK Ltd, Edinburgh
Printed and bound in the U.S.A. by Thomson-Shore Inc., Dexter, Michigan

Bloomsbury books may be purchased for business or promotional use.
For information on bulk purchases please contact Macmillan Corporate
and Premium Sales Department at specialmarkets@macmillan.com.

Indocilis privata loqui

One

Bishopstone Halt

Let me try this for an opening.

There's a boy, standing on a railway track. He's a little boy – he looks eight or nine years old at the very most – and he's rather small and slight for his age. He is standing with his hands held straight down by his sides, and his feet are clamped firmly together. Seen from behind, he seems to be staring defiantly straight ahead at something, but we shall see in a moment that his eyes are in fact screwed tightly shut. He has oddly muscular shoulders, clumsily cropped hair, and is almost naked; he's wearing a pair of worn linen underpants – nothing else – and just the one hastily laced-up leather shoe, on his right foot. He's as brown as a berry, all over. The railway track stretches away in front of him in a long straight line, and its rails are hazed with the mist of a fine English mid-September morning as they disappear into the distance.

As if it had been ruled across a map, this track more or less exactly bisects the brown and overgrazed field it runs through, and immediately beyond the scrubby blackthorn hedge on this field's southern side, divided from it only by a half-dry ditch of dead reeds, is a beach, a great slow curve of shingle that looks as though it reaches along the shore for at least a mile in both directions, east towards the yellowing cliffs of Seaford and west (behind the boy) towards the mouth of the river at Newhaven. There seems to be no sand at all on this beach – all you can see are black, grey and dark grey flints, going on for ever, with barely a pale stone among them.

Almost exactly halfway along their two-mile curve the stones rise to their highest point, and there on the crest of the shingle is perched a strange and lost-looking collection of white-painted concrete and timber huts, lifted above the stones on squat brick bases. These huts look as if they might be a hospital, or perhaps a school – a sanatorium, even – but it's hard to say for sure; there are no signs up anywhere, and it looks as if there is no one about to ask on this particular morning. All the windows are shuttered closed, and across the stones beneath them the English Channel stretches away to France as flat and cold as a well-sharpened knife. There are no boats about to give scale to its horizon, and no gulls either. There is hardly any wind, and no waves to speak of. A soft swell lifts and clatters the grey stones right down at the water's edge – and because the wind is so light, and because there seems to be nobody about, the whole scene is very quiet. Not even the reeds in that half-dried ditch are whispering. It is so quiet, in fact, that you can hear that the little boy is not crying.

His chin is up, his shoulders are pushed back as far as they'll go and his eyes are as tightly closed as those apparently abandoned windows (you can see that, now). His mouth is clamped shut, too – and now, as if he were getting ready for something, the boy spreads his legs and crosses his fists in the small of his back. Near-naked as he is, he seems to be standing 'at ease', sticking his elbows out to the sides and pushing his bony little chest forward as if he were expecting a medal. Or perhaps as if he were trying to meet some dreadful blow halfway – as if his infant breastbone were the breastbone of some defiant and easily smashed little bird, one of those softly feathered species that explode in the air when the shot or hawk hits them . . . Whatever he's doing, his feet are now spread slightly too far apart for comfort, and because of the way he's standing you can now see what you may not have noticed at first, which is that there is something not quite right about this little boy's legs. The left one is a fair bit shorter than the right, and thin enough to make his foot look several bones too large; the left foot itself is turned markedly inward, as if his ankle had been attached in not exactly the right place. He's holding this left heel – the naked one – a good two inches clear of the weeping tar of the railway sleeper, as if he'd just trodden on a nail. The foot is shaking slightly. He still isn't crying. There still isn't a train.

And now there is.

And now the shouting starts.

A Mr Bridges, who in the calm, sunlit autumn of 1939 was living alone in the cottage which then stood next to the tracks at Bishopstone Halt (an unmanned concrete platform on the Hastings to Lewes branch line which had recently been constructed in case it should ever be necessary to get troops to the beach in a hurry), has spotted the tiny figure through his kitchen window. Fortunately, Mr Bridges has a clock above his sink, and he doesn't need to waste any time calculating in order to know that the next train is due past his window in less than three minutes; they run so close that they rattle his china, and their noise divides his solitary day into such regular parcels of time that he always knows when the next one is on its way. He also knows that this particular train isn't scheduled to slow down or stop. First he shouts and bangs on his kitchen window; then he wipes his hands on his dishcloth and runs out of his front door, shouting as he goes.

The little boy doesn't move. He doesn't even seem to hear.

As Mr Bridges runs, the oncoming train is still so far away from the two of them that it doesn't seem to be moving at all – east of Bishopstone Halt, the track runs dead straight towards Seaford for nearly a mile, and the distant blurred dot of the engine is barely visible at the vanishing point of the converging rails. It seems to shake slightly, even to *hover* in the distance, but not to be getting any closer. Mr Bridges knows that this is just an illusion. He knows that pretty soon the rails will begin to sing, the dot to swell, and before you know where you are it will be upon them. That's why he keeps shouting as he runs, calling out at the top of his voice and cursing his middle-aged legs for not moving as fast as he needs them to in this emergency. The spacing of the tarred sleepers forces him to clip his stride, which makes him swear even more – they are placed just too close together to let him break into a full run, and he knows that if he misses one and hits the clinker then a turned ankle will more than likely bring him down. Best as he can, he half lopes and half hobbles towards the boy, and, of course, straight towards the train. The dot hovers, and shakes, and begins to swell.

And now, right on cue, the rails begin their dreadful song; that strange, silvered, high-pitched music that can seem sinister at the best of times, and which now makes Mr Bridges want to vomit as he hears it change key and grow louder. He sees that the little boy – still thirty sleepers away, and with his legs still locked and spread – can also apparently hear or sense this change of key, because as the train approaches the child stretches his puny arms up and out to make himself into its target, and his fists seem to clench themselves into even tighter balls. The pain is starting to tear at Mr Bridges's sides now. His breath is drowned out by the rails. And now comes the whistle –

Cut.

And now the boy is in his arms – under him, in fact; pinned down under him in the wet and stinking grass by the side of the track, because some instinct has made this middle-aged man cover the boy's body with his own as the train flashes by in a thunder of light and dark less than four feet from his head, wheel after wheel, rim on rail, metal on metal, less than four feet away from his wet, astonished, staring face (tears of relief, are they, or is that just sweat?) with his ragged breath still tearing at his chest and the pain in his side so sharp that he thinks he must have broken a rib. Did he really scoop up and then throw down this intransigent bundle of flesh so hard? And then, when the train has passed, and the rails have spun out their song into its final dying whisper and the dot is getting smaller now and going away in the other direction, around a bend and away into the September haze as it heads for Southease and Beddingham and Lewes and eventually Brighton, Mr Bridges gasps his breath back into his aching chest, and gathers himself. He gets up, and looks down at the bare-skinned creature lying half crushed in the broken grass between his feet, and he yanks the child upright with one big strong hand. He's furious. He starts to slap the child, first on the back of the boy's knees and then right across his sunburnt face, making a furious attempt to get him to open his eyes, or to speak – or something. Anything. And also to relieve his own feelings, I shouldn't wonder – yes, that's it; it is a mixture of shock and anger that is making Mr Bridges treat this little boy who he doesn't even know so badly, making him shout at the boy – making him bend right down so that their two very different faces are almost nose to nose, the big, red, wet, angry one and the little, screwed-shut, frightened and frightening one, making Mr Bridges roar right in the little boy's face between his great rib-tearing breaths, shout at him what the bloody, fucking, what the bloody fucking *hell*, and what if I hadn't been in my kitchen, eh? Eh? You little fucking. Well you can speak, can't you? Fuck.

No waves. No people. No boats.

Empty water.

Shuttered windows. Screwed-shut eyes in a burnt brown face.

No wind.

And still no tears. None.

Not yet.

Two

Wimbledon Broadway

I

The next time we see this dry-eyed little would-be suicide he will be hurling himself – as if risking or welcoming collisions was somehow a constant in his life – down the wet, windy and about-to-get-crowded eastern pavement of Wimbledon Broadway, just before dinner time on a showery Thursday in late March.

There are several important pieces of information I should probably pass on about him before we continue – that he's now grown up, for instance, but that you wouldn't necessarily know it to look at him; that the polio he had as a child has marked him out as different from other young men, but not so different that *everybody* stares; that, courtesy of a broken-down number 47 bus, he's rather late for work. There's much more I could say about him of course, but what I want you to concentrate on just now, as I introduce you to young Reggie, in this, the twenty-third year of his life – sorry, I should have said that earlier, that's his name; Reggie, Reggie (please don't laugh) Rainbow – as I introduce you to Reggie and encourage you to watch him closely as he makes his not-untroubled way down this particular strip of south London pavement, what I want you to notice most of all is how Reggie carries himself. It tells you a lot. I don't mean just his limp and his disproportionately strong shoulders or the built-up sole on his left boot – all of those are pretty obvious – but rather the whole impression Reggie makes as he levers himself through the thickening dinner-time traffic. He makes it look as if that slight and oddly proportioned body of his is some kind of badly wrapped parcel, and one which he seems fiercely determined to deliver on time – and without troubling anyone else for directions, thank you very much. Clearly, carrying it around is some kind of an effort, because even when he hits his stride on a clear patch of pavement he keeps his eyes down and his forehead furrowed; at times, the parcel seems to be about to slip clumsily from his grasp, and he'll pause for a moment, take stock, and reposition the two-sizes-too-large Harris tweed jacket he's wearing, wrapping the front of it protectively around his chest like a sheet of brown paper before continuing on his way.

Perhaps it's just the threat of a returning shower that makes him do that, but there is something about the way Reggie clutches and tugs at this unbuttoned jacket of his that has a very particular effect. It makes him look as if he's determined to protect whatever he's wrapping up so carefully from something more than just the chill March air. Of course, he *could* be doing this just because of the cold, as I say – that white shirt under the jacket looks thin, and worn – but the vehemency of the gesture combines with his short stature (Reggie is five foot three if he's an inch) to make him look oddly vulnerable. In fact, if you weren't able to catch the occasional flash of that downturned face – sharp-featured, bright-eyed and strikingly dark-skinned (weathered, I think would be the exact word) – then you might well be hard put to tell from your first impression if Reggie was an adult or still a child.

Whether he was a man of twenty-two or a boy of sixteen. Or even fourteen, at that height.

Not that I want you to feel sorry for him, not for a minute. He doesn't feel sorry for himself, and never has done, not since he was eight or nine – not since that morning with the train, in fact. He hates pity likes a dog hates cats, does our Reggie; hates it, in all its forms and sizes.

That's why, when he reaches the junction of the Broadway with Russell Road – where the shoe shop is – young Reggie comes to a sudden and clumsy halt. Standing on a plinth just outside the entrance to the shop is a dummy made of painted and varnished papier mâché, and although Reggie has made the best job he can of ignoring the sight of this unpleasant object for several mornings in a row recently, on this particular morning he suddenly finds himself unable to keep up the effort any longer. The dummy depicts a four-foot-high little boy. His hair is an unlikely yellow, his lips a cheery cherry red, and the whites of his turned-up eyes look like they've been slicked on straight from the tin. Dressed in just a pair of shorts and a neat blue jumper, he's wearing a leg-brace – complete with carefully painted-on brown leather straps – and has a crutch jammed into his left armpit. With his right hand – and this is the point of his whole existence – he is holding out a bright red loaf-sized collecting box whose slot is just the right size for a copper – or even, more optimistically, for a fat half-crown. If you're a passer-by then this little boy's blind stare is meant to make you smile sadly and fish in your bag for some change, but that's not the effect it has on Reggie. In fact, if he thought he could get away with it, Reggie would have picked up a brick from a bomb site one morning this week and cheer-fully smashed the face off the thing. Yesterday, he'd caught a shopper in the act of dropping her coin and then patting the boy's head with her gloved hand as if it belonged to a dog or well-behaved pony, murmuring a few well-chosen words of approval. This morning, there is no lady – thank God, other-wise I think there might have been some kind of a scene – but there are some raindrops caught in the boy's painted hair, and that, together with the memory of that murmuring, pale-gloved woman and her dropped coin – of the hollow noise it made – is what has stopped Reggie, late as he is. He knows exactly how it feels to be shivering in shorts and a piece of clumsily strapped-on aluminium on a cold March morning. He knows what it feels like to have wet hair, and to be small. He knows exactly how it feels to be looked down on.

He stares.

For a moment, his mouth works as if he wanted to spit, giving us a glimpse of some stained and pointed teeth – but then, without looking round to see if anyone is watching, Reggie takes a lurching step towards the sightless little effigy and reaches out and strokes the figure's hair himself, carefully chasing each and every one of the raindrops out from the grooves between the painted curls. When they've all gone, he steps back, and says out loud, *There, that's better.*

He stands a moment longer, staring at the boy some more, and at his crutch, and then, apparently remembering where he is – not to mention what time it is – he twists out a thin-lipped little grin – a grin with which you're going to become very familiar, I hope – and mutters *Sod it*, to himself this time, but loud enough to make a passing housewife grimace and tut as she tries to get past him and into the shoe shop. Ignoring her stare, Reggie wraps his parcel back up again with a quick one-two rearrangement of his jacket; a darting look at the black-and-white enamelled clock on the front of the Co-op opposite confirms that it's now gone twelve, so he lurches back off down the Broadway to deliver it at double time, pounding the pavement with that built-up boot of his as if he was angry with them both.

When he's up to speed, this young man can thread himself through a thickening lunchtime crowd as surely as a darning needle can pierce silk, and I have to say it's quite an act. Every

14

human step is a fall from which we save ourselves, they say, but in Reggie's case that's even more true than normal; head down, he stabs the toe of that built-up left boot of his down into the paving stones in a kind of regular, staccato *demi-pointe*, making it the pivot over which he then levers the rest of his top-heavy self, catching himself just in time. Only once does his technique falter, and that's when a puddle makes him misjudge his launch off the kerb at the corner of Southey Street – the kerbstone here is part of a botched-up repair to some bomb damage, and it tilts. He stumbles, and the two-sizes-too-big tweed jacket flaps open in the cold wind, revealing another underwing flash of white shirt. With the swiftness of habit he grabs it and rewraps himself, and the threat of an undignified tumble soon passes. Once he's steadied himself, he taps himself on the chest, twice, right where the inside breast pocket of his jacket is, and then lurches on.

That breast pocket is where Reggie keeps his ration book – he's always on the lookout for anything sweet, is our Reg, and confectionery is still on points in the spring of 1953. It's also where, during the day, he keeps his knife. It's not a big or dangerous blade, being merely a two-inch penknife with a delicate mother-of-pearl handle – a lady's knife, really – but nonetheless, he never leaves his digs without it. He taps at his pocket like that quite often, without even realising he's doing it, just to make sure the knife's still there – either that, or for luck, I suppose.

Reggie's destination? A black-painted door with a black-and-white sign over it, hidden down an alley just off Montague Road, which is only two more corners away. His employer? One Mr Edward Brookes Esquire, known in the profession as Ted or Teddy. His job?

Well, more of that later. It's all about timing, this business. Timing, and –

2

Under the harsh glare of a single pair of floodlights, a dark-haired man in his late thirties is stepping out onto the stage of an empty theatre. The auditorium is silent, but the man strides on exactly as if he was cutting his entrance through an anticipatory swathe of applause. *His* jacket is an impeccably cut and close-fitting double-breasted wool-mixture dinner jacket, satin-lapelled. He is wearing white gloves with a single pearl button, and showing a full inch of starched cuff. His hair is carefully side-parted. His feet are accented in black patent, his trousers have a black ribbon side-stripe, and he's carrying a black top hat in his gloved right hand; in delicate contrast, the lighting is turning the thin coating of dust on the unswept boards of the stage into a soft, powdery silver. There's a fringed ivory silk evening scarf draped casually around his neck (the two horizontal lines of fringing are *perfectly* level) and a snowy linen handkerchief juts in two crisp peaks from the appropriate pocket. Even his eyes are black and white. There's something very classic and even pre-war about the whole look – a touch of the Café Royal – and he's a hand-some devil. The kind of man who looks as though he smiles for a living, if you know what I mean.

For now his face is pale, and deeply shadowed by the overhead floods, but you can easily imagine what the finished effect will be like when the warm glow of the footlights is doing its job and he's properly made up; you can just see how, when he shoots his cuffs and suddenly glances up at the house like that, the forbidding black glass of his eyes will shine and melt. I wouldn't be at all surprised if several women in the audience find themselves shifting slightly in their seats as his gaze brushes theirs – but then I would imagine that's the whole idea.

The man takes a pace forward, and stops. In the middle of the stage is a large object about the size and shape of a telephone box, draped in some kind of silver silk or satin-like fabric. He looks at it, and then at a wristwatch that he pulls out of his jacket. Then he walks offstage.

Then he walks on again.

He does this three times in a row.

From the way he walks, it would seem that there's some kind of imaginary music playing in this man's head. Something that he's trying to time his moves to, and that only he can hear.

The fourth time he makes his entrance he seems satisfied, and the frown that was beginning to collect on his forehead is ironed away. He hits a mark just down left of centre, about four strides away from the silver-draped box; then, still clearly timing each move to some imaginary music, he swings his top hat from his right hand smartly up onto his head and taps it into place. Turning sideways to show the stalls his profile, he raises first one hand and then the next, smoothly unbuttoning each of his gloves in turn. He removes them – all the while keeping his eyes moving along the rows of darkened seats in the stalls, one eyebrow ever so slightly raised – and then turns square to the audience again and cradles the gloves in his now-bare hands. He looks at them tenderly, as if they were a pair of innocent creatures that he was about to restore to their well-earned freedom. Then with a swift, jerking flourish, he brings his hands sharply down level with his crotch – and immediately flings them up and out to his right and left. Inexplicably, they are now empty, and the pair of white doves which ought to be circling high above his head in noisy bewilderment are nowhere to be seen.

He leaves his hands hanging in the air for a moment, and raises that black and questioning eyebrow ever so slightly higher. Then (without pause or explanation) he makes a pair of devil's horns with the pinkie and first finger of his left hand. He inserts these fingers into his full-lipped mouth, and mimes a loud, commanding wolf whistle.

This silence produces a sound.

A young woman enters, upstage right. She is wearing slacks, three-inch black *glacee* heels – the source of the sound – a tight powder-blue sweater, and an even tighter smile. She's short – five foot two, I would say, if she took off those shoes. She ignores the large box and walks straight to her mark with exaggeratedly tiny and hip-swinging steps, as if her knees and ankles were tightly hobbled. She's looking distinctly ill-at-ease under the heavy foundation she's wearing, and the harsh overhead lights aren't doing her scraped back bottle-blonde hair any favours.

She waits.

Without looking round, the man pulls the silk scarf from his neck and prepares to throw it over his head. The woman gawkily prepares to catch it, clearly unsure of whether she'll be able to manage this simple task. The man's eyebrow goes up again – straight to the lads in the gods, this time – and with another quick flash of his hands he tosses the balled scarf high in the air, upstage right. His assistant's eager fingers splay and reach, but instead of gathering an arc of flying silk, they find only air; his hands, meanwhile, are once again elegantly empty. The young woman looks confused, but he doesn't wait; already his top hat is off and twirling in his hands, the oval of its scarlet lining a sudden and demanding mouth. As if he were playing with a favourite dog, he makes two slow swinging right-hand passes across the front of his body, clearly indicating that he is going to toss the hat stage left for the woman to retrieve. She anxiously totters across the stage behind him, readying herself for her task. He keeps his eyes on his audience – and then on the third swing turns his well-tailored back on them and converts the pass with the hat (which he now swaps deftly into his left hand) into a slow upward diagonal. He does this twice, moving very slowly and clearly for everybody's benefit – the dog's included – and still exactly in time with his silent music. Neither he nor the woman has yet looked at the draped box. The hat is now down right of his body; suddenly, he double-times his gesture, flashing the hat up and down and up again, keeping strict time with three peremptory accents from an unheard snare drum – and as the girl stumbles forward to catch it on the expected third pass, both of his hands are suddenly up and to his left and empty again. The hat, of course, is nowhere to be seen; upstage, the girl gives a pantomime flinch of female failure to the sound of an accusing stroke from an imagined cymbal, and the man is already turning downstage again, with both eyebrows raised this time. He brings his empty hands slowly down, making a dismissive shrugging gesture that displays just how well cut that dinner jacket of his is across the shoulders. There is a momentary pause, in which he snaps the snowy linen handkerchief from his breast pocket, wipes the sweat from both his hands and then in three swift successive folds and one sudden landing swoop tucks it back whence it came, its two crisp peaks apparently – and inexplicably – as immaculate as they were before. All of this happens a bit faster than the eye can quite follow, but then his hands slow down again, as if they were considering what to do next. He shifts his attention back up to the gallery again, and then back down to the circle, and then finally to one particular seat in the middle of the stalls. His expression, though still officially deadpan, seems to shift; he flashes a look upstage at his assistant, and then back out at the empty seat. He is making, it would seem, a choice.

She, meanwhile, tries to look foolish and unconcerned at the same time.

In response to this slight shift in his expression – his brows furrow again, ever so slightly – it would seem that the silent music has just changed key. The man reaches slowly into his right trouser pocket, and quite matter-of-factly produces a small coil of rope; soft, and scarlet. Snake-like. He looks down at it as if this prop were an old and valued friend, and gestures elegantly towards it with his other, empty hand. Then, having now apparently decided what to do about his problem upstage, he once again shapes the relevant fingers into a pair of horns and inserts them into his mouth. Evidently the wolf whistle is louder and even more commanding this time, because the problem springs nervously into action. She spins, and looks upstage. She doesn't do it that well, but you can see that she is pretending that the mystery object under the silken drapes is now being wheeled on from the wings. You can also see, from the way that the man now strides smartly across to downstage right, uncoiling and coiling the rope as he goes, that the music has changed tempo as well as key – something warmer and brighter seems to be suggested; something a bit more *promising*, if you know what I mean. The girl steps slightly to one side; clearly, whoever is wheeling the mystery object on from the wings is rotating it as it comes, and she needs to keep out of their way. As soon as it has come to a halt, and the man has coiled and recoiled his rope to his satisfaction, he beckons her over, indicating that she should hold out both her hands in front of her with her wrists pressed together. She hesitates, and looks a little worried, but then does what she is told, spreading her fingers out in a double fan. Without hesitating, the man swiftly and efficiently binds her wrists – twice round clockwise, once over and through – and then –

Then, the music seems to falter.

The man stops, and stares straight into the girl's face. You can see straightaway that this gesture isn't part of the act; an imaginary drumstick clatters to the floor, and nobody in the pit dares to pick it up. An awkward silence installs itself on the stage, and the dust has time to settle across the boards like sifted flour.

Slowly and deliberately, the man in the dinner jacket removes the rope from the girl's wrists and starts to re-coil it. He takes his time, not giving either her or the empty seats out front any hint as to why he's stopped. Unsure of how to respond, she lets her body go slack; her hips push slightly to one side. Specifically, she seems unsure whether she ought to keep her wrists held out or not. She lets her eyes drop down to the floor and shifts from three-inch heel to three-inch heel, and for the first time in the proceedings begins to look like an actual woman. She relaxes her face and attempts a smile, revealing that she's really quite pretty under all that make-up – but then she thinks better of it and snaps her mask back on, because the man is setting to work on her with the rope again now, looping it tightly round her wrists and quickly making her helpless. Again, he stops short of the final knot, and stares at her as if she ought to understand why.

This elaborate routine of threat and deferral happens four more times in a row. The silence intensifies.

If the seats out front are empty – and they undoubtedly are – then who is he doing all of this for? The stare before the missing knot gets stonier each time, and the repetition is beginning to look less like rehearsal and more like a punishment. Is it for something the young woman has done, or merely for something that she *is*? It is only when the man performs the move for the seventh time – the magic number, you might say – that the reason for this threatening hiatus in their routine emerges.

Despite herself, the girl's stuck-on smile has started to fray, and the insides of her wrists have started to sweat. She always tries very hard to get everything right for rehearsals with this bastard – she even rinsed her rehearsal jumper out in the sink last night, thinking he might have noticed she was making an effort – but stupidly, today of all days, she has forgotten to powder her wrists before starting work. She could kick herself, but it's too late now, and as the man starts to repeat the rigmarole with the ropes for the seventh time she once again shifts her body weight nervously from one three-inch heel onto the other, and rather too abruptly. This makes her unpowdered wrists slip one against the other, just at that vulnerable spot where the pulse beats under her skin, and – *hey presto!* – the two inches of spare red silk which are the crux of the trick, the hidden two inches of scarlet slack which the man has tucked swiftly between her wrists under cover of her splayed fingers and which need to be kept firmly pressed between in place if the trick knot is to work, slip, and are suddenly revealed, spilling out from their hiding place like blood from a wound. From the frozen expressions on both of their faces (one angry, one afraid) it feels as if the soundtrack at this point shouldn't be just the clatter of one dropped drumstick, but instead the brazen din of some awful enamelled dinner plate or silver-plated tray being dropped loudly in the wings.

The woman waits, sqeezing hard between her legs (she has just realised that she urgently needs to pop backstage to the

Ladies – her bladder never does behave itself, not at the best of times) and he, of course, makes her wait. He re-coils his rope with conspicuous slowness. His voice, when it finally comes, is in lots of ways just like his face: handsome, clean-cut and effortlessly threatening. Without apparently raising it at all, and concentrating the whole time on his hapless, wronged and now-flaccid little scarlet friend, he says:

'Shall we try that move just the *once* more, Sandra?'

Of course, she daren't reply.

'Just the once more . . . and without one *iota* of fucking feeling – if you wouldn't mind, my darling.'

Sandra keeps her nerve, and for some odd reason remembers at that exact moment that high above her head there is another woman also trying to keep her poise under difficult circumstances. The dome that topped the New Wimbledon Theatre's facade was (and still is) crested with a great gilt angel, the woman whose job it was to herald the attractions of the place with blasts from a silent, golden trumpet. For just a moment, Sandra wonders if her employer's is really the kind of language the angel is supposed to be advertising to the passing shoppers, but she knows better than to express any such thought. She tells herself to concentrate. In particular, she tells herself not to think for even a second about the things which this man's hands can and have and undoubtedly will again do to her on other and less professional occasions. She readies the backs of her wrists by giving them each a drying wipe across the sides of her thighs, and gets ready to spread her fingers and hope for the best. The man in the dinner jacket coils the scarlet silk, lets it drop and coils it again. The next time he lets the rope fall, he passes the fingers of his left hand across his forehead as if trying to iron out that recalcitrant frown, and now he's biting his bottom lip, which Sandra knows from

23

experience is *really* not a good sign. She wonders whether to try saying something, and once again decides against it.

Clearly, things are not going well.

Sandra is, in a way, the least of this smartly dressed man's worries. Time was when even a low billing at a respectable south London house like the New Wimbledon would have pretty much shoehorned you into a few more useful bookings; this time around, however, the usual week-before-closing phone calls to his agent have failed to produce anything except a possible two-from-the-bottom return visit to the Bradford Alhambra – and that not until the middle of May, would you mind, when this was still the week commencing March the twenty-third. Everybody knew the touring game wasn't what it used to be – but that was bloody ridiculous, and he'd said so. The houses at the New had been thin all week, and then there'd been the old Queen dying, and then – just to depress things even further – there'd been that very unpleasant splash across the front page of the *Mirror* about the bodies found papered up in a cupboard in Notting Hill, which had sent all the girls backstage into a proper twitter, and more to the point was hardly designed to put any of his normally appreciative female punters in the right frame of mind to enjoy a second-half spot billed in scarlet letters as 'The Missing Lady'.

To make matters worse – if that were possible, which he was beginning to doubt – at the end of the first house yesterday Sandra had tapped on his dressing-room door and enquired with a quite unnecessary edge to her voice if he was planning to take her out for a quick bite somewhere between the shows, an enquiry that came just when he was in the middle of brushing his teeth in expectation of a backstage visit from one of his regulars, a very well-put-together bank manager's wife from Tooting who quite often turned up when he played south of the river, and who was always good to be touched for a new pair of cufflinks or a small cheque after they'd done the business. This error in timing had led to strong words between himself and Sandra, and then to a quick over-the-chair dressing-room seeing-to that had been meant to get her off his back for the rest of the week but in fact only served to remind him of how terminally dissatisfied he was getting with this particular set-up. There were bones, quite frankly, in all the wrong places. Then – to *really* add insult to incompetence – in the second house, when she'd held out her wrists for the ropes on the key change and was supposed to be looking straight out front and pulling focus with her very best 'Innocence Wronged' impersonation, misdirecting the house away from the double finger-spread that masked the false tie, she'd looked straight across-stage instead and winked at him, would you mind, actually bloody *winked*, completely putting him off his stride and almost causing him to lose the knot. Unrehearsed business like that from a girl was not something he would tolerate at the best of times – hence this bad-tempered lunchtime rehearsal – but in a week of unresponsive houses and tricky phone calls it was almost the last straw. In fact – amazing how things can come to a head over one tiny little detail, isn't it, and all this over a faked rope tie which ought to be one of the absolute basics – it was making him think that the whole bloody situation was in need of an overhaul. What with all the forthcoming celebrations, he'd fancied a summer season somewhere, but the chances of something like that coming in looked like they were receding fast. What were they calling it in all the papers? *The New Elizabethan Age?* – well what was he supposed to do? Come on dressed as Sir Walter fucking Raleigh and drop his cloak for some bloody tart to walk all bloody over? Would that get him a booking somewhere decent before the end of the month?

Instead of doing what he felt like doing, which was to forcibly remind Sandra that there were plenty of other girls in south London who'd be grateful to be got rid of twice nightly if she didn't fancy the job any longer – three times on Thursday and Saturdays – the man in the dinner jacket re-coiled his rope, took a concealed deep breath and slapped his working face back on. *Every inch the gentleman*, that was what they all said about Teddy Brookes Esq., and who was he to disillusion anybody? His voice sharpened to match the smile.

'Wrists a bit higher this time please, Sandra. And our eyes are house front at this point in the act, as I'm sure you remember.'

'Certainly, Mr Brookes.'

He wished he could pull the rope tight, make it bite into her skin and remind her to get the misdirection fucking *right* this time, but you can't do that with a faked wrist loop; the hidden two inches of slack have to stay just that, otherwise the knot can't be dropped when she gets to her quick change. He compromised by flashing the rope round her wrists nearly twice as fast as he did in the actual act. Thank goodness, this time, it worked; her eyes stayed wide and the blood stayed hidden. He stepped away, apparently to admire his handiwork but also to check the time again on his watch.

'And where's our little limping wonder got to, do you reckon?' he snapped, baring his teeth in a snarl as stagy as a circus tiger's. 'Eh, Sandra, my roped-up lovely? What do you reckon's become of our little *Reggie*?'

Yes, that's right; there's my *reveal*, as they say in the business. Reggie is Mr Brookes's disappearance boy. And what with being late because of the number 47 bus – not to mention the probable atmosphere he knows he's about to walk slap bang into, because Reggie's no fool when it comes to Mr Brookes and his women – quite frankly, as he rounds his final corner into Montague Road, ignoring as he does so the patronising and golden gaze of the second sightless effigy of his day; as he swings left down a side alley and thumps his way into work under the sign saying *Stage Door* with barely a nod through the window to Mr Gardiner, the door's keeper; as he heads, head down, into the labyrinth of white-tiled and white-walled corridors that will finally lead him onto the bright, dusty stage – quite frankly, as he does all of that, *disappear* is just exactly what young Reggie Rainbow wishes he could sometimes bloody do.

3

It's a funny sort of job description, isn't it? Faintly disreputable. But then I suppose most ways of earning a living that don't begin until all the lights have gone down are, one way or another.

To explain; the disappearance boy is the member of the act who the public never sees. The one – if the act is any good – that they will never even suspect is there. To qualify for the job the boy in question has to be small enough to hide in less space than anyone would think ordinarily possible; the muscles of his arms and shoulders must be strong enough to let him cling to the back of a swinging cabinet door, and his fingers must be deft enough to bring off a quick change in almost total darkness. He has to be sharp-minded enough to know *exactly* when to pull a hidden lever, and he has to have a taste for invisibility. For obvious reasons, the disappearance boy never – ever – takes a bow.

As it happens, Reggie has all of these qualities. You might even say he was born that way – or at the very least that his early life could almost have been designed to equip him for this particular and strange employment.

To explain:

You already know that it was a disease with a beautiful name that had made him so slight and short. *Poliomyelitis* – the word is striking, no matter how ugly its meaning, and on difficult days Reggie still finds himself repeating its musical syllables under his breath when he's out on one of his pavement-pounding walks, turning them over and over in his mouth, and still wondering why they had chosen him.

He'd once looked the word up in an encyclopedia, and read there that his story wasn't at all uncommon. According to the fine print of the relevant entry the virus had probably claimed him as its own courtesy of somebody's unwashed hands, and most likely entered his two-year-old body through the mucous lining of his throat. It had stopped short of its usual objective – destroying the motor neurons that connect the spinal cord to the muscles of the lungs, and murdering its host – and in his case contented itself with merely delivering what the entry called *Acute Flaccid Paralysis* to his legs. Then, he knew, he'd got lucky.

In the decade of Reg's childhood the accepted treatment of infant paralysis was something called *casting* – the immobilising of the afflicted limbs in heavy moulds of plaster of Paris. The process was thought to encourage recuperation, but often had the effect of wasting the very muscles it was meant to salvage, and sometimes even ended up condemning the child to life in a wheelchair. Reggie was spared this entombment by a simple accident of circumstance. He'd spent the first two years of his life in a ward on the third floor of the London County Council's National Children's Home up at Highbury Barn, and as luck would have it, it became official LCC policy at the end of that second year to farm out any child considered unlikely to ever become a suitable candidate for fostering to an independent charity. The now-twisted Reggie fell heavily into that class of unfortunates, and once he was out of immediate danger he was simply sent away. He'd already been given his new name – *Reggie* because by law every abandoned child the Home received on its wards had to be christened, and because Reginald was a popular name in the autumn of 1930; *Rainbow* because a sudden whim on the part of the Home's registrar made him hope that a little alliterative good luck might somehow rub off on such an optimistic surname's squalling new owner. Now he was given a new set of clothes for the journey, and the names were written out on a brown-paper label and tied to his wrist; then he was wrapped in a blanket and put on a train with a nurse. A taxi met them at Seaford Station and took them down the bumpy unmetalled road that led past Mr Bridges's kitchen window, and then turned left along the timber track that led out across the shingle of Bishopstone beach itself. Reg made the entire journey in silence. He was one of the youngest children ever to have made it, and he lived out there on the stones for the next seven years.

It must have been a strange place. The Home for Poor Brave Things, it was called, and it cared for a small but constantly replenished community of orphaned or abandoned children with disabilities from whenever they arrived until they reached the age of sixteen. The most striking of the surviving images of how it looked in Reggie's day is a photograph showing nineteen little boys lined up in a row out on the black-and-grey pebbles in order of their height, seven of them on crutches and one in a wheelchair. All of them are scowling at the camera and all of them naked except for their institutional linen underpants. They are all shockingly dark-skinned, and seem to be about to be herded into the sea by a pair of nurses in gull-like headdresses and heavy overcoats – evidently, the morning when the photograph was taken was a cold one, despite the sunshine that defines every detail of the boys' bodies. Nobody looks as though they think there is anything odd about children being forcibly immersed in freezing water, neither the boys nor their guardians. They just look cross with the photographer for interrupting their routine.

Thalassotherapy, sea-bathing for invalids it is called now – another beautiful word for something harsh – and though some commentators at the time labelled its pioneers barbaric, it has since been recognised as a perfectly legitimate therapy for wasting diseases like polio. There was much talk at the Home for Poor Brave Things of the light, air and salt water of the beach *cleansing* the Home's infant charges, of *stains being washed away* – as if disability, like being orphaned or illegitimate, was a sin rather than a fact – but that (I suppose) we must now forgive, as we must forgive the Board's choosing the Home's remote location so that the sight of its inhabitants shouldn't offend anybody. What matters now is that the doctors and nurses were at least to some degree right in their belief that self-help, fresh air, constant exposure to sunlight and above all repeated immersion in salt water could help repair their variously damaged and stigmatised charges. The regime certainly rescued Reggie. Being constantly half naked under the nurses' watchful eyes gave him the defiance he needed to survive; the painful daily slide down that bank of unforgiving flints and the screaming kicks against the beach's icy water strengthened his 'useless' leg, and the necessity for hauling himself across the floor of a chilly dormitory soon gave him a new and compensating set of muscles in his shoulders and arms. By the time he was seven, the metal brace that had been kept strapped to his leg for six hours a day as an infant was judged no longer necessary, and he swung and dragged himself from place to place using just a pair of crutches. He learnt how to live with bruises, and how to lie awake at night with no company except the moon slicing in through an open window, and no sound except the chatter of distant stones. Perhaps more importantly still, he learnt how to keep his head down, and to take off on his own the moment his nurses' backs were turned. Even before he could walk entirely unaided the young Reggie had learnt how to squeeze himself and his unusual body away in the gaps in other people's attention – and to be at home there.

Without meaning to, the Home even equipped him with the cabinet-clinging fingers that make him so invaluable to Mr Brookes, and the teeth that make him so reluctant to smile outright. The peculiar combination of strength and dexterity in his hands came not only from handling his crutches, but from the apprenticeship in metalwork that the boys were given three afternoons a week in the largest of the Home's huts. It was Reggie's allotted task to twist and trim wires which had been gripped in a vice, and it was a task he performed with grinning relish, nipping, jerking and clipping as if the bright metal deserved to be shown who was boss. The grin itself came about courtesy of the Home's kitchen sugar-cupboard. Once a week the ranges in the kitchen were used to manufacture boiled sweets which were then sent away for sale in a tea shop in Seaford; once a week, young Reggie would sneak in and wait for the cook's back to be turned. He loved the colours in their little stoppered bottles – bile green, rose pink – and the cyanide smell of the fake almond essence. He loved watching for the moment when the muscle-thick sugar threatened to blacken in the pan – and he loved to steal. Sugar quickly became his favourite food, and he still has the rotten teeth to prove it. His twenty-three-year-old self still keeps his lips sealed when he grins, lest they give away what he wants to keep hidden – and he still thinks of sweetness as something you have to steal when nobody's looking.

Every Sunday morning, the children were crocodiled over Mr Bridges's level crossing and onto a footpath that led over some fields to Bishopstone's tiny flint-walled church. Reggie didn't mind the walk – in fact, he always thought of the expedition as a treat. The windows of the church were full of stained glass, and on sunny days watching their colours come and go on the stone floor reminded him of the cellophane wrappers from his favourite sweets. One window was more brightly coloured than all the others, and he would always try and sit where he could see it. *Just like your name, Reg,* one of the nurses whispered, seeing him staring up at it. He grinned at her, lips closed, and looked back up. Sunday by Sunday, colour by colour, this window taught Reggie a lesson that wasn't directly stored in his body, but which nonetheless was planted so deep inside him that no surgeon's knife could ever have reached it.

He couldn't remember *when* the nurses had told him his mother was dead, but he was quite sure he had always known it as a fact. It never occurred to him to worry about the lack of detail in their story – the why and where and how – but instead he latched on to the good news in the tale, which was that she was now watching over him, and during his seventh summer, when every Sunday morning seemed to be sunny, and his favourite window always bright, this idea of being continually spied on and cared for began to take a very concrete form in Reggie's mind. The window featured a pair of bare-armed creatures swooping down from on high on outspread wings, all indigo and violet and parrot yellow – the source of the colours on the floor – and it was in exactly this gaudy and muscular shape that Reggie began to imagine his absent mother. The creatures in the window were smiling as they gazed down at the world, and as he stared up at them Sunday after Sunday it occurred to him that that was what she must be doing too. Admiring their muscular arms, he concluded that she would be well capable of turning up and carrying him away at a moment's notice should a dramatic rescue ever be required, and like a stolen sweet tucked in the

33

roof of his mouth this secret thought would sometimes keep him grinning to himself all week. That thought was why, two years later, when at nine o'clock on a fine but hazy mid-September morning the staff and children were told by a flustered and scared-looking young doctor that instead of heading to the workshop for their metalwork training they were all going to be something called *evacuated*, young Reggie knew almost immediately what it was that he had to do.

The doctor – a junior – was in a state of shock. He'd only been given twenty-four hours to empty the buildings of the Home – Seaford Bay was thought to be a prime potential invasion site, and had been designated for immediate clearance and fortification by the Ministry of Defence – and had snapped out the phrase *or stay here and get shot* at one of the nurses when she had raised her hand and asked him if the Ministry really needed the children to leave quite so soon, making her cry. Although Reggie understood very little of the rest that was said, he knew he was in peril, and by the time the nurses had begun ushering their charges back to the dormitories to pack their cardboard suitcases he had already hit on his idea. He waited for his supervising nurse to be distracted, and then – even though he was stripped to his underpants, because the children had been told to change into their Sunday best for the journey – he ducked under his metal cot, grabbed his crutches and shoes and dragged himself out of sight across the floor and out through a door.

The back of the dormitory led out onto a concrete sun terrace, and then down onto the beach. After working his way round to the rear of the kitchen block on the stones – falling twice in the process, and hurting himself quite badly – Reggie squatted on a doorstep to lace on his right shoe, and threw the left one out onto the beach; then he slid his hands and forearms into the biting aluminium supports of his crutches and began to propel himself furiously down the concrete path that led out onto the timber road. When he reached it, he swerved right – not looking back once – and swung himself away from the Home, his bare foot alternately dangling and dragging on the tarred timbers. Fighting his way through a ragged gap in a blackthorn hedge (he fell again at this point), he climbed the slippery grass of the embankment, threw away the crutches, and picked his spot on the line. As he drew himself upright on his chosen sleeper, he closed his eyes, not because he was frightened, but to help him listen out for the next sound he was sure he would hear; the downward rush of his mother's rescuing, rainbow-bright wings.

What actually happened next, you already know.

Being swept off the line into a pair of unknown arms just as the scream of the train was drowned out in the thunder of its wheels taught that desperate little boy a powerful but contradictory lesson. In the moment between being knocked off his feet by the force of Mr Bridges's final lunge and the shock of landing under him in the long rank grass by the side of the tracks, Reggie really did think that he was being carried up into the air by his mother. By the time he finally opened his eyes – by the time they had been forcibly smacked open by Mr Bridges – he knew that he was on his own. I'm not saying that his childish self knew it in the same conscious way that his twenty-two-year-old self now thinks he knows it – he could never, for instance, have been able to put the thought into an actual, word-by-word sentence – but that was undoubtedly why the nine-year-old Reggie kept his eyes screwed tightly shut as Mr Bridges roared right into his face, and why he didn't cry. He needed time to think, and time to scrawl a pledge to himself across the back of his blood-dark eyelids. A pledge that he would never ask for anybody's help ever again – time to write it, sign it and seal it shut.

That promise is the reason why everybody backstage in Wimbledon agrees that Reggie's a young man who *knows how to keep his head down*. It's the reason why – from the methodical way he lays out Mr Brookes's props to his own cheerfully and filthily tight-lipped way with words – everything about our Reggie is pretty much self-contained. It also explains why Reggie was keeping his eyes so firmly fixed down on the pavement as he ducked round the corner into Montague Street. He's still allergic to rainbows, and to people with unfurled wings, no matter how golden or high up or obviously ludicrous they are.

When Mr Brookes looked up and saw Reggie finally limping out onto the stage that morning – jacket flapping, face twisted into that odd little tooth-hiding grin of his – he completely forgot to be angry. Typical Reggie, he thought – slipping on like a fox through a letter box, jaunty as all get up and without a trace of apology on his face.

'Ah, Reggie,' he said, re-coiling his rope one more time. 'So good of you to join us.'

'Sorry, Mr Brookes,' replied Reggie, pulling his lips even tighter, surreptitiously tapping his breast pocket while he did it.

'That number 47 was being a right pain in the arse again. Where've we got to then? D'you want me inside the apparatus?'

4

Illusion acts are always rehearsed without witnesses; as with certain other bits of life, it all has to happen behind locked doors. In order to describe how this particular rehearsal continued I'm obviously going to have to break with that convention, but I don't want anyone to accuse me of taking the magic out of the proceedings. So first I'm going to describe the act as it will be tonight when all the lights are up on the six thirty house, and then I'll go back and show you how Mr Brookes does it. All I'd say by way of a warning is that you need to remember that a magician is not someone who deceives, but someone who keeps his promise. Which is to deceive.

All right?

Sandra is just about to be lifted up onto a chair to have her ankles secured as firmly as her wrists, and the band are already on their fourth chorus of Ray Noble's 'The Very Thought of You'. The lights are starting to get properly warm. As I promised you earlier, Mr Brookes is looking even more the handsome devil than ever – now that it's show time, he's wearing a strong foundation, surprisingly firmly pencilled eyebrows, pulpy red lips and enough mascara to make sure that that penetrating gaze of his reaches right up to the cheap seats. Sandra, in comparison, is still looking quite pale under that pulledbacked scrape of blonde hair of hers. She's smiling, of course, and doing her best to make the most of her costume

– back-seamed stockings, matching black satin skirt and blouse, starched collar, cuffs, cap and apron – but after her afternoon ordeal it can't be said that she's looking quite as pert as a French Maid is usually paid to look. The satin of her skirt is so tight that it makes it difficult for her to move. When Mr Brookes walks round in front of her, however, squeezes his hands onto her hips and gives her a quick lift, she's suddenly up on the chair in one straight-from-standing jump – and if you think that's easy, just you try it in three-inch heels and with your wrists tied. She wobbles slightly, but Mr Brookes moves swiftly on; another coil of scarlet rope appears from nowhere, and this one is deftly looped and knotted around her ankles. Mr Brookes gestures dramatically to the flies, and to the sound of a smartly timed cymbal-crash a spotlight hits the exact centre of the stage, outlining in silver the mysteriously draped object that has been waiting so patiently for its moment in the limelight.

Now we seem to be getting down to the point of these elaborate proceedings.

Leaving Sandra stranded on her chair, Mr Brookes prowls around the drapes as if they concealed a familiar adversary. In the pit, the band vamps admirably. Mr Brookes stoops, and gathers a handful of silk. Up on her chair, Sandra – still smiling – shifts her weight nervously from hip to hip, and with (thank goodness) her wrists and ankles pressed firmly together. Then, preparing himself exactly as if he were about to execute that old chestnut whereby the conjuror pulls a tablecloth away without breaking a single plate, Mr Brookes whips the drapes away with a matador flourish, and sends them flying – silver, suspended, gone-in-a-flash – into the wings.

What is revealed is exactly what you would expect under the circumstances.

It's looking pretty battered, but the harlequin paintwork on the cabinet still shines in the lights – and at just short of ten feet tall, it's impressive. Mr Brookes's hands respectfully request that we inspect it closely while we still have the chance. The sides of the box are smooth, except for a strip of moulding about two feet off the floor; it has six small brass handles, one set just inside each of the corners about five feet off the ground and two on a pair of wardrobe-like doors set in the front panel. For some reason, these doors don't reach down to the ground, but stop short just above the line of moulding. Drawing our attention to this feature, Mr Brookes once again spreads his lips with two swiftly licked fingers, and in the pit the percussionist once again provides the loud serio-comic rip of a wolf whistle; right on cue, two embarrassed-looking stagehands in spangled waistcoats wheel on a small set of functional brown-stained wooden stairs, which they proceed to carefully if a little clumsily slot into the empty space just below the doors. Mr Brookes glances over their handiwork, then ascends the steps. He checks we are all with him by means of a quick questioning look over his shoulder, and then dramatically throws open the doors.

The interior of the cabinet is mirrored, and (of course) entirely empty.

Mr Brookes looks across the stage at his accomplice. She smiles courageously in response, and then keeps her grin clamped firmly in place as he hurries down the steps, crosses the stage and sweeps her off the chair and into his arms. Carrying her for all the world like a bride across a threshold – albeit one bound hand and foot – he swings her high-heeled feet delicately down onto the bottom step of the stairs; using his proffered hand to steady herself, she hops up them in three neat, determined and heels-together jumps. Mr Brookes sweeps round to the opposite side of the stairs, indicating as he does so that his lovely assistant is now going to take her rightful place inside the cabinet. This she does, grinning with apology for the little backwards shuffling move she has to make to do it. Multiplied in the mirrors, she looks out at us from inside her sparkling new home, clearly unsure as to what is going to happen to her next.

We don't have to wait very long to find out.

On a cue from Mr Brookes, the pit switches to an uptempo rendition of that much-loved classic 'Goodnight, Sweetheart'; he flies up the steps, and closes the cabinet doors on Sandra's smile. Dipping his hand first into his left pocket and then the right, he produces a short length of chain and a padlock, and before you know where you are he's got those doors locked tight and the key tucked in his breast-pocket handkerchief and safely stowed away in his left-hand trouser pocket – clearly, whatever else happens tonight, that girl of his is going *nowhere*. He comes jauntily down the steps, beckoning to the waiting stagehands to remove them as he does so. Then he reaches out and seizes hold of the now free-standing box by two of its corner handles and begins to spin it, turning it fast and hard on its castors – three times clockwise, three times anticlockwise, and frowning with the effort of shifting the body trapped inside. Then he suddenly steps away from the still-spinning apparatus, leaving it to settle. Smiling again, he reveals from behind his back a rather sinister-looking silver-topped walking cane – something that he seems to have plucked out of thin air. He moves stage left of the box, evidently considering his next move, and smartly taps the side of the box with the cane, twice – and quite hard. Then he steps to the right, and strikes it twice again. The first two blows are accompanied by the percussionist's military-sounding snare drum, but the second pair land with a proper deep thump from his foot pedal. Mr Brookes lets that noise hit home, then steps to the left again, clearly preparing himself for a third and final assault. The percussionist gives him a good proper build-up; Mr Brookes shoots his cuffs, takes a deep breath, raises the cane, steps back a pace, and then, as a cymbal crashes, decisively strikes the air.

In a puff of smoke, the four side panels of the cabinet fall simultaneously open. A rough-edged question mark of pink and orange rises into the lights, writhes, and spirits itself discreetly away. The cymbal-stroke fades too, and the lights strike nothing but an empty cross of mirrors.

As you can see, the Lady is indeed missing.

And now comes the part of the act which I think Mr Brookes always does best.

Taking his time, he casually smooths a stray lock of Brylcreemed hair back into place. Then he simply stays where he is, looking straight out front and with that one black eyebrow of his just ever so slightly raised. *Well*, his look seems to be suggesting, *are you saying she didn't deserve it?* Teasingly, he glances back upstage at the remains of his exploded apparatus, inviting us to check that there can't have been a mistake. Inevitably, he makes us wonder if he can't somehow still have Sandra locked up in or under its ruins. Then, with a rotation of his left wrist, his cane suggests that we might want to remove our attention from his elegant person, and direct it more towards the stage-left wing.

His right hand rises, and he clicks his fingers. Skin sandpapers skin, the follow spot swoops down to the edge of the proscenium and there – large as life and twice as bold, sweeping on to the sound of another cymbal-crash – is Sandra – Sandra, but different.

Sandra, entirely transformed.

Maid no longer, Sandra is wearing a burgundy satin ballgown from a Bond Street couturier, and her neck is stacked with rubies. Her blonde curls cascade onto a white fox drape, and as she strides on she is pouring Mr Brookes a nice glass of something from a freshly opened bottle of champagne. Now we know why it specifies *Lady* on the bills – and no wonder the band sails into a jauntily uptempo reprise of 'The Very Thought of You' to welcome her back. Mr Brookes, ever the man about town, appears not at all astonished by what has happened to her in the few seconds since he saw her last – one might even think he planned it, he stays so debonair. He accepts the proffered *coupe* of bubbly, sips, and returns the glass. A quick kiss, followed by three quick spinning turns and a final throw of his magic cane up into the air, and he re-equips himself for a night out with this glamorous creature – the gloves, scarf and top hat all reappear in their proper places, and after one last adjustment of that recalcitrant lock of hair he offers his lady a suitably gentlemanly arm. She, of course, takes him up on the offer – but just before he sweeps her off to whatever upmarket entertainment venue he is escorting her to this evening – is it to be the Café Royal, I wonder? – Mr Brookes pauses. His hands pat all of his pockets in turn. Is he looking for his wallet? His watch? At last his fingers find what they were seeking, and he pulls out the handkerchief in which we previously saw him wrap that all-important padlock key for safe keeping. He deftly unfolds it – and lying there is not the key at all, but the red silk ropes that we last saw twisted around his lady friend's wrists and ankles. Mysteriously, they are freshly coiled, and apparently unused. Sandra looks on politely, suggesting that in her new incarnation she has no idea what such things might possibly be used for. Mr Brookes weighs the ropes gently in his hand, and looks out front for one last time. Once again, those pencilled black eyebrows rise in suggestion. *Oh well*, they seem to be saying, *you know how it is, gentlemen. Always best to be prepared . . .*

Sandra's smile falters for a second. But no one notices – because Mr Brookes slides the ropes back into his pocket, twirls his cane, flicks his eyes up to the flies and bids us a smart and entirely proper goodnight by flicking his white-gloved fingers to the brim of his black top hat. The band launches into a swift two-bar button, and the curtain descends. The happy couple reappear for one last time, knocking out a briskly professional double-dip bow with one reverse, and then a stagehand behind the drapes pages the curtain back so that Mr Brookes can hand Sandra off in truly gentlemanly fashion. A rather charming skip from her, and one last smile and a wave from him, and they exit, looking for all the world as if he's planning on booking the honeymoon suite some-time rather soon. Thank you, and goodnight!

So here's how it's done.

First things first. The biggest and broadest trick in Mr Brookes's act is that he makes you think that he's the one who's doing it. Everything about him is designed to make you think that he is the one who's making everything happen, but in fact, the body (so to speak) of the act is accomplished by Sandra, by the two stagehands and by our young Reggie.

Secondly, what he *does* work hard to achieve, he makes you miss. *Misdirection*, it's called; the art of leading your punters' attention astray. While one hand is flying dramatically upward to the sound of a cymbal-crash, the other set of fingers will be busy palming or pocketing something, unnoticed. And never mind your eye – every detail of the act is designed to draw your *mind* away from how hard those well-trained fingers of Mr Brookes are working. The tight white gloves with the pearl buttons, for instance, the ones that you see him so conspicuously unfastening and loosening finger by finger at the beginning of the act, just before he palms them into his waiting left-hand cuff – the buttons are only there so that when he tricks the gloves back on at the end their sudden restoration will seem bewilderingly effortless. You can't work out how on earth he has managed to do up such a pair of fiddly buttons again without you spotting him do it, whereas in actual fact the final gloves are a different, much looser and buttonless pair, loaded inside two concealed pochettes set either side of the extended back vent of his dinner jacket, and specifically designed to be slipped on in a moment. The exactly level edges of the silk scarf which is pulled up into his other cuff by its pre-rigged elastic – what the business calls *a visible vanish* – the scarlet-and-black top hat that collapses as it is knocked flat against his chest and then slipped inside his jacket – everything is contrived to make him look as though he's a man of leisure, whereas in fact the only genuine gesture in the entire act is when Mr Brookes pauses to quickly wipe the sweat from his hands on his handkerchief. Those elegantly deceiving digits of his ache, every night.

Of course, if Mr Brookes were alone up there while he was doing all of this your eye might well catch him out, especially if you had been duped by a man dressed like him before. But he isn't alone, and at every crucial moment that suspicious eye of yours is cleverly distracted. Sandra's high heels and hobbling skirt may make her seem gangly and insecure, and she may have to be handed up steps and carried from one place to the other – but all of this makes you completely miss the fact that each of her moves is expertly timed and delivered, drawing your eyes away from Mr Brookes's deceptive hands just when you should be watching them closely. Likewise, the apron and cap and cuffs all conspire to make her maid's outfit seem quite fussy and elaborate, whereas in fact everything she has on is rigged to be ripped off in a moment. It's all, as they say, an act. The demure high neck of the blouse is only there to conceal the rubies she's already wearing underneath, and the cap isn't there to tell you she's a hard-working domestic at all; it conceals the fact that her own hair is already pin-curled flat, ready for her to get the blonde quick-change wig pulled on over it in the wings in one neat tug. It also usefully combines with her three-inch heels to make her seem nearly as tall as Mr Brookes, so that you believe she almost fills the just-big-enough magic cabinet (the mirrors help with that too) – and therefore couldn't possibly squeeze herself into anything smaller.

And what about Reggie? What's he up to? When the two stagehands wheel on the draped cabinet in reponse to Mr Brookes's first wolf-whistled summons, they rotate it. This is quite unneccesary, but demonstrates that there is no one clinging to its outside. As soon as he has undraped it, Mr Brookes opens the doors at the front, thus showing you straight away that there's no one inside either. This is of course all more deception; Reggie was inside the cabinet when the stagehands were showing you the outside, and outside when Mr Brookes was showing you the inside, slipping through a panel hidden in the mirrors and then clinging like a monkey to the back of the cabinet by means of those two conveniently placed handles, toes perched on that otherwise unneccessary strip of moulding. The minute Sandra is in the box he flips open the panel again, and they start working as one. The rope round her wrists goes between her teeth; the one round her ankles is passed out to Reg, together with her cap, shoes and quickly ripped-off skirt. Then, while she lifts herself momentarily up using two hand-grips hidden in the ceiling of the cabinet, he opens the trap in its floor. The now bare-foot Sandra drops down through the open floor and then, via another opening panel down in the base of the cabinet, folds herself into the open back of the flight of steps. Again, it's not easy, but bending is how she makes her living – and with enough practice and determination it's surprising just how small a space a person can fold themselves into. She pulls her knees to her chest, braces herself with her hands and bites down hard on the rope between her teeth.

As she is doing all of this – and as she's then being wheeled off into the wings by the two stagehands – you quite naturally think she is still tied up in the cabinet; not because you are stupid, but because having seen how clumsy and constrained she is, you cannot imagine her doing anything skilfully or fast.

Because the steps are brought onstage by two stagehands who look like nice boys, and who clearly aren't part of the act proper at all, so couldn't possibly be part of any deception.

Because the steps are so bloody small – or rather, cleverly insignificant, compared with the painted and glittered and spotlit cabinet.

Because you're too busy watching Mr Brookes do lots of urgent, impressive and entirely unnecessary things with a chain, a fake padlock and a key.

And because no one ever quite guesses how things are going to turn out, do they? No one ever quite realises just how heavily things are rigged.

The most exposed part of the routine is when Sandra is being wheeled away in the steps. Reggie is back inside the cabinet at this point, bracing himself against the mirrors and giving the box the weight it needs as Mr Brookes sets it off on its final spin. Once it comes to a stop, he has only seconds to get himself down through the trapdoor and curled up out of sight before pulling the lever to release the sides of the cabinet – but as those seconds tick away you're so busy imagining Sandra still trapped and shaken between her mirrors that it never occurs to you to wonder why the stagehands are wheeling the steps off instead of simply picking them up and carrying them. Then, when Mr Brookes produces his cane, plucked from its hiding place in the black trelliswork outlining the cabinet's diamond paintwork, it's once again the girl you think of, and how she must be flinching away from those blows in the dark – never for a moment imagining that she could be already running and ripping and zipping in the wings. When the cane pulls back for the final strike and the drum begins to roll, you never stop to wonder why Mr Brookes feels he has to threaten her with his cane *three* times, only to wonder what kind of state she'll be in when you see her next – while down inside the cabinet what is actually happening is that Reggie is swearing like a trooper and praying that Sandra doesn't mess anything up in her change in the wings, cursing the high heels digging into his chest and groping for the lever and switch that operate the spring release and the smoke.

When the cabinet has fallen open, and there is that odd moment of silence in which Mr Brookes casually looks upstage at the clearing smoke, Reggie always hold his breath. A *force*, they call this bit – the trick of making you ignore all other explanations except the one the man in charge wants you to think about. Of course, if anyone in the audience genuinely believed that they'd actually just watched a woman get roped, stuffed into a box and made to vanish, they'd scream. But instead, Reg knows, they are watching the smoke wreathe its way into nothingness over Mr Brookes's head, concentrating on him and his magical powers, missing entirely the fact that Sandra is busy transforming herself *herself*, and somewhere else entirely.

Why do people never spot how the world actually works? Reg sometimes wonders, as he lies there in the dark, trying not to cough with the smoke. *Perhaps they're paying us to* – but he never gets to the end of that thought, because there's always a sharp rapping knock over his head from Mr Brookes, letting him know that the tabs are down and it's time to uncurl and clamber free.

The rest is just nuts and bolts. The finesse with the reappearing ropes – the *finesse* is the final grace note of an act, the twist that makes you smile – is in fact achieved with the crudest trickery of the whole routine; a second handkerchief with two fresh ropes inside it is already set in Mr Brookes's right-hand trouser pocket from the moment he walks on. The magical plume of smoke from inside the locked cabinet is produced by two teaspoons of flash powder mixed with a quarter-teaspoon of powdered magnesium; the flick of Reggie's switch connects an inch of fuse wire in the powder tray to a six-volt lantern battery, and the heat of the wire does the rest. The mirrors inside the cabinet are actually polished zinc; the silver satin drape which shrouds the apparatus is salvaged parachute silk, but with its hems weighted with lead fishing weights so that it will fly like the real thing. Sandra's ball gown isn't from Bond Street at all, but from a retired wardrobe mistress in Forest Hill. Her white 'fox' fur stole is a length of remodelled angora rabbit. The champagne she's pouring is French's Ginger Ale, and the gold-foiled Moët & Chandon bottle she's pouring it from so elegantly gets washed out and reused every night. Her freshly brushed-out blonde curls are a wig, as you know, and her radiant smile at the curtain call –

Sandra's smile has been getting a bit harder to keep in place recently, and this afternoon's rehearsal hasn't exactly helped. Although she does still fancy Teddy – and God know he's better on the job than some she's chosen in her time – after six weeks, she knows a little too much about what those hands can do to her ever to be fully at ease in their company. Grin and bear it may be the routine onstage, but that does have its limits. She's really not sure — well, let's just say she's really not sure how much longer she can put up with transforming herself whenever he clicks his fingers.

Clearly, Reggie isn't the only thing that's invisible in this act.

'I think we can leave that there for now,' said Mr Brookes, coiling his rope for the very last time and finally declaring the rehearsal over. He stowed the rope carefully back in his pocket, and started wiping his hands on a clean white handkerchief. 'If I might have my practice mirror now, Reggie — oh, and Sandra . . .'

'Yes, Mr Brookes?'

'You could afford to wear your fur a bit lower on the return tonight at the six thirty, I think. We might as well give the poor deluded sods their money's worth, mightn't we?'

Watching Sandra's thin face as she tried to decide whether to try answering back or not, Reggie reckoned he'd give these two until about Friday. *Please God she doesn't just run, like the last one did*, he thought to himself as he was clearing up afterwards. *Because then we'll really be up the fucking pictures.*

5

The mirror that Reggie was asked to fetch at the end of that rehearsal was a pier glass in a battered mahogany frame. Its mirroring was blown and spotted in quite a few places, but Mr Brookes superstitiously refused to replace it – it had been with him for years. As Sandra hung up her gown on the back of her dressing-room door and congratulated herself on having got through all of that without once making Teddy properly lose his temper, and as Reggie collected the parachute silk from where it had landed in the wings and dragged it out into a backstage corridor so he could check the hem for tears, Mr Brookes tilted his mirror and spread his hands into two well-boned fans, making sure they were properly lit. He inverted them, inspected them, bit a nail – and then began the chore of repeating each produce and vanish in the act six times. He repeated each move three times watching his hands, and three times staring himself straight in the eye. As always, he paid particular attention to the production of his smile. He never blinked.

Sometimes, Mr Brookes feels tired – of the repetition, of the telephone calls and arrangements, of the twelve shows a week plus matinees, and of the women. He knows what he's like, though, and let's face it, he's been doing this all his life.

He looked in his clouded mirror, and smiled for the forty-second time.

That's more like it, he thought. *Teddy Brookes. Esquire.*

Again, he didn't blink.

6

There was still no news of a booking by Friday lunchtime, and so that night Reggie came in early to make sure every-thing was ready to be packed up into storage after the final three shows on Saturday. After he'd cleaned the pier glass rather more thoroughly than was strictly necessary, and laid out Mr Brookes's make-up, he went down into the wings to catch the curtain coming down on the six thirty first half. The Rigoletto Brothers – the trampoline duo who closed the first act – were one of his favourite turns on the circuit, and he knew he was going to miss rubbing past them in the corridors and popping down to watch them whenever he felt like it. Tonight, when their big finish came, the younger of the two brothers arced so high over the stage in his white tights that Reggie found himself involuntarily tapping his breast pocket for luck. The sweat came off the twisting figure like a spray of diamonds, and when the house applauded, so did Reg. He stayed all the way through their bows – he liked that bit as much as anything, loved the fact that now they were back down to earth you could see how hard they'd been working to fly like that, their thick black Italian hair shining, both of them dripping and gasping for breath, their matted chests heaving – and he trotted off backstage with a grin on his face, ready to check that everything was shipshape for the act. His night continued pretty well. Both houses were good, and there was a very respectable round at the end of the second Friday night showing of 'The Missing Lady'. It wasn't until after the curtain came down at the very end of the night that their final weekend in Wimbledon began to go wrong.

Reg never knew exactly what had happened – Mr Gardiner hinted that there had been some kind of a scene at the stage door as the two of them went home – but whatever it was, the incident had obviously led to trouble between them later. Mr Brookes's customary skill with close-up handwork must have let him down for once, and when Sandra turned up for the Saturday matinee not even the thick layer of Superior Pancake No. 3 she was wearing round her mouth could conceal the split in her lip. The show, predictably, was rotten; her timing was all over the shop. Reggie knew better than to get between them, but after the curtain he did go round to Sandra's dressing room to ask if she needed anything fetching for her tea between the two evening shows. She said she didn't, so he left her to it, but he certainly wasn't looking forward to the rest of the night.

Sandra may not have felt like being fetched a sardine sandwich, but she'd certainly felt like a drink. Years of touring had taught her always to keep two things close at hand whenever possible; her self-respect, and a quarter-bottle of Gordon's. Now, after the language Mr Brookes had just used to her on the stairs back up to the dressing rooms, she was in need of both. She locked her door, filled her glass, stared at herself in the mirror for a bit and then got to work. An hour later, she emerged from her dressing room for the first evening show with her smile freshly painted and its edges sharper than ever. Nothing had been said, but she knew that after last night's set-to and the bite of his signet ring into her face the chances of Mr Brookes keeping her on as either his Lady or his current piece of skirt were slight, and while she was redoing her slap she had decided to go out with a bang. No one was knocking her about for a hobby, thank you very much, no matter how good a screw they were three times a week.

There's nothing like suspecting you won't have a job to go to tomorrow morning to make you feel like pushing the boat out, and by the time Sandra made her high-heeled entrance in that week's final evening show her maid had acquired a definite sense of well-oiled bravado. A positive volley of wolf whistles from the second circle greeted her energetic jump-from-standing onto the chair – her skirt got very fetchingly hitched up, and she saw no need to smooth it down – and when the ropes went around her wrists her wide-eyed dismay got a *very* appreciative chuckle from two middle-aged gentlemen sitting together at the front of the stalls. She showed no signs of flagging, either, despite Mr Brookes's warning stares; her backward hops up the steps were more provocative than they'd ever been, and the audience's final sight of her framed between her mirrors was as pretty as a very particular and sometimes quite pricey kind of picture. Once the doors had clicked shut she slipped her ropes and lifted and dropped and folded herself quicker than Reggie had ever known her do it – so quickly, in fact, that they almost lost their timing. Then, of course, she slid into the steps, and he had to leave her to it. That was when she made her mistake.

The dangerous moments are always when you think you're home and dry, aren't they? – when the body lets down its guard.

When she sailed back on after her quick change, Sandra's smile was frosted with triumph. However, in her tipsy determination to show Mr Brookes that anything he could do, she could do better (she'd always liked that song), she'd failed to notice that the zipper of her ball gown hadn't caught properly. Three paces onstage, she let out all the breath she had been holding in during the tension of the change itself, and as her ribs deflated under the corsetry of the dress it slipped. The toe of her leading shoe caught in its front hem, and she tripped. She stumbled, grabbed at her slithering fur, and sent half the *coupe* of ginger ale splashing down the front of her burgundy satin. There was a laugh from some men in the audience, but it died; Sandra recovered as best she could, hitching the fur up over her breasts and letting out a high-pitched little giggle of her own, but by then the damage was done, and the applause which had greeted her entrance pattered away into nothing. The band, of course, carried on regardless. Mr Brookes took the half-empty glass, glared at her, and tossed back the ginger ale as angrily as if it were a neat and punishing vodka.

Then he just stood there. He looked for a moment as though he had half a mind to smash the glass at her feet – never mind the orchestra's eyes, in the pit – but instead he punished her much more simply. Cutting all of the final business entirely, he let her struggle to keep her stained dress up over her breasts for a full sixteen bars of music; only then did he deign to give the cue to the flyman to bring in the tabs. Adding injury to insult, he deliberately left it to the very last minute to grab her by the wrist and tug her upstage of the descending wall of fabric. She staggered, tripped and almost fell again, and the laughter of the audience grew into ragged, jeering applause.

Reggie knew that something had gone badly wrong as soon as he crawled out. The band was still blaring out the music for the call on the other side of the curtain, but Mr Brookes was standing stock-still and with his face in shadow, his back pointedly turned. One hand was dangling the empty champagne glass, and the other was clenching and unclenching itself. Sandra, ten feet away, was shifting anxiously from foot to foot, one hand straying up to her wig, her shoulders and the tops of her breasts eerily white in the between-the-acts twilight. Mr Brookes turned.

'D'you know what you are, Sandra?'

The words slit through the music on the other side of the tabs like a razor. She bit her damaged lip, and stuck her chin up bravely as he moved towards her.

'No, Mr Brookes,' she replied. 'At this particular moment, I have no flippin' idea who I am at all.'

'Well, then, I'll tell you,' he said, gouging his words into the remaining space between their faces exactly, and ignoring the half-lit chaos around them.

'You're a girl in a million, you are. The one fucking girl in a million who can't walk straight even *before* I've fucked her. So why don't you sod off back to whichever agency it was I got you from and take your wan little tits with you? Your money's at the stage door.'

Reg could see that she would have liked nothing better than to have signed off by raking her nails across his face, but she hesitated – and at that exact point, after a hurried bar's rest, the band on the other side of the curtain launched into 'The Sun in Old Toledo', and the next act's lighting blazed on up in the flies. The sudden overhead wash of pink and blue put the blood back into Sandra's cheeks, and she almost managed a smile.

'Well,' she pronounced, tugging her fur up and dodging the stagehands who were coming on to clear the cabinet, 'it's been lovely working with you, and I do hope something comes along for you very soon, Mr Brookes.'

She kicked the satin of her falling ball gown out of the way, turned, took three strides, and then turned again at the wing, delivering her exit line over one still-bare shoulder like a real pro.

'Like a lorry doing sixty miles an hour through a red light, for instance.'

A stagehand guffawed. Reggie wouldn't have put it past Mr Brookes to lose it at that point – especially when the stage manager started hissing *Places please, everybody*, and tapping his clipboard at them – but all he did was stand there, still clutching that ridiculously empty glass, and watching Sandra stalk away. The stagehands set to work with a vengeance to get the cabinet offstage in time, and the two dancers of the Spanish speciality act dodged them in a swirl of ruffles and took up their places. The stage manager hissed again, and to Reggie's astonishment Mr Brookes, still standing there, took the time to let his face melt into a wide, handsome and white-toothed smile – a real one. In desperation, the stage manager shouted into the flies, and the curtain began to rise. Mr Brookes turned crisply on his heel, and Reg lurched off after him, making it into the wings just in time. The lights got brighter, Carlita arched her spine into the cradle of Carlos's well-muscled arms, and the band played on.

It was only when the curtain was down and the theatre was dark again that Reggie had time to think, and realised why his employer had smiled like that. He'd just got exactly what he wanted . . . And maybe it was the shadows on Mr Brookes's suddenly cast-bronze face, or the way his dark red mouth had prepared itself for that smile with a quick, flicking wipe of his tongue – but Reg didn't think he'd ever seen him look so bloody handsome.

His last packing-up job was to sort out Mr Brookes's make-up. A smudge of black had somehow got onto the No. 7, but two deft flicks with the thin blade of his penknife and a quick wipe with a rag soon sorted that out. Once he'd got the greasy silver-papered sticks all in order, he cleaned his hands, then wrapped the sticks in a hand towel and carefully stowed them away in the bottom of the old biscuit tin that was their home – the mice had got at them once, and he'd had the devil's own job to replace them. The mascara and Rachel powder and the two-pound glass jar of Pond's Remover went in on top. Reggie glanced up into the mirror again as he collected that last item – the women here at work never really took all their slap off, did they, just plastered more on, especially if they were meeting someone after. *Good luck to each and every one of them*, Reggie thought, and snapped the lid on the tin. He breathed on the mirror, and then wiped it clean with his sleeve, momentarily grinning at his other, dark self. *Good luck to each and every bloody one of them, the bloody tarts*. All he had to do now was to check the label on the laundry bag one last time, double-check round the sink and under the furniture, and give one last final flick of the switch to kill the light bulbs.

Heading back down the corridor, he stooped to pick up a pair of damp wool tights that had slipped off one of the radiators. He lifted them to his nose, momentarily collecting a trace of coal-tar soap and sweat, and then draped them back over radiator, straightening a leg that hung stubbornly crooked. He'd heard from one of the lads who'd helped him with packing the cabinet that the Rigolettos were being held over for an extension week, and as he rearranged the crooked leg he wondered if one evening next week he might even get the number 47 back over one night and pay to watch the act from out front for once. Treat himself – why not? He even started whistling their music as he limped on down the corridor – 'The March of the Slaves' it was called, apparently. Reggie was a lousy whistler, and knew it, but now that everybody else had gone home it didn't really matter. He turned up the volume, and enjoyed making the concrete floor and white-tiled walls ring with his unapologetic noise.

Mr Gardiner was a Scot; the kind of man who was never without his regimental tie during office hours, and who believed in keeping people's spirits up. He did this mostly by sharing a civil phrase or two with every single artist or artiste who passed through his door, no matter what their standing in the profession – and regardless of whether they returned the compliment or not.

On this particular Saturday night he was occupying the time before he could fulfil that duty with regard to the very last of his week's guests by rereading a story on page four of the *South London Gazette*, a story which was headlined STAR GUEST BURGLED THROUGH LOCKED DOOR. He had just reached (for the third time) the paragraph describing how the victim had woken to realise that there was a man standing over her bed – the silly girl – when he heard Reggie's tuneless approach; reluctantly, he folded his paper and laid it aside, reminding himself as he did so that professional standards in the theatre had to be kept up at all times.

'Anything nice Sunday, Reg?' he barked, opening his window and accepting the proffered dressing-room keys. His eyes briefly strayed back down to the photograph in his paper as he turned to find their places on his board of numbered hooks. Reggie tried not to smile. The woman in the photograph looked a bit like Sandra, he thought – blonde, with a big white fur.

'Nothing special, Mr Gardiner. Might take myself off for a nice walk somewhere I thought. The river at Richmond or something. You know.'

'Oh, *very* nice, Richmond,' said Mr Gardiner, finally dropping the keys over their allotted hooks. Order had been restored. 'Do give it my regards.'

'I certainly will,' said Reggie, crossing his jacket over his chest against the night and pushing open the stage door. 'Well . . .'

It was always odd, saying goodnight at the end of an engagement.

'Well, take care then, Mr Gardiner. Until next time.'

'Take care, young man,' barked Mr Gardiner, as the door swung closed and the cold air brushed his face for a moment. He congratulated himself quietly for not having alluded to the young man's imminent lack of an engagement – that had been rather nicely handled, he thought – and then, as he put on his brown dustcoat and collected his bunch of locking-up keys, he found his eye caught by the folded paper once again. For a young lady who'd just had her jewels stolen, he thought, she didn't look too put out at all, and since there was now finally no one left hanging about to hear him, he felt free to offer her his pennyworth of advice out loud.

'Locks and keys, miss,' said Mr Gardiner, doing up his last three buttons in time to his phrasing. 'Locks . . . And . . . Keys. I think you'll find that's the motto of this particular story.'

As Mr Gardiner sets off on his nightly round, preparing once again to seal up his theatre in its own particular darkness and put it to bed with another week of sweat and laughs and deceptions all done, I think it's only fair to tell you that Reggie's statement about where he was thinking of heading the next day was a lie. *Misdirection* – you see, it really is that easy when you know how. It helps, of course, if your subject's attention is already halfway up the garden path with a young lady at the Savoy, as Mr Gardiner's had undoubtedly been at the time. Reggie's sum-total experience of *The River at Richmond* was limited to having once seen that phrase stretched across the bottom of an old London Transport poster, revealed when he'd been watching a young workman clearing a hoarding before slapping up an advertisement; he'd no more

59

actually been there than Mr Gardiner ever had. But he'd guessed correctly from the tone of their nightly goodbyes that a bracing walk along the Thames was exactly what an old stickler like Mr Gardiner would think was the proper way for a semi-unfortunate like himself to work off his surplus energies on a Sunday afternoon. It conformed to his views about what an otherwise nice young lad like Reggie *ought* to be getting up to in his spare time.

Funny, what people assume.

Reggie's real plan for his Sunday is something quite different. Just like he did last Sunday, and the Sunday before that – ever since he discovered the place, in fact – he is going to get the first bus that comes along that will take him up to Clapham, and then on Clapham High Street he's going to change onto a number 28, and then onto a number 3 to Dulwich. Getting off at the bombsite at the bottom of Gipsy Hill, he'll then take the steep walk up to the gates of the Dulwich and Sydenham Municipal Cemetery, only stopping twice to lean on the wooden handrail to the right of the path and catch his breath.

7

He stands still, listening to the bell of a nearby church tolling for the service. Then he listens to it stop. He's quite warm after his climb up the hill, but the day itself is cold – there's a weak March sun struggling to emerge through some clouds over his head, and it hasn't quite made it yet. He wraps his jacket across his chest. The graves over here on the far side of the cemetery by the railway are relatively recent, and Reggie stops occasionally, looks around, and then stoops to inspect one of the bunches of flowers laid on or by the still-white stones. Several times, he just stops and looks around anyway.

A small bunch of sugar-pink florist's roses catches his eye – it's the brightest thing here – and Reg kneels down to see if there's a label attached to the cellophane. Just as he does this a young woman in a headscarf surprises him by coming round the corner of the gravel path, and as Reggie hurriedly stands up and brushes off his knees she gives him a brave little smile. Her coat is dirty, Reggie notices with some embarrassment. The bunch of daffodils jammed into the top of her basket is wrapped in newspaper, and the expression on her face makes her look as though she needs to hurry to get back to the house whose garden they came from and get everybody's Sunday dinner on. Reggie returns her smile, keeping his teeth hidden, but the young woman doesn't stop.

Reggie watches her go, and then moves slowly on down his chosen row of stones. Three doors down (so to speak) from the grave with the bunch of roses, he comes to a halt.

Once again, he stops and looks around, apparently checking to see if anyone is watching him. He stares at the stone, and seems to be on the verge of saying something; he rests a hand on it. But that exchange of smiles with the young woman in the headscarf has evidently unsettled him, and he doesn't stay long. He limps on (how odd; his limp seems to be more pronounced this morning – perhaps it's the cold), and right at the end of the path he's chosen he arrives at what seems to be his second destination, a black-painted cast-iron bench almost hidden within a stand of overgrown holly. This seems to be more like it, and he relaxes a bit. From here, he can see all the way down the path should anyone approach, but no one can easily see him. A train goes past on its way round to Blackfriars and Farringdon, and as its sound dies away Reggie gets out a tin of tobacco and rolls himself a cigarette. He lights it, and then drags on it – like a schoolboy imitating somebody he's seen at the pictures, he cups it in his right hand as if protecting his fag from the still-chilly air. Then he looks at his watch. He exhales a wreath of smoke, and jams his other hand into his pocket; he leans back, and lifts his face to the appearing sun – the clouds have just parted properly for the first time. He even closes his eyes. With both his legs stretched out for once and his left hand thrust deep in his trouser pocket, he looks as though . . . as though, I suppose, he just wants to have a quiet moment alone with his thoughts. That's what benches in cemeteries are there for, after all.

Two cigarettes later, the sun gives up and goes in again, and Reggie shivers and checks his watch. Hearing footsteps on the path, he quickly tucks his legs away under the bench, hiding his boot, and busies himself with rolling a new cigarette. The footsteps belong to a young man in a dark jacket, but Reg doesn't look up as he passes. He hunches his shoulders, clearly willing whoever this young man is to walk on by.

Only when the coast is clear again does he uncurl his legs and light his finished fag.

A cemetery is a strange place to spend a Sunday morning, isn't it? – especially a morning when the displays of spring flowers are coming into bloom in all the parks of London, and you could easily have a taken a bus to one of them instead. A strange place to sit on a cast-iron bench with your Sunday-best tie on, smoking, looking for all the world as if you were waiting for some stranger to come and find you.

8

On his first day without work, Reggie spent the afternoon in the library, ploughing a solitary furrow through all the papers. He read (among other things) about how a florist in Kensington was preparing to fly eighteen boxes of white orchids in from the South of France *to meet the extravagance of the anticipated demand during the pre-Coronation Season*. I'd like to see that, he thought. On the Wednesday, he went back and went upstairs to the reference section, and looked up the entry headed 'Coronation' in his favourite encyclopedia – he'd been too young for the last one, after all, and wanted to get a better idea of what was actually going to happen on the day. On Thursday he did what he always did on Thursday, which was to check his mantelpiece money-tin. He reluctantly agreed with himself that he'd probably better not trek over to the Broadway that evening to treat himself to a ticket for the Rigolettos, and just went out for a good pavement-pounding walk instead. On Friday and Saturday he caught up with his darning, found a cake shop with a window display of special-occasion icing which he promised himself he'd return to after Mr Brookes had got their next booking, and had tinned fish for his dinner, twice. On the Sunday he walked to Clapham High Street to save the fare and only got the bus to his cemetery from there.

It was rather crowded that morning, because the sun was properly out now, and the woman with the daffodils reappeared and unsettled him further by speaking to him, so he didn't stay long, spending barely half an hour on his bench.

On the way home he treated himself to a saccharine-glazed bun from the Gipsy Hill Station buffet by way of compensation, but when he got back to his room he looked in his savings tin again and reminded himself that the second week of resting between bookings was never quite so much fun as the first, and that he needed to pull in his horns.

The next week passed slowly; the weather improved, but not much else. At six o'clock on the Saturday, there was a knock on his door.

He could hear Mr Brookes's voice buzzing out of the receiver on the hall table even before he picked it up. Apparently – Reg didn't get quite all of this, because Mr Brookes was in a pub, and having to shout – apparently something had turned up. The spot was third on the bill at the Brighton Grand, starting on Monday week – there'd been an accident – second-act only, and the management was hoping to string out the bill for three weeks, God help them. He'd have to find a new girl of course, and there was nothing much that could be done in that department on a Saturday night, but he'd keep Reg posted, and with any luck they'd be able to –

At this point, Mr Brookes was cut off by someone saying they needed to use the fucking telephone, if he didn't fucking mind. Reg explained to his landlady as best he could what the situation was – she'd stayed to listen – then had his tea, and then went to bed early. At ten o'clock, he was woken by another knock at his door – an angry one, this time.

Mr Brookes, still shouting, said that he'd struck lucky, and wanted to know if Reg could meet him at Victoria Station in time for the five nineteen train – yes, Reg, the five nineteen on *Monday* – because they'd be rehearsing in Brighton, on bloody stage, would you bloody believe? Then he rang off, laughing and shouting that something needed taking care of straight away, and that he'd explain everything else on the train.

He'd have to forget the cemetery tomorrow morning, was Reg's first thought – there'd be too much to do. Why did everything with Mr Brookes have to be so bloody last minute?

What with a rush-hour jam on the way to Victoria, a forgotten valise and a final limping dash to check that the skip and apparatus had been loaded safely together in the same luggage car, the phrase turned out to be literal for once. Reg barely had time to get a word in with Mr Brookes at the station, and it wasn't until just gone eighteen minutes past five – eighteen minutes past five on the evening of Monday the thirteenth of April, to be precise – that Reggie finally hurled himself, panting, into the crowded front compartment of the five nineteen to Brighton.

I don't know if you remember them, but the step up into those old-fashioned single-doored Southern Railway compartments was high, and there'd been a real tangle getting on; Reggie almost fell, and Mr Brookes was shouting something at someone behind them, and people were staring. Doors banged, whistles blew, and when the train jolted into life it lurched forward so violently that Reggie had to grab at his seat and concentrate for a moment on not swearing out loud. He was also trying not to stare too hard at the strikingly turned-out and well-built (if not exactly tidy or clean) young woman who'd managed to leave it even later than they had to squeeze herself onto the train. She trod on someone's foot, and caused several male eyebrows to rise as she reached up to stuff her coat and two bulging suitcases into the overhead luggage rack. In the opposite corner, Mr Brookes was smiling at the spectacle, barely even pretending to open his *Evening Standard*. Once she'd shoehorned herself into a seat, the woman opened a large and scuffed-looking red leather handbag, tossed back her roughly cut hair and proceeded to dig around in the bag for her compact.

'Oh dear, that was close,' she said, smiling at herself in the mirror — as if all that rushing about had been somebody else's fault — and checking her teeth for traces of her dark red lipstick. Then she snapped the compact shut, and extended a red-nailed hand across the space between them. The nail polish was chipped.

'You must be Reggie,' she said. 'I'm Pamela. Pamela *Rose*.'

The voice was friendly, and trowelled the sound of Soho over what could have once been Kingston upon Thames — or perhaps vice versa. She accented the second part of her name as if it was a clue to something, and as Reggie took her hand and more or less shook it — what else could he do? — he became aware that it was her perfume that was adding such a strong and suggestive grace note to the warm fug of the compartment. Talcum powder, he decided; that was it, talcum powder, with sugar around the edges — and a great big bunch of roses somewhere smack in the middle, to go with her name. He liked it, and smiled. She smiled right back, keeping hold of his hand. She was wearing a boldly fitted black-and-yellow tweed two-piece that had seen slightly better days, and a black roll-neck sweater; apart from the lipstick, her face was almost bare. A crowded charm bracelet jangled softly on her left wrist, and two ropes of pearls swung above her breasts. As the five nineteen lurched with a bump over its points onto the Brighton line and began to pick up speed, she tilted her head briefly to indicate the now occupied Mr Brookes, and winked. The train slid over the Thames.

'It's all right,' she said, in a conspiratorial stage whisper, and leaning forward slightly to make her point, 'I knew he wouldn't have told you.'

She leaned forward again, making her pearls swing.

'I'm the new girl,' she said.

Three

North Road

I

Everybody fancies something a bit different when they come
to the seaside, don't they? And according to that Monday's
Brighton Evening Argus and Gazette you would have had quite
a choice. There are thirty-seven adverts on the entertainents
page including all the variety houses and the roller rink as
well as the cinemas and theatres – so this may take some time.

First up, you could have tried *Chloe et Cherie* at the
Continental Cinema down on the seafront – not that I'm
suggesting for a moment you would have picked something
from that particular class of entertainment as your first choice,
or that you would have been fooled by the picture in the advert,
which I'm sure was more suggestive than the actual film itself
– or – moving down the column a bit – you could have sampled
Barbara Stanwyck in *All I Desire* at the Essoldo (highly recom-
mended), or Jean Simmons in *The Actress* at the seafront Odeon
(competent, but a bit dull). If you fancied something live by
way of a change, then I could have offered you the lovely Miss
Vanda Godsell in *Separate Rooms* out on the Palace Pier, *Relative
Values* with Gladys Cooper at the Theatre Royal if you felt like
being respectable, and the brand-new *Follies of 1953* in the
Pavilion Ballroom at the Aquarium if you didn't – the chorus
down at the Aquarium was mostly local in the spring, filling in
before the professionals took over for the beauty pageants and
Lido shows of the summer season, and had a reputation for
being rather more easily impressed at the stage door than the
out-of-town girls, if you get my drift. Of course, down at the

very bottom of the page, last but not least, 'for one week only' – as if it was ever for anything else – there was always the touring production of *Rose Marie* on ice up at the Sports Stadium, still doing the rounds after all these years – but why go for the old-fashioned, when you could have had the new? I'll leave the choice to you, obviously, but all in all you'd have to say that there was pretty much everything that the discerning spring visitor could reasonably require by way of diversion on offer that week – and all with prices starting at just one shilling for the back balcony at the Continental, should you have decided to give that disreputable old fleapit a go after all. And if – by any chance – none of that tickled your fancy, then you could of course have just saved your money and stayed in the lounge of your hotel. There you would have had the choice of listening to the pianist – if you were paying full whack at the Bedford or the Metropole – or, if you were staying somewhere a little more modest, to the BBC Concert Orchestra on the Home Service. Playing Delius, I shouldn't wonder. I can just picture you, sipping your gin-and-mix and taking a quiet look at the evening paper, skipping the one or two items about the troubles in Kenya like the rest of us and concentrating instead on the centre spread, the one outlining the plans for the Big Day itself, all the parades and fireworks and so on – the big day, when the beautiful Princess and her even prettier unmarried sister would be riding to the Abbey in those fabulous coaches of theirs, ready to give us the biggest and best-dressed pageant of loveliness of them all.

Or you could have just turned your back on all of that – on all that choice and chatter and well-upholstered romance – and decided to take a walk along the front as the sun went down. That was what Reggie did, when all the rush and fuss of arriving was finally over. Like him, you could have chosen to just go and lean on the rusting promenade railings for a bit and have a good quiet stare at the sea, letting that two-page centre-spread Coronation guide from yesterday's paper blot up the grease from your bag of cooling, vinegary chips. You could have let the lights of the town all come on behind you without even turning round to have a look, deciding that what you really needed was just to be on your own with your thoughts for a bit before walking all the way back along the front and hauling yourself up the five flights of stairs to your new bed. Just to think back over the last twenty-four hours and get them in some sort of order.

Most people don't notice it, but the steady slope of Queen's Road as it descends from Brighton station to the promenade is quite pronounced – and especially if you've got a heavy case to carry. In the last-minute rush, the brown-paper parcel containing a three-week supply of flash powder had somehow ended up in Reggie's, and as he'd lurched towards the front it was clipping his knee at every second stride. When he reached the Clock Tower a cold breeze blowing up the street slapped his face as if it had been instructed to greet this latest visitor personally, inviting him to look up and get his first proper sight of the sea, but he ignored it. Mr Brookes had booked them into a cheap hotel by the station for their first night in town, and they'd nearly got stuck there – it had taken him until nearly twelve o'clock on the Tuesday to find all three of them proper digs on the phone, and because they hadn't booked ahead, when he did, they were all over the shop. Mr Brookes himself was right out in Hove – the posh bit – Reg down along the seafront and Miss Rose somewhere up back behind the station with a Mrs Brennan or Brown or something. It fell to Reg of course to help her with her bags, and although the room when they finally got there was all right, with a proper window and even its own sink, the place itself was rather further than they'd been told, which meant that by the time Reggie had set off back into the town to pick up his own suitcase and head off down to the seafront to find his digs it was already well past one – and Mr Brookes had said he wanted them both back at the Grand at three o'clock sharp to sign in and walk the stage. Pamela had looked surprised that they were starting work straight away, which showed just how little she knew what was in store for her, Reg reckoned.

Come on, look on the flippin' bright side, he thought, lugging his bag round the corner of the Queen's Hotel. *She certainly looks like she knows how to look after herself. And let's face it*, he told himself, shrugging off whatever point the seafront air was still trying to make as it had another go at his face, *she'll bloody have to; six days from now she's due to go missing fourteen times a week.* He paused, sniffing the burnt-sugar smell of candyfloss coming out through the turnstiles of the Palace Pier. The breakfast at the hotel had been shocking, and he hadn't eaten since. Getting his breath back, he took the opportunity to look across the road and stare at the customers ensconced behind the salt-fogged windows of the Royal Albion's dining room.

'Murray's Cabaret, Beak Street,' he said, out loud this time, giving his pockets a quick rummage for anything edible he might have forgotten. 'Sounds a proper enough place to have worked. Shame she's never done any actual box work before, though.'

A promenader buttoned up against the breeze stared at him, obviously wondering what he was talking about. He ignored the man, picked his case up again, swung it into his other hand, and wondered how much further his digs were. All Mr Brookes had given him by way of directions was a bit of thin blue paper with the words *Seaview*, *26* and *Fitzroy* scrawled across it. Just keep going along the seafront until you see the sign, the man at the hotel had said, it's not that far.

Fitzroy Place turned out to be a good twenty minutes away. It was a gloomy street, set back off the seafront at the end of narrow cul-de-sac; the black paint on the panelled front door of number 26 was thick and fissured, and Reg had to bang twice to get a response. However once he was up the front steps and inside the hallway looked all right – it wasn't *too* dark, with a skylight up at the top – and he was pleased to see that the stairs had kept their grand mahogany handrail. Stairs were a challenge for Reggie when there was a suitcase involved, and his nicotine-stained landlady had taken one look at his built-up boot and asked him sharply if he realised the vacancy was on the top floor. Fortunately, Reggie had met plenty of landladies like this one before; his best tooth-concealing grin was quickly produced, and he assured her that he'd manage.

'Oh, you'd be surprised, Mrs Steed,' he said, quick as a knife, having read her name on the broken bell. 'Managing's my middle name. Has to be, in my line of work.'

She looked him up and down, and apparently made up her mind he'd do. She was used to *theatricals*, she said, leading him up the stairs.

'Live and let live, I always say.'

Reggie smiled, hauling himself up the next step.

'Mind you, no overnight guests. Not even cousins. No cats, no dogs, no birds. No use of the front door in either direction after midnight . . .'

She paused and wheezed, clutching the banister.

'And no fried food in the rooms . . .'

The room turned out to be right up under the roof. The lino was bare; there was a bed, a chair, a mean-looking wardrobe and a small mirrored washstand on a chest of drawers. But it looked pretty much as clean as Mrs Steed claimed it was, and had a window, and that was quite good enough for Reggie. Baths were on Fridays, she said, and all damages were to be settled immediately; Reg assured her he thought he would be comfortable, pocketed his key and promised that he would sign her book on his way back down. Apart from the wallpaper, which was all roses, and hideous, there was nothing that he could see that was going to be too much of a problem, not for the few short weeks that he was going to be staying here at any rate. The air in the room felt stale, so the first thing he did was to try the window – the sash felt as if it had been painted shut, but Reggie applied his grip, and was soon rewarded with the loud crack of something giving way.

There it was again – that cold sea air, pushing its way into the room and demanding to talk to him, telling his London skin that he definitely wasn't playing Wimbledon Broadway any more, not this week.

Reg leaned out, surprising a gull on a neighbouring roof, and almost shouted himself. The end of the grey-stuccoed street framed a sudden, shining, vertical slice of the English Channel, bright and hard under the April sun. He'd had no idea . . . He held on to the half-rotted window frame and cantilevered himself right out, far enough out for the breeze to properly catch at his hair as he craned his neck. *So Seaview it is after all, Mrs Steed*, he thought – *so long as you don't mind getting a grip and craning your neck*. He filled his lungs, hauled himself in, and slid the window half closed, leaving the curtains to stir. Looking around, he decided that the room would do very nicely, five flights of stairs or not. At least there'd be no one walking over his bloody head – and there was a street lamp across the way, and the window ledge was wide enough to keep a bottle of milk on. He bounced a bit on the bed, and stared at some length at the wallpaper with its slow-moving riot of grey roses on a dull red background. They definitely weren't going to help with getting up in the mornings, but he was sure he'd get used to them.

He kicked his case under the bed, and wondered why that smell of the sea was still bothering him.

Twenty past two. Blimey, time to head off for work already.

The Brighton Grand is gone now. The doors finally closed for business in 1955, and the building memorably burnt to the ground in 1961, but on the afternoon that Mr Brookes and Reggie and their new girl first arrived its facade was still making a reasonably convincing job of promising the pedestrians who passed it on their way up North Road a good night out. Plastered Italianate pillars divided up the windows of the first floor, a couple of gesturing ladies still flanked the pediment at the top, and either side of the front doors – grand affairs with ideas well above their station, all bevelled glass and big bright handles – two framed bills proudly listed the current show's attractions in scarlet and blue lettering. These changed every two or three weeks – weekly in the winter – and this week, underneath headliners Lauri Lupino Lane and Madame Valentine's 'Nudes de Montmartre', they announced by means of a pasted-on slip that third on the bill was one Miss Burstone, the Talented Vocaliste. This, Reggie guessed, was the act that had been hurried on to replace whoever had been injured, and who they'd be replacing come Monday. He couldn't see the name of anyone he'd ever shared a stage with before – and certainly no Rigolettos – and running his eye down the rest of the names he couldn't help but smile. The management – Mr J. Clements, Sole Prop – definitely wasn't making its money by underestimating anybody's taste. The Three Karloffs; 'Ramena' and her Exotic Dance; Suzanne De Wynter, Aerialiste Extraordinaire; Paquita and Pascale; George Truzzi; The Lovely LORRAINE; Mr Paul Clifford and his Orchestra – in other words, a few laughs, a couple of specialities, a touch of skirt and quite a bit of skin towards the top of the bill. It looked as though The Missing Lady should be right at home, so long as they could get her up and running in time.

They didn't go in through those glittering front doors, of course – they carried on up North Road and ducked off to their left, going in the back way.

Round the back, every expense had been spared. The stage door itself was concealed at the end of a plain brick alleyway that led down the side of the building, and once inside, the bareness continued. The stage-door keeper here was called Mr English, and his window and pencil-on-a-string and board of keys all looked rather depressingly familiar. But he looked like he might be a nice old bird underneath, Reg thought, easier to thaw out than Mr Gardiner, and once Mr English had reached their keys down from his board and explained rather prissily who was going to be put where he offered to lead them down the sloping, concrete-floored corridor – its floor slightly ridged so that the pantomime ponies wouldn't slip as they made their way from the street to the stage – and into the darkened wings. Then it was down three steps and round to the back of the metal pass door that led out into the auditorium.

They're almost all gone now, these buildings, but if you're trying to imagine what one of them would have been like to live and work in, then I suggest you start with the smell. It never quite goes away, in a theatre: breath, sweat, chocolate, clothing – and cigarettes, lots of them, in those days. The distinctive top note of a coloured gel which must have caught last night in a lantern frame; the scorched red silk of the lampshades on the front of the dress circle; damp chiffon and powder, from 'Les Nudes de Montmartre'. The slight acidity of accumulated laughter – if laughter has a smell – something just rancid enough to fog the gilding and darken the engraved Stalls Bar mirrors, all of it mixed and thickened by a night

spent locked in the dark and now just lingering in the drapes
and the upholstery.

Here we go again, thought Reg, sniffing. *Home from bloody
home.*

'Right,' said Mr Brookes, rubbing and twisting his hands
together. 'Shall we?'

Leaving Reggie and Pamela together in the middle of the
stalls, he slipped through a door leading out into the foyer.
Reggie was familiar with this part of the get-in routine, and
knew all he had to do was sit and watch and wait, but Pamela
clearly wasn't; as Mr Brookes headed off into the dark to find
his way upstairs, she looked around as if she wasn't quite sure
why she'd been brought along. A stained-glass panelled door
leading to the bar at the back of the stalls had been left propped
open, and a single shaft of daylight was raking across the scal-
loped backs of the seats in front of them, barely penetrating
the toothless mouth of the stage.

'Not spending much on the paintwork, are they?' she said
eventually, eyeing the quartet of bare-breasted ladies who
supported the boxes on either side of the proscenium. One
breast was fissured. 'Still, I expect it looks better with all the
lights on. Funny old places these, aren't they?'

Reggie had never really thought of it like that exactly, but
he could see she had a point. In this lighting, the Grand wasn't
looking very grand at all. The upholstery on the back of the
seat in front of him was greasy, and the swags of laurel leaves
that draped the proscenium looked more black than gilt. The
lingering smell of last night's house only underlined the
emptiness, and up above the rather-too-small chandelier that
was supposed to top the whole thing off you could barely see
a smokily painted midnight sky with a spattering of gold stars.
The clouds were cracked and starting to peel. Reg squinted

and tipped his head back. He could just about make out a constellation of stars that he didn't recognise down in the left-hand corner, seven of them, all in one gilt cluster, barely catching the light. What were they?

'I've played in worse,' he said, still squinting. 'Better, obviously, sometimes, but definitely worse as well.'

He'd have to look them up in an encyclopedia – not that there was much likelihood of there being time to get to a library this week. Why *did* Mr Brookes always insist on this get-in routine of using the girl to check his sightlines right up to the back of the gallery, when they could easily have had an hour off for lunch and a roam around instead? After all, it wasn't as if a house like this was ever going to sell much up beyond the second circle, was it? – not at this time of year.

'Reggie!'

He twisted round and up to see where Mr Brookes was calling from, but couldn't find a figure to go with the voice up there in the darkness. He shouted back anyway.

'Yes Mr Brookes?' It seemed right to be formal, somehow, with the new girl here.

The voice came echoing down again over the serried ranks of empty seats, dark and direct and no-nonsense. Mr Brookes knew that all this place needed to come alive was a few paying customers.

'Show Pam back through the pass door and get her to walk the reveal, would you, Reg?'

'Yes, boss.'

Pam, he thought, leading the way through the darkness. *Not Pamela, not Miss Rose: Pam. Doesn't waste any bloody time, does he?*

'What does he mean?' Pam was keeping her voice down as she picked her way behind Reggie along the row of seats – obviously she didn't want her new employer to hear her. 'Walk his what? Bloody hell that's heavy –'

The pass door at the Grand was a serious affair, an eight-foot-high contraption of sliding metal. Though the stage side of it was blank and black, the auditorium side was scarlet, and had NO ADMISSION TO THE PUBLIC lettered across it in six-inch-high capitals. Clearly whoever had painted them had very pronounced opinions about the dividing line between the two worlds it served to keep separate. Reggie helped Pam to hold the door open, and she squeezed herself through.

'Straight on from stage left,' he said, keeping his voice down too, 'and then hold centre two feet upstage of the footlights. He just likes to get an idea of what you're going to look like before he starts working. Helps him feel in control. Just up those steps and then left and you're on.'

Pamela peered ahead to see where Reggie was indicating.

'Does it now? Well who am I to get in the way of anybody's feelings? Right . . .'

Reggie let the iron barrier slide slowly closed behind her (it sighed, as if it was sorry to see her go; Persephone, returning to Hades), shuttering off her swinging backside as she picked her way up the three concrete steps to stage level. It would be just like Mr Brookes to bring a girl all the way down here to the seaside and then send her packing if she wasn't up to scratch, he knew that. But time was short, and with that figure, he thought she stood more than a fair chance.

'Is this it?'

She was shading her eyes as if it wasn't darkness she was looking up into but a too-bright light. Her other hand was reversed on her hip, knuckles resting lightly on the bone, fingers curled, elbow and shoulder perfectly relaxed. *Well*, thought Reg, *that'll show him.*

'Mr Brookes? You there?'

'Left a bit.' The voice echoed down from somewhere right up under the painted stars. 'Now right.'

'Sounds like the rifle range at the fair,' she laughed, obeying his instructions with a lazy cha-cha first one way and then the other. 'Not going to bloody shoot me, are you?'

'Not unless I have to. Right, that's bang centre. Think you can remember that?'

'Oh, I think so. I just need to line myself up with that door to the bar.'

She pointed to the back of the stalls. The half-light from the open door hid all of her nerves, and softened the lines of her hair and the black and white of her elegantly extended forearm. The gold charms on her wrist rearranged them-selves, and fell silent; one pointing finger sketched in the thought that somewhere out there beyond the bar there must be a street, and people, and a normal working life. You could see that it was true what she'd said on the train about work-ing in a floor show, thought Reggie. She hit every pose just right.

'But then, it won't be the first time I've done that of an evening.'

Her laugh rang out through her voice, and Reggie couldn't help but smile back at her from out in the darkened auditor-ium. He remembered what Mr Brookes had shouted down the phone at him over the noise of that pub, and decided that yes, they had struck lucky. Rehearsals with this one might even be fun.

The walking done to his satisfaction, Mr Brookes told them he'd see them bright and early tomorrow morning. He then headed off to find Mr Clements's office and introduce himself and clarify the arrangements for them rehearsing on the stage.

'Nine thirty, Reg, and everything ready by then please,' he shouted, as he disappeared back up into the darkness.

It was dark now; he could barely see the sea.

Replaying that scene with Pam onstage in his head, Reg smiled again. She was a bit smashing, he decided – apart from that one moment when they'd been getting off the train and he'd stumbled as he smelt the air for the first time, she hadn't looked or stared at his boot once, not in the whole two days they'd now known each other.

It was funny about that air. It had made him shiver when he'd first realised why the smell and taste of it had been bothering him, but now that he'd had time for a walk and a think and a bite to eat he'd calmed down a bit. After all, that was all years ago – lying in a metal cot and hearing the stones outside the window and smelling the salt in the air.

Watching the moon slice the dormitory wall into a black world and a silver one.

He leaned against the railing, and peered into the dark. Somewhere out there, beyond one of those two blinking, misdirecting piers, the stones must all still be there, piled up under the windows, waiting for his staggering feet. *Seaford 12½ Miles*, the sign on the seafront had read – hadn't that been the nearest town? But he never had been back, and he had no intention of even thinking about it now, whether the stones were five miles away from where he was standing or fifty – not even if there was a bus that went straight there along the coast. He was sure of that.

A courting couple passed behind him on the prom. The girl was laughing softly, and the boy looked ridiculously handsome in his open-necked shirt. Some music drifted towards them from somewhere, and for the first time Reggie turned round and looked at all the lights of his new town.

He scrunched up what was left of his chips in their newspaper, and threw them out on the beach for the shadowy, gathering gulls.

As it happens, Reg's first impressions of the new girl were mostly right. She very much *could* take care of herself.

In 1953, women of all classes were expected to dress, walk and talk as if they needed looking after, and although Pam could manage a reasonable approximation of that approach to life if the professional situation required it, it wasn't her mode of choice. The way she dressed, combined with that defiantly almost-bare face (just a lick of pale powder, a slash of dark red lipstick and invariably a cigarette), meant that few people were surprised when she came straight out and told them the kinds of thing that she mostly did for a living. She laughed often, and well – and not to impress. It was one of her trademark gestures, the ones her friends knew her by; shaking out her charm bracelet, rooting in that big red bag to see where her fags had got to this time and laughing, throwing back her head and tossing her unkempt hair out of her eyes.

That was exactly what she'd done when Mr Brookes had offered to buy her that second drink in the Golden Lion. Of course, she'd realised that he wasn't being entirely straightforward with her, and had already guessed that this act he was trying to sell her a job in would involve more than just parading a couple of frocks. However, as she now told herself as she got dressed for work, *How hard can being made to disappear be?* She'd needed a break, and that was that. Keeping things going with bits and pieces at the London Camera Club and whatever else the modelling agency could get her was all very well, but six regular guineas a week would make a very welcome change. Almost a holiday, in fact. She was going to take the money, get some air, enjoy the fact that nobody down here knew who she was and see what happened.

There'd been a lovely new shot of Princess Margaret out on the town in yesterday's paper, and as soon as she'd seen it she'd known it was just the right thing for sticking up on her dressing-room mirror – 'Margaret *Rose* Windsor', it said underneath, and the fact that they shared a name always made her feel better. Men were always looking up at Margaret in her pictures, never she up at them, and she liked that – it looked as though she had all the time and choice in the world. All the time in the world . . .

She clasped on her pearls and laughed at herself. Who was she trying to bloody kid? She was lucky if she got a bunch of lilacs from Berwick Street Market these days. She checked in her bag for change, and decided that she'd probably better pop back to that kiosk in the station for her fags before work – she'd find a more convenient place later, but at least she knew where that was.

She was lovely all over, was Pamela, but I'd say that the best thing about her was that smile of hers – the one she wore as casually and as well as that ever-present *eau de parfum*. It had a lovely gentle way of suggesting that it was probably the people around her who were the problem in life, not her, and it went with her everywhere. Even in the infamous contact sheets of her that were being passed around at the time – the one that showed her sprawled across a sunny bed in Berwick Street with just a cigarette for company, for instance, the one that the photographer who shot it swore he'd pass on to the soon-to-be-famous painter he knew from the French Pub, but somehow never quite did – her smile accompanied her in every single frame. It got wiped off occasionally, of course, but it always came back.

3

Mr Brookes had started very slowly. Reggie had come in early as instructed, and had got everything set up and ready to go on the half-lit stage – the costumes set out neatly on some chairs, the apparatus ready under its ghostly silver drape, the hand props all to hand as required. Then, working very methodically, and only going into as much detail as he thought wouldn't frighten her off, her new employer had talked Pam through the whole act, showing her the frocks, the shoes and the new brunette wig he'd borrowed for her first, and then the ropes, which he briefly uncoiled and asked her to test so she could feel how soft and manageable they were. Then he'd uncovered the apparatus and opened it up so that she could climb up through it and get acquainted with all its doors and handles. He showed her the bolt and switch inside the trap which Reggie had to operate, and the battery for the smoke trigger down in its corner, and stressed the importance of not knocking into or disabling any of them; he demonstrated the trap, and the all-important concealed opening down at the front that she'd be sliding through. Now, however, the preliminaries were over. He'd deliberately kept a blanket over the steps, and when he pulled it off to reveal them he did so quickly, to get it over with. Pam stared, then crouched down and inspected their insides, feeling for the two metal struts that would eventually stop her from falling out as she was wheeled away inside them by the stagehands.

'Bloody hell. What are you going to do to me to get me tidied away into that then? Chop me up?' she said. 'All right . . . don't bloody answer me, either of you.'

They didn't. Pam unclasped her pearls, and passed them to Reggie.

'Just show me. And gently.'

'Certainly,' said Mr Brookes. 'Let's start with the breathing, shall we?'

In a life class or photography session – both of whose demands Pamela knew all about – the trick is to keep breathing no matter how demanding the pose. For box work, the breath has to be punched out and *held out*; being empty is the only way a girl can hope to get her knees pinned sufficiently high up onto her chest or her chin pushed far enough down on her sternum, at least for the kind of conceal Pam had to achieve.

Mr Brookes started by stepping right in close behind her. He reached round as if he was demonstrating one of those manoeuvres they used to have pictured on charts in doctors' waiting rooms, and, without explaining what he was doing, pressed his fingers across her lower ribs. He told her to breathe out, and pushed her ribs in hard towards her spine as she did it; then he told her she had to hold her breath out until he got to the end of a slow count of six. When she'd got the hang of that, he stepped even closer in behind her to get a better purchase, and then he counted, and pushed, and counted, and pushed, raising the count for which she had to hold herself empty by one beat every time. In between the numbers he kept up a steady drip of information, explaining that as she pulled herself up on the hand grips in the ceiling for Reg to open the trap, and again before she dropped down through it to jackknife herself in under the steps, she would have to blast

87

every ounce of breath out of herself, keeping herself hollow even when her lungs started screaming.

Reggie watched the proceeding closely, sitting on a chair and waiting to be called. Her pearls had felt slightly warm when he'd taken them, and he remembered reading somewhere that that meant they were real. He wasn't surprised – you could see why people would want to buy this one proper presents. The fact that Mr Brookes had his chest pressed into her back seemed not to be bothering her in the slightest, which was a good sign, and only when the count for which she had to hold her breath out reached seventeen did she shift her position at all, lifting her hands up over her head and lacing her fingers through her hair to achieve the extra push she needed to get everything out. She was doing well, he reckoned.

Once Mr Brookes had got Pamela as far as being able to hold herself empty for a slow count of twenty-five, he removed his hands, and asked her to climb up into the cabinet.

'I think we'll mime the ripping off of your skirt for today,' he said, passing his jacket to Reggie, and rolling up his sleeves. 'Eventually of course you'll be doing the drop in just your stockings, but the waistband on those slacks looks perfectly practical for rehearsal purposes to me. Better use the actual cap and shoes, though – you might as well get used to passing them out to our Reg through the back. And we'll keep the apparatus doors open both at the back and the front for today, so that no one has to be working entirely in the dark.' He paused here, and smiled. 'Not at this early stage in the proceedings, anyway.'

Pamela allowed herself half a smile in response, and looked up over her head to locate the two looped hand grips hidden in the cabinet ceiling. Reggie positioned himself at the back and got ready to take her cap and shoes and imaginary skirt as she shed them.

'All right then,' said Mr Brookes. 'On my count. Nice and deeply in to start with. And remember –'

The opposing zinc panels multiplied Pam into an infinity of hoisted figures, black and white on silver. She tried to avoid her own face, but couldn't.

'Yes?'

'Remember that as soon as the doors click shut the rope round your wrists goes between your teeth, so that your hands are then free to deal with your ankles and shoes. So you might as well do this with your mouth full. Reg –'

'Christ. Don't want bloody much, do you?'

It took nearly five hours.

First she had to get the hang of lifting herself up on the straps right – that alone took twenty minutes – then the drop through the open trap, then the drop and curl and slide into the steps, then the whole thing together as one uninterrupted, breathless sequence. Then, of course, she had to stay jammed into the steps while Mr Brookes counted out the full length of time it would take the stagehands to trundle her safely into the wings. The first time she made it all the way through, Reggie handed out a woman white-faced with shock and effort, her heaving shoulders sheened with sweat – Pam had stripped off her black sweater barely an hour into proceedings, and was working in just her bra and slacks. She looked as though she'd been dug up.

'Thanks,' she said, tersely, taking Reggie's proffered hand to steady herself after she'd uncurled. 'Jesus. Well . . . so that's what it feels like when you go all the way.'

She was still fighting to get her breath back. Reggie stared at the scrapes and bruises that were already writing the apparatus's angry signature across her back and forearms; he'd been expecting them, but still, they were going to need taking care of later. There'd be others on her shins as well, where she braced her knees against the metal strut.

'I hope the music's nice and loud.'

Mr Brookes was only half looking at her, quietly looping and relooping a rope. It was Reggie who spoke up, filling in for Mr Brookes's silence.

'Why's that then?'

'Because,' she said, scraping her falling hair back out of her face again, and sucking in her breath, 'I do hate it when people can hear me scream while I'm working. And now . . .'

She blew what breath she'd managed to drag back into her lungs right out through her mouth, like a swimmer climbing back up onto the starting block. Turning to Mr Brookes, she somehow managed to both smile and grit her teeth at the same time.

'Now I expect you'd like to see me do that all over again, wouldn't you? As the lance corporal said to the bishop.'

'I most certainly would . . .' Mr Brookes's hands paused, and he let his mouth curl around the words as if he was tasting them. 'I would love to see you do that again. *Several* times.'

Whatever the thought was that was passing across his face, it went as soon as it had come; the hands went back to busying themselves with the ropes, and his working smile slid itself back into place as if the proverbial butter wouldn't melt. The transformation was so quick that Pam wasn't even sure if she'd seen the expression in his eyes and mouth darken or not – it was like that business he'd described with the scarf, making people think that they'd seen something, then straight away telling them they couldn't possibly have.

'But we'll cross that bridge in the morning, if you don't mind.' The rope resolved into a coil, and was tossed across the stage. 'The crew will be arriving for the matinee soon, and I'm rather a stickler for not being observed on the job, if you see what I mean. Now, Reg, do you think you might rustle us up a cup of tea from somewhere?'

They stopped a full hour before the crew and band started arriving for work every day for the rest of that week – Mr Brookes was indeed a stickler for ensuring that no one ever got to see the mechanics of his act. However, that still left seven hours' work with the apparatus every day. By the time Pam and Reg moved upstairs that Saturday lunchtime to work on her costumes in a spare dressing room Pam's fore-arms and shins were a map of bruises, and she'd used up nearly a quarter of a bottle of her *eau de parfum* to keep herself fresh while they worked. At the end of each session Reggie would boil up some tea on the gas ring in the laundry room, and she'd try to slap the blood back into her arms and legs while she was waiting. She could feel precisely where those two metal struts had pressed themselves into her skin, and for some reason it made her feel as if she'd been mauled by exactly the kind of man she'd taken this job to get away from, one of those Dean Street drunks who wouldn't take fuck off for an answer – and to be honest, even after four days of practice, she still wasn't at all sure if she was going to be able to do this. She hadn't said anything, but the dark drop down from the handles into the bottom of the cabinet made her stomach turn over every time; ridiculously, it always made her think of a drop into dark water, and the floor always seemed to hit her feet too late, making her terrified that it wouldn't be there at all. Keeping the ropes clenched between her ankles always made her feel as if she was going to totter over on her heels at any minute, and right in front of him – and these last couple of days, when they'd been running things, and he'd insisted on still talking her through it all the time, describing exactly what her drawn-up knees and stretched-out spine were meant to be doing, there was sometimes something about the sound of his voice that made her want to kick her legs, steps or no steps. She'd come here to get away from men telling her what position to take up next, thank you very fucking much . . .

The boy was good, though. Never dropped a stitch, never hurried her, never made her feel like she was in the wrong place. And he was doing a very professional job on the alterations to her outfits. Didn't talk much, but never mind.

When she woke up on the Sunday morning and checked herself in Mrs Brennan's grimy bathroom mirror, Pam saw that the bruises on her forearms had thickened. It looked as if someone had tried to take a stick to her face and she'd flung up her arms to protect herself.

Wrapping her grubby baby-pink dressing gown back around herself, she went back upstairs to her bedroom and dragged the bigger of her two suitcases down from the top of the wardrobe. Then she dug around till she found a pair of balled-up white evening gloves; sitting down on the edge of her bed, she pulled them on and tried out a few poses, pulling her dressing gown down around her shoulders to mimic the low neckline of the ball gown. It would be two more things to get on in the change, but God knows she'd got dressed in a hurry enough times in her life. Besides, he hadn't called them in for this extra Sunday room-above-a-pub rehearsal until half ten this morning, so she still had time for a bit of practice.

She slid the gloves off, balled them up again, and lay back on the bed. One last day of rehearsal today, then a run-through with a pianist tomorrow afternoon, onstage; she was almost there. She must remember to thank Reg for fixing the tear in that underskirt after she'd ripped it again in her change. And to find somewhere that sold her *eau de parfum* tomorrow. And to eat.

What was it that Brookes had said to her yesterday? *Don't make the mistake of trying to think. It's your body that has to do the work, not your head.*

She closed her eyes. Christ, she'd be glad when tomorrow night was over.

4

When it came to it, no one would have ever known it was her first time – if you know what I mean. The second comic had got the house nicely warmed up after the interval; the Karloffs went down very well with their slow-motion acrobatics, Lorraine and her mirror proved as effective as that sort of speciality always is if the presentation is first class, and Madame Valentine's girls got a very respectable round from the stalls at the end of their first number. All of this meant that Mr Brookes had plenty of atmosphere to walk on into, which always gave him a spring in his step. He was groomed as impeccably as ever of course – not a sign of nerves – and brought off the first visible vanish with the gloves especially neatly, getting the house's interest straight away. Mr Clifford kept everything good and lively in the pit, and the cymbals and drums and the first wolf whistle were all timed right on the nose.

Pam's French Maid was a bit hesitant on her entrance, but that more or less went with the character – and she looked terrific. The first rope went on fine, and Mr Brookes was pleased; no big laughs so far, but no discernible dip in interest either. Then, when he lifted Pam up onto the chair for the rope round her ankles, things started to pick up. Reggie's refitting of her black satin skirt had made it tight in all the right places, and as he looped and twisted the rope Mr Brookes could feel a definite sharpening of attention out front. Then came the lift, the carry, and the three high-heeled backwards hops up the stairs. It really isn't a move for an amateur, and especially not for one carrying that extra bit of flesh around the top and hips – however, good girl; not only did Pam manage it keeping perfect time with the band, but she hit her pose on the top step with real aplomb, eyes stretched wide and *Maiden in Distress* written all over her face. Only Mr Brookes could see the beads of sweat on her neck. She shuffled inside, and waited.

This was it, then.

Brookes had taken the precautionary measure of asking Mr Clifford not to hit the tempo too hard when the band cut into their key change, and when it came to the cue he closed the cabinet doors a tad more more gently than he would have done on its previous incumbent. He did it, you might say, *politely*. Pamela stayed as calm as she had always known she would have to, and when the darkness snapped shut around her, wasted no time. Using the muffled cover of the music to keep up a steady continuo of obscenities under her breath, she slipped the ropes, ripped off her skirt, passed her shoes and skirt and cap behind her to Reggie, hoisted her knees, punched her breath out, closed her eyes, counted to two for Reg to open the trap – and dropped.

The moment before she landed, the old feelings rushed up to meet her stomach; that there wouldn't be a floor, that she was going to drop for ever, and that there'd be dark water waiting for her instead of metal.

It was a long moment – but then the cabinet bottom smacked against her stockinged feet and her body barged all thought out of the way; working almost by themselves, her hands pushed open the hinged panel and found the two metal struts under the treads. An unidentified roaring in her head was threatening to drown out the vital guiding thread of the music now, but she made it. When the steps started moving, she almost threw up – the sudden lurch took her completely by surprise. But she

95

braced herself, hard, and next thing she knew a young stage-hand who she wasn't actually sure she'd ever met before was offering her a strong and very nicely turned arm by way of a lift up and out, and suddenly she was dashing down the stage-left wing trying to find her quick-change mirror, ripping open her blouse as she went and trying not to giggle as she suddenly and idiotically remembered another occasion entirely when she'd done that with her blouse and a mirror and a nice young man she didn't really know. She wished she could slap herself. The music seemed oddly slow and distant, and she seemed to be dressing someone else. She found herself muttering apologies as she stepped into the gown, clawed at the zipper, pulled her wig straight (was that right?) pulled on the gloves, swallowed, stamped her left foot into its shoe, grabbed the fur, grabbed the bottle, lifted the glass – and realised as she looked at the overdressed stranger in the pier glass that she felt completely, bizarrely and unnaturally calm. So calm that she hadn't even noticed that the only sound now ringing in her ears definitely *was* the sound of her own pumping blood, because the world around her had gone suddenly quiet.

The music had stopped.

The stranger in the cloudy mirror widened her eyes, apparently as surprised as she was that this point in the evening had arrived already.

She turned her head, and saw Mr Brookes's naked right hand dispersing a wreath of pink-and-orange smoke. One fingertip abraded another, and she didn't have time to think.

The lights slapped her as firmly across the face as the wind off the sea had slapped at Reggie; however, unlike Reg, Pam smiled. Then, as she felt the weight of the fitted maroon satin swinging from her hips, she realised that the clatter of applause she could hear was for her, and three paces onto the stage an exhilaration as strong as two double Scotches coursed across her exposed skin, making her face burn under her make-up and almost knocking her off her shoes. She resisted her natural impulse, which was to toss back her head and laugh, and leaned into her stride instead, lifting the *coupe* of ginger ale as she went, determined not to fuck up at the last minute. As he took the shaking glass from her outstretched hand, Mr Brookes's eyes clipped hers with a blaze of warning, telegraphing an exactly judged mix of encouragement and threat. She got the message, sobered up, turned front, shared a suitably decorous variety of smiles with the ladies and gentlemen in the stalls and circle while Mr Brookes did his stuff with the gloves and cane and hat and ropes, then took his proffered hand and brought off her last four moves like a real pro – dip, change places, dip and upstage turn; gloves smooth, rubies bright, hair shining, fox clutched, chin lifted and lips softly gleaming throughout – everything, in fact, as it should be, from that well-turned ankle to those perfectly moulded collarbones. Miss Pamela *Rose*, would you mind, out on the town for the evening with her gentleman. Bloody marvellous. I thank you!

The applause continued after the tabs had hit the deck, but Pam couldn't hear it. She could only hear the sound of her own unsuccessfully stifled laughter as the relief hit her like a train. She gasped.

'Thank you – I – God – I –'

'Not bad for a first show,' said Mr Brookes, plucking a clean handkerchief from its black wool-and-mohair lair and busily wiping his hands. He lifted his empty champagne glass to Pamela with a small nod of appreciation, which wasn't something Reg had ever seen him do before, not with any of the girls.

'God, it happens fast once it starts –'

She tried turning upstage to thank Reggie, but that was all she had time for; the stagehands were already folding up the cabinet and wheeling it away, the drapes that hid the Montmartre backdrop were flying, the lights were changing to their allotted French twilight and the Maureen O'Hara lookalike who led Madame Valentine's thirteen Parisian love-lies was mouthing a not-quite-genteel *Would you mind, dear?* at Pam and pushing her out of the way as the girls found their marks for their second spot in a flurry of talc and damped-down drapery and not a lot else. Suddenly Pamela stumbled; Mr Brookes caught her and guided her through the melee to the wings, one hand at her elbow, the other in the small of her back. Reg's eyes flicked between the two hands. He'd been worried about getting that dress to fit, especially around her top half, but although he said it himself his hard work with the pressing iron had paid off, and she and Mr Brookes made a fine pair. The curtain rose, the syrupy rendition of Rina Ketty's 'J'Attendrai' headed for its first chorus out in the pit, and the lights spilling into the wings caught at Pam's bright, wide eyes.

'Ah, Reg,' said Mr Brookes, releasing her and wiping his hands again. 'A little easier on the flash powder for the second show if you don't mind – any more smoke, and I'd have been buggered on the set-up for the reveal.' Then he shot his cuffs, and headed into the darkness as if he had a taxi to hail.

'Blimey, don't get much out of that one, do you?' panted Pam as she stared after his back, her breasts still rising and fall-ing as the music swelled.

'Trust me,' said Reg, grinning, and forgetting to hide his teeth, 'you do if you get it bloody wrong.'

Of course, exhilaration doesn't last – and once it goes, the pain seeps in to take its place. Reg knew that, and after the second show he limped his way upstairs to make sure his new colleague was all right. He'd left it a good twenty minutes, but found her still staring at herself in her mirror, the ball gown ballooning up around her in a froth of underskirts. That newspaper clipping from last week was still pinned up on the mirror frame, Reggie noticed.

'I thought those gloves might need a rinse,' he said gently. 'Want you looking your best again tomorrow, don't we?'

Pamela groaned.

'Oh Christ, I'm tired. Twice in one night.'

She was looking at herself as if she was trying to work out who she was. He knew that look – the one where your body won't move.

'Want me to unzip you? – that satin creases rotten when it's sat on too long.'

'Sorry . . .'

He helped her up.

'Don't worry. Once you hear that music again tomorrow it'll all kick back in. That's how it works . . . Wig first. That's it –'

They worked together just like they did in the act – but slower now, and gently. Pam pulled off her wig, Reggie found and released her zipper, she steadied herself on his shoulder, then he held the bodice down and open so that she could step free of its bones. The room was small, and hot, and soon she was just in her shoes and underwear, but Pam had had too many men watch her undress in the course of her life to mind about that. Besides, this was work, and she was tired. It was nice to be with someone who knew how to lift off a frock for once. She prised off the shoes, then reached back and unhooked her bra.

'Run me some hot water, would you, Reg? There's a bowl and some Dettol under the sink.'

For his part, Reg was unembarrassed too. He didn't stare, but he didn't feel that he shouldn't be there. He liked that she didn't mind him helping.

Pamela checked the worst of her scrapes, and wrung out a hand towel in the steaming, milky water. The reassuring smell of the disinfectant filled the room. Dragging the cloth along an outstretched arm, she inspected herself. The dark flaws in the alabaster would fade once she'd learnt how to avoid knocking herself so often, she knew that, and soon she'd be back to her trademark whiteness. There was no major harm done. But the long gloves looked good, actually, especially with that fur over the dress; white on white on white, with the burgundy underneath. Maybe she'd keep them . . . She glanced up at Margaret Rose, and when she did that she could see Reggie at work behind her in the mirror. He was reaching up and flattening out the underlayers of netting, making sure the gown was hanging right on the back of the door and that nothing needed steaming or pressing or stitching before tomorrow. He cared more about that bloody dress than she did, she thought – and she must remember to lift it when she was coming up the backstage stairs between the shows, because she'd nearly caught her toe again tonight.

'Thanks for fixing that hem again for me, Reg,' she said, wringing the rag out. 'I promise I'll get the hang of the step-in soon.'

The water dropped through the bright light from the bulbs around the mirror; mislaid rhinestones, falling. Tears.

'You're welcome.'

Watching him work, it occurred to her that it was funny how she still thought of him as a boy even when you could see that he wasn't one at all, not when you were alone in a small room with him. Somehow he didn't seem to have any of that hardness men always seemed to acquire – the ones who earned their living around women, anyway. Maybe it was something to do with his foot. It did make him . . . well, *special* was the word that came into her head, though she couldn't really say why. Silly word – you couldn't say that to his face, not without him thinking you were treating him like a kid. She draped an arm up over her head, wiping the sweat out of her blue-stubbled armpit and from under her breast with the dribbling rag. Reggie had turned now, and was watching her. She didn't mind; for once, the light from the naked bulbs seemed kind. They were both looking tired in the same way, she thought, she under her slap, he under that odd gypsy tan of his. The water ran down her skin into her lap. When she spoke, it was gently.

'Does your mother know what you do for a living, Reg?'

He must have been surprised by the question – even Pam didn't really know where it had suddenly come from. But he didn't particularly show it, and the pause before he answered her was very short.

'Not really.'

His eyes flicked away from the mirror and down onto the floor. There was the suggestion of something in his voice that she hadn't quite heard before, or at least not quite so clearly. Avoidance, perhaps, or defence.

'Why d'you ask?'

'I just wondered. Why's that then?'

There was another pause, longer this time, and then Reg told her his story.

He didn't tell her everything, of course. There were parts of the story he wasn't really sure of himself, after all, so to keep things simple he just said that his mother was dead, and that most of the people who'd looked after him had been as kind as they knew how to be at the time. He didn't mention The Home for Poor Brave Things by name (I wonder if he even knew it by that name himself) or the wet black stones of its curving beach, or the train. He tried to end his account of himself with a bit of a flourish, saying that he'd never really much minded where he lived anyway, and that this was a good job as jobs went so long as Mr Brookes was having a good day. It wasn't a tale he'd told very often, and the clumsiness showed.

She was gentle, too.

'And what about your dad then?'

'Oh . . .'

The foot twisted.

'I never knew him. And I'm not sure that my mum did either, if you know what I mean.'

The eyes flashed back up into the mirror on that one, and the grin was back in its twisted place – but only half back, as if to indicate that he knew that that old story wasn't much of a joke really, not if you were on the receiving end.

'I do, as it happens.' The last thing he'd want was sympathy, Pam knew that; when she eventually smiled back, it was quite matter-of-factly.

'Well, I'm sure she'd be proud of you. You're very good at your job, and I like that. It's always better when you know where you are with a . . . well, with a . . .'

The water from the towel dropped brightly onto the litter of her dressing table. She didn't want to say *a man*; it could have spoilt everything. She squeezed the hand towel out again, and noticed that Reg had shifted his position slightly in the mirror, marking the beat of her hesitation with another downward flick of his eyes. But then he completed her thought for her.

'When you know where you are with the other half of your act?' he suggested, still looking at the floor. It was very quietly done, and she was grateful.

'Exactly. Took the words right out of my mouth, Reg.'

She stood up and inspected herself. The combination of the black stockings and suspenders left over from the maid's costume with her naked top half made her look like some sort of dreadful old-fashioned dirty postcard she thought, just the sort of work she hated, but then again, all things considered, not bad. Not bad at all – and at the end of a demanding double session. If you know what I mean.

She put one stockinged foot up on her chair.

Reggie really was staring now. Their eyes met in the mirror.

'Well,' she said, holding his gaze, 'I suppose I'd better give downstairs a wipe as well if I'm going to keep myself respectable and fragrant for my public. So you'd probably better fuck off while I do that, if you wouldn't mind.'

That restored the full grin, and seeing him framed in her mirror and smiling made Pamela realise how striking-looking the boy was, if and when he stopped moving long enough for you to get a proper look. He had lovely eyes when he shared them, and the sharp features all worked together somehow when his grin came out. They went with who he *was* – and she'd always been a sucker for strong shoulders on a man. The legs were a let-down, however, and the teeth were shocking.

Now it was her turn to be caught staring.

'See you when you're all nice and clean then, Miss *Rose*.'

He winked, and was out of the door before she'd even got half her laugh out. There was a lot more to that boy than met the eye, that was for sure. And what a story about his mum – she wondered if it was true that she was dead. They told the kids that sometimes, didn't they, to make it less dreadful . . . She'd have to ask him some more sometime – after this week was over. She dunked the hand towel back in the bowl, looked up at Margaret Rose, laughed again, and unhooked her second suspender.

5

By the time she'd got herself changed it was late, and they were the last two out of the stage door. She'd done her best with a lick of powder, but had all too clearly just thrown her shabby man's camel-hair coat over her sweater to go home. She looked as though she badly needed a drink.

'I know,' she said. 'Not so glamorous now.'

'I've seen worse . . .'

Reggie was handing their keys over to Mr English and scribbling their names under *Out* in the book.

'Bloody cheek. Thanks, Mr English.'

'Goodnight, Miss. And welcome to the Grand Theatre, Miss, after your very first night.'

You silly old bugger, thought Reg. *It's not the bloody Palladium.*

'Thanks . . .' She was trying to make the words as kind as she could, but it was hard when you were this tired. 'I'll do my very best to keep your punters happy for you while I'm here, Mr English. Five to six tomorrow it is.'

When they got outside the town was already falling quiet, and the night growing chilly. Even up here on North Road, a good seven streets away from the promenade, you could sense the closeness of the sea. Pamela stopped for a moment in the alley to button her coat, and while she did it she raised her face to the night with her eyes closed, trying her hardest to let all the tension of the evening go. Then she breathed out, and slipped her arm through Reggie's without even looking at him.

'Walk me home, Reg,' she whispered.

They set off together, his limping feet beating a soft one–two variation on the steadier rhythm of her heels as they headed down the narrow brick alleyway, the two sounds linked together like their two arms, their breaths just visible in the cold April air.

6

There was one very tricky moment with a dropped shoe inside the apparatus on the second evening house of the Thursday, but apart from that the rest of their first week went well. Mr Brookes seemed to think he was getting his six guineas' worth, and some of Pam's bruises began to fade. She even got her first few wolf whistles from the back of the circle. Reggie began to look forward to their nightly walks home together, and they soon became as much a part of his routine at the end of the night as wiping down the zinc panels inside the cabinet or checking the lead weights in the hem of the silver drape. There was an overgrown laburnum tree almost filling the front garden up at Mrs Brennan's, and they got into the habit of saying their goodnights under the street lamp at the end of her road. Reggie would stand and watch her safely disappear round behind the tree – a tangle of black branches, just beginning to show the neat emerald stitches of its new leaves – before he turned and headed home to his bed of roses.

They didn't ever talk much on these walks – they both seemed to enjoy a spot of quiet after all the noise and lights of work – but they soon became important to him. And to her. There always seemed to be a pair of catcalling sailors who would spot Pam as they made their way up the Queen's Road towards the station, laughing and asking if she fancied making them miss their last train back to Portsmouth; sometimes she would laugh and shout back, sometimes just ignore them, but always she would squeeze Reggie's arm, as if she was grateful for his protection.

Reg had planned to have enough time by the end of the week to finally go and visit his new local library. However, as part of his clearing up after the show on Friday he'd discovered that he was about to run out of the wire wool he used to clean the terminals on the smoke trigger, and by the time he'd dealt with that it wasn't until after the matinee on Saturday that he had time to go and make his visit. He delivered the between-the-shows sandwiches (meat paste for Mr Brookes, mock crab and cress for Pamela) and then set off at a pace – the library was just down at the bottom of North Road as luck would have it, just next door to the Pavilion, and he was sure he'd have time to find what he was looking before before he was due back if he got a move on.

Reggie had been to a fair few municipal libraries in the course of his touring life – they were always one of his main sources of occupation when he was on the road – and so knew when he'd chanced upon a good one. The exterior had already struck him as promising when he'd been passing earlier in the week – the Indian-looking window frames reminded him of the Bradford Alhambra – but he was even happier when he actually got inside and up the flamboyantly tiled stairs to the reference library. The books were ranged along the walls of a splendid old high-ceilinged room that was as full of quiet as it was of light, and – for a Saturday – it was gratifyingly empty of customers. Up on the end wall, under the clock, he could see straight away that they had exactly what he liked most, which was a whole proper shelf-full of encyclopedias.

Pulling down the first volume of the set bound in heavy dark blue linen – the *Britannica*, his favourite – he rifled quickly through the small-print pages until he found an entry headed 'Astronomy, Comparative'. The article itself was much too long to be a quick read, but three pages in he found just what he needed, which was a set of four white-on-black maps showing the constellations as they appeared at four different times of year. He quickly ticked off the names of all the shapes he recognised – *Cancer, Cassiopeia, Cygnus* – and then hunted for the one he didn't. It didn't take him long; there they were, on the chart for Spring, hiding right down in the bottom left-hand corner, just like they were up on the smoky ceiling out front at the Grand.

'*The Pleiades*,' he read. '*Named after the seven sisters of ancient mythology, they are one of the brightest stellar objects visible to the naked eye. Visible for only half the year, their appearance above the horizon has always been treated as an auspicious sign . . .*'

An auspicious sign – he liked the sound of it, but was unsure of exactly what it meant; hefting the enclopedia onto the reading desk, he walked along the shelf to where the dictionaries were – he could always use a brand-new word, could Reggie.

'*Betokening success*,' the dictionary pronounced, much to his satisfaction. '*Giving promise of a favourable issue . . .*'

Looking up, he checked that he still had the whole place to himself, and then, grinning, filled the sunlit room with his voice.

'Lucky For Some,' he enunciated, letting the words ring just like Mr Brookes did.

'Written in the Fucking Stars.' The grin widened.

'All that bollocks . . .'

Glancing up at the clock on the end wall, he realised that he had less than ten minutes before he was needed back at work. Restoring the dictionary and the encyclopedia back to their respective places – Reggie was never one to leave a book lying about open – he headed quickly back downstairs, swinging himself round the strange oriental-looking banister finial on the stairs in his hurry.

On his way out, Reggie stopped for a moment at a small table positioned just by the library door. Picking up one of the copies of a pocket-sized book that were stacked there in a pile, he looked briefly at the front cover – which showed a traffic roundabout decorated with blazing red and yellow flower beds – turned it over to glance in the back, and slid the book into his inside breast pocket next to his knife. He checked to make sure that the woman at the desk hadn't seen him do it, then slipped out of the door.

7

There are six cemeteries marked on the fold-out map at the back of Brighton Council's handily pocket-sized *Welcome to Brighton* guidebook for 1953 – seven if you include the Jewish burial ground off the Ditchling Road, and eight if you add the *chattri* commemorating the Indian servicemen who died in the Pavilion while it was being used as a military hospital during the First World War. It took Reggie until nearly four o'clock on that Sunday to find the right one of the eight for his purpose, but when he finally got there, it turned out to be perfect.

As its name suggests, the Downs Road Cemetery was out on what was then the farthest northern edge of the town, just where the new housing estates were starting to bite into the edges of the countryside proper. The overshadowed paths of its bottom section were old, and meandered around the kind of squat nineteenth-century brick-and-flint mortuary chapel that now looked more like a suitable setting for a second-rate horror film than for anybody's grief. Further up the hill there was a more recent extension that had been laid out on what had previously been open downland, and up here there was light, and air. Connected to their older neighbours by a metal kissing gate let into a high wall, the gravestones in this exten- sion were laid out in orderly straight lines, and along its northern and eastern reaches the smooth asphalt paths grid- ded stretches of still-untenanted grassland. On a breezy spring day like the one Reggie had chosen for his visit this unmown turf rippled silver and green, and from the slight rise in the centre of the graves there was even a view right across the town to the matching waves of the distant and glittering sea.

Once he had passed the big black gold-lettered sign with all the cemetery's opening times on it and swung in through its impressive, brick-pillared entrance (the walls on either side were high, and topped with broken glass), Reggie limped purposefully through the blackened monuments that greeted him. When he got to the wall that sealed off the top of the old cemetery he thought he'd reached its limit, and not having found what he was looking for, was about to head off somewhere else – but some instinct for where things might be hidden made him follow the wall eastwards and through a thick stand of acrid-leaved privet and bay. That was how he found the gate.

The metalwork gave out a strident warning creak as he pushed his way through it – that felt wrong, but as soon as Reg got clear of the trees and shaded his eyes to survey the view he knew that this was going to be more like it. The lack of obstructions and the way the paths stretched away from him in straight lines meant that up here he could see straight away if anybody was about. Now it was simply a matter of being diligent, and putting in the time, so he began to work his way along the first path, heading further out into the flower-starred grass.

It's a strange business, talking to the dead – but if you've ever done it, then you won't need me to tell you that.

Reggie had first done it when he was nineteen, on a wet Sunday afternoon in Wolverhampton. He'd actually wandered into the cemetery looking for something else entirely, following a young man in a raincoat who'd looked conspicuously over his shoulder at him from a nearby bus stop. Then, when he'd got no more than a couple of rows of stones inside the gates, he'd had to stoop to retie his left-boot bootlace, and had lost sight of his quarry while he was down there. He stood up, steadying himself on the nearest gravestone, and while he was searching for the vanished young man happened to look down and read the name and dates on the stone. The second half of the inscription – the date on which the grave's occupant had died – was obscured by his hand, and he shifted himself so that he could read it. As if they'd been waiting for him to do just that, the letters and numbers spelt out the words *15 September 1930*. Not surprisingly, this stopped Reggie in his tracks, because that was the exact date of his birthday.

Staring at the numbers on the stone made him remember what he'd been told by the nurses back at the Home, that there'd been a death when he was born. As he stared – the young man in the raincoat now completely forgotten – he found his eyes drawn away from the carved numbers and down to the empty vase which lay on its side at the base of the stone. As he looked at it lying there, a hand gripped his throat. The vase looked as if it had been empty for some time. Didn't this woman have any children? Didn't they care? Not even really realising that he was doing it, much less why, he found himself mumbling to this stranger – words that were part apology, part appeal for information – and even wiping the rain off the top of her stone with his handkerchief.

That was how it had all started – accidentally, in other words – but now, whichever town 'The Missing Lady' took him to, finding a cemetery and visiting it had become as much a part of his routine as finding the library and a cafe for his breakfast. He didn't always quite feel sure what exactly what it was that he was looking for when he went to one of these strange places, and sometimes he would be interrupted, or fail to find anyone who had the right sort of date on their stone – and even if he did, he didn't always manage to put what he wanted to say into words. Sometimes – as you've seen – he would give up trying to speak, and just sit somewhere and close his eyes. Recently, he'd started dressing up for these visits, putting on a clean shirt and a tie and polishing his boots to a Sunday shine.

Why was this happening at this particular point in his life? I couldn't honestly say. Perhaps it was just time.

That's right; Reggie visits cemeteries in order to talk to his mother.

He was spoilt for choice today; bizarrely, there were two ladies with appropriate dates resting quite close together on the same tarmacked path. After spending some time limping backwards and forwards between the stones, out of his two possible choices – a Doreen and a Maria – he chose Doreen for his partner at this particular matinee. Her name felt warmer than the other one – more *touchable*. That feeling had come into his head as soon as he'd seen her stone, and as definitely as if he'd looked her name up in the big heavy dictionary at the library.

'Hello again,' he said.

His voice was tentative. It sounded as if he wasn't quite sure of being remembered. The wind from the distant sea tried to embarrass him by ruffling his hair, but he smoothed it back. The dance of a lemon-yellow butterfly distracted him for a moment, and led his eyes back round to the sea. He squinted, shielding his eyes with his hand, and then returned to his task.

'I actually thought about writing it all down for you this week – you know, putting it all in a letter and just leaving that for you to read later . . . but then if somebody found it, somebody who actually knew you – I mean, not you, but her,' (he gestured at Doreen's name on the stone), 'that would be confusing for them, wouldn't it . . .? They'd think some unfortunate had been up here and got themselves confused.'

His voice trailed away and his left foot shifted; then he stood up straight, like a schoolboy being reprimanded, and took his hands out of his pockets.

'So anyway, I'll just have to tell you the news out loud, won't I?'

He hated the fact that it was always him who had to start the conversation, hated it — it set things up as if she were asleep, or poorly, with her eyes closed and her hands outside the crisp white sheets of a bed, which was never how he imagined her at all.

'Sorry about not coming last week, but it's all been a bit hectic. And the week before that, it was that woman with the daffodils, interrupting me again. You know I can't do it properly if there's anybody else around.'

He swallowed twice, and winced. The lump in his throat was a familiar enemy, but that didn't make it any less annoying.

'Hope you're warm enough.'

As if the idea of his mother being cold made him angry, Reggie's foot seemed to twist of its own accord; he kicked at the ground with the toe of his boot again. It was never easy, but today it seemed especially hard to get things going. He took a deep breath and plunged on, talking fast to help himself keep going, and with his eyes turned half away from the stone.

'So anyway, quite a bit of news for you this week. The new girl is fine, no better than she should be if you know what I mean but we're getting on OK. Pamela. Miss Pamela Rose — she's never worked in this bit of the game before but she's a worker, I'll say that for her. Mr Brookes hasn't said much since we opened, surprise surprise, but I think he's happy. The houses have been all right, more or less. My digs are fine, the breakfast isn't up to much, but there's a place just back from the seafront where I'm going now in the mornings. Italians. The landlady carries on a bit, and the wallpaper keeps me awake sometimes. At night. What with the street lamp and everything coming in through the window. The air. Well, you know how it is. So all the usual really. All the usual . . . The stage-door keeper's called Mr English, funny old bird, changes his cravat every week.'

'The library's lovely . . .'

He trailed off and stopped, and looked around at the sea. He squinted, like he always seemed to when there was too much light. His throat was hurting again, and after getting all of that out in a rush he seemed to have hit a wall. But Reggie was nothing if not determined; he kicked his boot at the turf again so hard that he scuffed it, and that gave him the excuse he needed to stop for a moment and collect his thoughts. Kneeling down, he spat in his handkerchief and started to polish the scuff out. He frowned with concentration – and just for a moment heard a voice talking somewhere in the back of his head, snapping out the phrase *Yes, that's right, matron, all present and correct*. He looked down at his handkerchief, which had been clean when he set out and now was smudged with spit and grass cuttings and dubbin. That Sunday voice had been in his head earlier, when he'd got the handkerchief out of his drawer – and he heard it again now, clear and sharp as a clip on the back of the head, accompanied with the flash of a white headdress: *Got your clean hanky for church, Reggie?* . . . He folded the memory up with his handkerchief and put it back in his pocket. That nurse or matron or whoever it was in his mind wasn't who he was here to talk to, and the old days on the stones weren't what he was here to talk about. He got up – or at least he almost did, but something stopped him.

'No,' he said suddenly – and much more loudly, looking directly at the stone with a sharp, angry glance. Whoever he was answering, their question was obviously one he'd been asked just one too many times.

'No, there's still nobody special. I've told you that before.'

There was an awkward silence, which he tried to fill by clambering upright and kicking at a tuft of grass. He seemed to be sorry for raising his voice like that; when he spoke next it was still sharply and clearly, but much more quietly.

'Not *yet*.'

Another silence. Clearly she hadn't heard – hadn't heard, or didn't want to. His voice insisted:

'I said, *not yet*. Honestly, that must be the tenth time you've asked me that . . .'

Silence, again.

The breeze that had been tousling his hair dropped a stray lock back across Reggie's forehead, and he knocked it away again. He straightened himself up, screwed up his eyes at Doreen's name for a final moment, and brushed his hands clean on his trousers. For whatever reason, that seemed to be the end of the conversation.

'Right then,' he said, in the determinedly cheery voice of somebody who has just been told that visiting time is over. Scanning the nearby graves, he spotted a china jug holding some blue Dutch irises; they didn't look very fresh, but they'd do. Leaving the jug to its rightful owner, he laid the flowers out on the turf below Doreen's stone in a tidy fan, then wiped his hands.

'Cheerio then,' he said, after a long moment of thought. 'Best be off, I suppose. I'll see you next Sunday – we're going to be here for three weeks.'

Reggie reached up and patted the knife in his breast pocket, twice.

'But then I expect you already know that.'

Bending down one more time to adjust the alignment of his flowers, he turned, and went – down the path, under the trees, out through the gate, down through the gloomy shrubberies and back down into the town via the Lewes Road. He walked fast, and clutched his flapping jacket to him like he always did, swallowing away the remnants of that bruising lump in his throat and keeping his head well down. Nobody who saw him could possibly have guessed what he'd just been doing.

8

Having been its only witness, I wonder what you think of this strange Sunday rigmarole of Reggie's. I wonder if you're thinking *Well yes I can see that he's upset, and I can understand why he might be, but it's all an illusion, isn't it, talking to the dead? I mean, when you think about it, isn't he doing exactly what Mr Brookes is persuading the punters to do fourteen times a week down at the Grand? Imagine that there's a woman in an empty box.*

A woman Reggie seems to think can somehow give him the advice he needs. A woman he seems to think he can turn to to help him sort out his still-young and oddly angry life.

All an illusion. I couldn't have put it better myself.

9

Pamela, up at Mrs Brennan's, was restless. As you do on a Sunday night, she was staring at the pool of light that was cast up from her bedside light onto the plasterwork rosette on the ceiling, and slowly smoking the last cigarette of the day. She'd tried reading a magazine, but now she was thinking back over the week, trying to sift the pictures into an order that would let her go to sleep. She couldn't say she thought much of an April Sunday in Brighton, that was for sure. The piers had seemed noisy and cold – all that pointless shrieking – there was nothing she really fancied on at any of the pictures, and window-shopping for other women's opinions of how she ought to look had never been her favourite way to waste an afternoon. For the first time since she'd arrived, she was missing the noise and arguments of Soho. She was thinking about Reg, too. That foot was hardly an attraction, obviously, but he was a sweet boy, and surely he didn't *have* to be such a loner. His sort often were, of course. One of Madame Valentine's girls was local, and was bound to know the places people talked about – the ones where the Reggies of the town went. Maybe she'd even suggest an outing for a drink together one evening. She'd have to be careful about asking around, though; she'd never had a problem with that side of things personally, but you never could tell who was going to be funny about real life, even backstage in a theatre.

As for herself and her new single life down here by the seaside, well, the smoke rising from her cigarette into the lamplight was making her think of the pink-and-orange smoke from the apparatus, and Mr Brookes raising his right hand. He was certainly quite a looker, this Teddy, if that clean-cut way of doing things was your style – and he had some lovely manners, too. On the Friday, they'd met on their way out from work, and he'd been all done up for a date in a clean shirt and tan gloves and a cashmere; after she'd signed out, he'd held the stage door open for her exactly as if she was about to step into a taxi or a posh restaurant. She'd even got a proper *After you, madam.*

She stubbed the cigarette out in a flowered saucer by the bed and told herself to stop it. Being alone in a single bed would do her just fine for the present, thank you very much. She'd enjoyed putting it about in her time, but now she was going to try the other thing for a while. She told herself to remember the way she'd suddenly felt when she'd walked on in that maroon dress for the first time, with the white gloves and the fur. She could get used to passing for a lady, she thought. Bruises aside, it rather suited her.

As Pam turned out her light and rolled over, Mr Brookes, in Hove, was already gently snoring. It was really only when he was asleep that the professional mask finally ebbed from the muscles of his face and now, with just a smudge of moonlight coming in through the curtains to catch them, they were for once unguarded. Even his hands were relaxed, and one lay fallen open beside him on the flowered counterpane. A bathroom light had been left on in the hall, and the pillow next to him on the double bed carried a few stray blonde hairs; he stirred and stretched, his body clearly enjoying the space in the bed. His limbs instinctively liked it when his overnight guests did the decent thing and got themselves off home before the morning. He smiled.

Reggie, perhaps unsurprisingly, couldn't sleep. He lay awake until half past midnight, gazing at Mrs Steed's roses as they ran riot behind the washstand mirror. He had that question that his mother had asked him up there in the cemetery running round and round in his head again tonight, and was wondering if he was ever going to be able to answer it. As you do when you can't sleep, he was blaming himself, running through all the things he'd done in his search for an answer so far; all that stupid staring at a pair of black-haired acrobats in white tights or at the young Italian cook in his breakfast cafe, all that broom-handled following boys from bus stops into cemeteries. He recalled in detail the last time when things had gone a bit further, which had been in Bradford last year during the run at the Alhambra; he'd spent forty-five minutes in a thin-walled boarding-house bedroom with somebody who the next morning had let his eyes slide off Reggie's face like a knife off a plate. He wanted to know when one thing was finally going to lead to another, and he was going to actually spend a whole night with someone – spend the night with *someone special*, as his mother always put it. He wanted to know when he was going to kiss the same person goodnight when the lights went out and then hello again the next morning when the sun came up. He wanted to know how he was ever going to make that happen.

Perhaps this is why Reggie's face and body are so hard to pin down – why he can look like a young man one moment and a damaged boy the next. It isn't his limp or height, or his strangely pinched and weathered face, but rather the fact that at the age of twenty-two he still has the dreams of a sixteen-year-old. Like a sixteen-year-old's, his body is aching to catch up with his heart, and his heart to catch up with his body.

Take his fingers, for instance; look how they're behaving tonight. The effort of clinging to the window frame as he leaned out for his last goodnight stare at the darkened sea has reminded them of the ache involved in clinging to the back of the cabinet, and that, involuntarily, is now making them recall and relive all the other times when they have flexed and clenched in the solitary dark. As he lies there with his eyes closed, they stretch and splay across the thin blanket that Mrs Steed has provided, and take on a life of their own. They think for themselves, and lead young Reggie astray. First, they dig into the blanket; then they push back, so that Reggie's back is flattened against the flowered wall. They hold him there. In that position, lying on his side, with his knees drawn up and his breath coming slowly and gently – a variation on Pam's position under the stairs, in fact – Reggie begins to firmly press each separate vertebra of his spine in turn into the rose-strewn wallpaper. He counts the bones off, calling to them by their proper names: *Cervical; Thoracic; Lumbar*. One by one, he persuades the muscles of his back that it is not him pressing his bones into the wall, but the roses themselves that are doing the pushing. It is a very exact sensation, and eventually resolves itself into the illusion that there is another, matching spine just beneath the wallpaper, pushing back against his. If he concentrates sufficiently, Reggie can even tell from the slight warmth that collects across his shoulders that the man lying behind him is also wearing pyjamas; if they had both been naked (Reggie is sure that he knows this) then the heat from their matched bodies would have been more fiery, more intense. Then, once – and only once – this sensation or illusion of a matching spine is fully convincing, Reggie goes on to the next stage.

This is to imagine that the stranger who owns these bones rolls sleepily over, and clasps him from behind. When this happens, Reggie grins, with his eyes still closed, and thinks about how easy it has been to smuggle this companion up into his room without anyone suspecting a thing. When Mrs Steed heard his solitary, slow one-two come thumping up her uncarpeted treads tonight she must have thought no more about it, never even thinking to stick her head out into the hallway and thus catch the owner of the second, clever, silent pair of feet following him up the stairs. *That'll be young Mr Rainbow*, she would have muttered to herself, sitting in her chair with her ashtray. *Such a shame about that, you know, little difference* . . . Well, let her. Let her think what she liked.

Being able to smile felt good, and Reggie now brought his routine to a close. Barely mouthing the word, he whispered his imaginary lover a quiet *Goodnight*, floating the word out into the night air of his bedroom as if it was being produced by Mr Clifford's percussionist with the softest possible stroke of a drumstick across the edge of a cymbal. The fourth time he whispered it, the charm worked, and – hey presto – he slept. As peacefully as he once used to sleep out on that beach at Bishopstone, with only the sound of the stones for his lullaby, or of a distant train.

10

Now that the dusty gilt fringing of the Grand's curtain was safely rising on the second week of their run, Mr Brookes knew that he had to get a grip. The act was going down well most nights, and Pam was certainly bringing some much needed life to the old routine; however, he had to face the fact that after this booking ended the diary was still looking pure blind empty, and the bills meanwhile would still be coming home to roost as regularly as the starlings of Leicester Square.

This situation meant that Mr Brookes's days were much more crowded than those of either of his colleagues. Besides the daily phone calls to his booking agent in London and the fixed daily preparations for the act – his solitary sessions in front of the pier glass, the make-up, the hand-wiping – he was now also obliged to get dressed in his slacks and blazer every morning and head out and do the rounds, dropping in on all the other theatre managements in town and leaving cards, enquiring if anyone knew of any likely openings. He made it all look as if it was the easiest thing in the world of course, but no one was fooled. Everyone knew that an act was only as good as its last booking, and while appearing as a second-half stopgap in what was basically a seaside skin show wasn't the worst billing in the world, it was hardly the best either. There were times during the week when his fingers began to itch with frustration as badly as Reggie's, and one too-direct query from Mr English as to whether there were any new engagements in the offing for that talented Miss Rose of his almost made him lose his temper with the old duffer. Despite his long days of smiles, phone calls and gins bought for strangers in hotel bars, there really did seem to be nothing about.

Mr Brookes kept track of all these meetings in a little pocket notebook. It was a slim, black, leather-bound affair with pages of thin blue paper that made it look as if somebody had been razoring up airmail letters – it was on one of these pages, torn out, that he'd scrawled Mrs Steed's address for Reggie. The pages at the back were filled with neatly pencilled lists; every drink that he bought, every name that was mentioned and every potentially useful telephone number he managed to prise out of a saloon-bar conversation was jotted down in double columns. Once listed, the names were then memorised – he'd learnt from experience that there was nothing like immediate recall of a name to impress a manager who would long ago have forgotten what distinguished Teddy Brookes Esq. from a dozen other illusion acts on the circuit. Always flattered to be remembered, they were. In the front pages of the notebook there was another list, and this one consisted entirely of female Christian names, some of them followed by telephone numbers, and some of them by brief one-word notes such as *Twice, Children* or *Ginger*. Occasionally, a name would have been scored out so vehemently that the pencil would have cut right through the thin blue paper.

This second list, I suppose, was another kind of record of just how hard Mr Brookes had to work to keep up his act.

Towards the end of this second week a cluster of pages in the otherwise empty middle of the notebook began to fill up with other, less obvious jottings. These notes were also in pencil, and were hastier and less formed than the orderly lists of names and addresses in the front and back, as if they'd been made in a hurry. *Brought To Heel* ran one, with the word *finally !!!!* scribbled underneath. *Decided to make a respectable woman out of her, did you?* ran another. The next page was taken up with a small scribbled sketch of what could have been a woman's body or dress hanging from a hook inside a travelling trunk or upright coffin – or, of course, inside the harlequin-painted apparatus, reduced to its most childish form of four blunt strokes. Some dashes and arrows seemed to indicate that the cabinet was going to be spun or opened in some different way than it was in the current routine; it seemed to have more doors, for one thing, and possibly some extra handles. On the most crowded pages, the notes were sometimes almost illegible; one set of musings seemed to be headed with a phrase that could have been read as either *box + stairs GONE* or as *boys staring GOOD.* Underlined and circled next to this was the single word *Shoes?*

It's hard to say whether this scrappiness – surprising in a man so otherwise fastidious as Mr Brookes – was in fact deliberate. Men are often funny with their lists and notes, aren't they, often resorting to code – and of course no illusionist of any kind wants his secrets to be legible to a stranger. To somebody who's managed to get their hand into his trouser pocket in an off-guard moment.

However, even if their details weren't clear, the jist of these scribblings was; prompted no doubt by the arrival of an unexpectedly marketable new assistant, Mr Brookes was starting to think about changing the act. The current routine had been on the road for eight seasons in a row now, and while he'd been doing the rounds several potential bookers had recently asked him whether he'd got anything new up his sleeve. He couldn't afford to buy anything entirely novel in the apparatus line just now, but a few alterations, a couple of different produces in the set-up, some suitably abbreviated and up-to-date re-dressing for the girl and he was sure he'd be able to give the current outfit another round of outings under a new title. People never seemed to get tired of telling him *It's 19 fucking 53, Teddy; nobody wants the old stuff any more* – but he knew different; what the punters really wanted was business *exactly* as before, but tarted up a bit so that nobody's wife or girlfriend could complain about things being old-fashioned. A spot of dazzle to hook their attention, some skin in the main body of the act and then a good strong finish, that was what was required. *Hook, Skin, Finish* – he even jotted it down.

In between the lists at the back, the lists at the front and the scribblings in the middle, some thirty-six pages of this little blue-paper notebook were still empty, and nowhere did it appear to contain any indication that he'd mentioned this new act he was planning to either of his colleagues.

What with settling into a new town, and getting used to being so tired last thing after work, the second week neared its end without Pam ever quite getting round to asking Reggie out for that drink. She'd planned to, and had even got as far as tactfully asking a couple of the other girls backstage if they knew what the pubs near the theatre were like; one of them had mentioned a place just off the seafront, the clientele of which reputedly had (as she warily put it) *a rather colourful reputation*, but that was as far as the plan ever went. On the Saturday, she ditched it entirely. This wasn't because Pam had become suddenly shy of broaching the subject of his single-ness again with Reg, but rather because of something she'd seen him do.

As she was arriving for the matinee that Saturday – late, and running, hair flying – she'd spotted Reggie ahead of her down on the other side of North Road, apparently waiting for the traffic to clear so that he could cross over to the stage-door alleyway. He didn't seem to have seen her running down the hill, and she was just about to wave and call out to him to get a move on and cross over when she realised her mistake; he wasn't standing still because he was waiting for the traffic to clear at all. Following his gaze, she saw that he was watching a young man who was walking away down the road past the front doors of the Grand. The young man wasn't anyone she recognised, but from the way Reg was staring after him he certainly seemed to be someone of significance.

About twenty yards down North Road, the young man stopped, and started inspecting something in the window of the ironmonger's on the corner. Pam caught a glimpse of a face in a collar and tie, topped with a quiff of bright black hair – nothing remarkable, she thought, but reasonably well put together so far as one could tell. Reg, when she looked back at him, was still staring. It was only when the young man in question straightened up and continued on his journey – having apparently decided that he didn't actually need whatever piece of metal it was he'd been staring at – that Reg seemed to pull himself together and start to look out for the traffic. Then she did wave, and call out his name. Reg looked, but blankly, as if his thoughts were somewhere else entirely – and then he smiled, and lurched straight over to meet her, making a woman coming down North Road on her bike swerve as he almost dodged himself straight under her wheels.

Pam knew better than to ask Reg who the young man with the Italian-looking black hair had been. If that was the way he liked to try to meet people, then good luck to him, and let's hope he was being careful and having fun.

'Come on,' she called across the street as he half hopped to meet her, reaching out to grab an arm to get him up the kerb. 'You know what that Mr English is like if we sign in late.'

The second show that night went down a storm. Mr Brookes had told them he wanted a good Saturday-night show to end the week, and that was exactly what he got. Smiling, he placed his hand in the small of Pamela's back to usher her offstage at the end of the calls again, placing it right where the waist seam sat on the top of her hips, and Reggie couldn't help noticing the proprietorial way that the fingers spread themselves. Pam laughed at something Mr Brookes whispered in her ear as they wove their way across the stage through the arriving nudes – it was something funny, obviously, but Reggie was too far away to catch what it actually was.

11

After he'd rearranged the dead irises, Reg coughed, wiped his hands and started with the usual. *Hello again*, he said, then *Hope you're warm enough* – but neither of them seemed to work. He stood up straight, coughed and trotted out some stories from his backstage week, making the best job he could of making them sound like news, stopping occasionally to look around and see if there were any spare fresh flowers nearby that he could lift to replace the irises. He told his mother how the houses had been during the week – poor to start with, but building by the Friday, like the weather; about how silly Mr English got with Pam sometimes, treating her like she was a cut above the other girls – *She's the real thing, that Miss Rose. Never gets her tone wrong, if you know what I mean*, he'd said to Reg one evening – and all about what a good round they'd got for the act from the third house last night. *Enough to shake a bit more gilt down off those stars on the ceiling, I shouldn't wonder*, he said. *Mr Clements Sole Prop will have to get the decorators in if things carry on like this, the old skin-flint* – and so on. As he continued, he became more and more aware that he wasn't talking about what was really on his mind. He'd woken up with Pam in his head this morning – Pam in the alleyway, Pam laughing, Pam with Mr Brookes's hand in the small of her back – and now all of that seemed to be sticking in his throat and making the familiar lump worse. When he got to last night itself, with Pam walking away from their lamp post and disappearing round the laburnum tree, he stopped and fell silent. A plane – a rarity, in those days – was ruling a metallic line over his head, but he didn't look up to watch it.

Well, we all have visits that fail, I suppose. Reg tried telling himself that it wasn't his fault that he didn't feel in the mood to talk, but it didn't work. It was that hand in the small of Pam's back again that was the problem – that was what was stopping him talking. He'd seen that before, and now he didn't know what to do about it. Not at all. Even as he tramped back into town to meet Pam for their Sunday-afternoon date at the Essoldo, he still couldn't get it out of his head.

There were lots of other things that Reg didn't mention, of course – as I'm sure you've noticed. He didn't mention the boy with the black hair that he had stared at yesterday morning on North Road – it was the chef from his breakfast cafe, as it happened, the Italian one – or talk about what his feelings were now that he was going to be heading back to London pretty soon, back to another single bed in a top-floor room. In other words, he didn't talk about *himself* at all.

Mothers can do that.

12

'Strand?' said Mr Brookes.

Mr Clements Sole Prop refused the proffered cigarette, but reached across his desk and took a cigar from the open pewter box with a thick-wristed hand. Mr Clements was only forty, but well past his prime – think of Eric Morley in an unsympathetic role, but with more weight and less breath. He sniffed his cigar before lighting it, and paused, ostensibly for thought. Mr Brookes let him take his time; he didn't have to be back downstairs for the matinee half for another ten minutes, and Mr Clements knew that.

'And you're going to feature this new girl of yours again, are you?' Mr Clements asked, sniffing again – as if the tobacco he was rolling between his fingers might contain some faint trace of the lady in question.

Like the door to the bar at the back of the stalls, Mr Clements's mahogany-panelled office up at the back of the second circle also had stained glass in its window. That, combined with a general dustiness, made it a dingy place to do business on a Thursday afternoon, but Mr Brookes wasn't going to let that cramp his style. He was pretty sure he'd aroused Mr Clements's interest; now all he had to do was finesse that into a booking. He took his time – he knew that the last thing you ever needed to do in these conversations was to sound like you were desperate for work. It was all, as always, a question of timing. Slow on the build-up; quick on the produce.

'Well, you saw yourself how well she goes across when you were kind enough to drop in and catch us on Saturday night, Mr Clements, especially with the lads upstairs,' he said lazily, making it sound as if he had six other offers in his pocket already – and as if he hadn't personally invited Clements to come and watch that particular show. 'Basically, I'm thinking about really going to town on the costumes for this one, and then putting her in something abbreviated for the finale. Of course –' he paused strategically – 'Of course if I *do* decide to open the act here then that would all depend on what sort of a bill you might be thinking of putting together for the celebrations. Where are you heading? Naughty, or nice – that's always the choice in this business, isn't it?'

'Oh, I think we'll be staying naughty, Coronation night or not,' said Mr Clements, keeping his eyes on the coiling smoke from his now-lit cigar. He instinctively mistrusted illusionists, and this Brookes character was giving him even more of the creeps than usual with his well-oiled patter. 'People can always get nice at home. I've got a new girl troupe lined up for the double spot at number two – Marie Devere's lot. They've just been supporting Max at the Leeds Empire. Though if I know Marie, there'll be a couple of strategically placed Union Jacks in the finale just to keep things proper.'

'So a double number-two spot for the girls with a fast turn-around in between that needs covering, just like on this one?' said Mr Brookes quickly, but looking airily down at a fingernail all the same, just to keep up appearances.

They both knew that that was the real point. The art of putting together a good running order for a variety show is a very practical one, and having found a formula that worked, Mr Clements was reluctant to change it. The ladies in the audience had to be kept happy with the comedy and the occasional well-turned-out gentleman, while the men in the audience had to be kept in their seats with the promise of seeing the goods at the end of the evening. That meant that the two outings for the troupe of underdressed young ladies who were always the number two attraction at the Grand had to be held back until the second half and then put on close together under the headliner, and that in turn meant a very nifty change from near-undress to near-illegal in between their two spots, with a new backdrop to go in upstage as well. The problem was always finding the right third-from-top filler to cover this change – too saucy, and it stole the nudes' second-spot thunder and killed the build-up to the headliner; too straight that late in the evening, and it was bound to get the bird.

'Yes . . . that's one possible idea. I still haven't made up my mind, of course. There are nearly four weeks to go . . .'

Mr Clements released a throatful of smoke into the colour-stained air as he said it, watching the blue and purple mix and turn slowly muddy as if to emphasise his point. His face was mask of heavy-jowled neutrality. *Good*, thought Mr Brookes, *he's going to bloody book me*.

'And of course I'd be happy to stick a Union Jack anywhere you fancy on my Pamela if that's what it takes to make her fit the bill, Mr Clements. You just say the word.'

There was another exhalation of smoke, another winding together of blue and purple.

'Got a title?'

Of course Mr Brookes had a title; it had been in his little black notebook since teatime on Tuesday, inspired by a tea-shop encounter with a youngster who'd told him she'd just had her first row with her husband. Just as he had imagined doing with her, Mr Brookes took his time.

'Well,' he said, giving a fair impression of a man in need of a fellow artiste's professional opinion, albeit with one raised eyebrow. 'I'm still not *quite* sure . . . but how does "Teddy Brookes: Respectable At Last!" strike you as a billing?'

Smoke snorted out of Mr Clements's nostrils as he laughed, and he held out his fat right hand across the desk for Mr Brookes to shake.

'Very clever. And does the young lady in question know what she's in for yet?'

'I think you can leave that to me, Mr Clements.'

'I'm sure I can.'

He could have winked, but he didn't need to. The business part of the meeting concluded, he shouted through the half-open door behind him.

'Florrie!'

A thin plain woman with a bun and a notepad squeezed herself in sideways through the connecting door, and took up what was clearly her usual seat in the only other chair, pencil poised.

'Yes, Mr Clements?'

'Contract,' Mr Clements barked. 'Two weeks in the Coronation Special with one week extension to be confirmed; June second kick-off, same rates, new title, billing as agreed. Cash in hand after the first house on Thursdays, et cetera. And if we might have that pot of tea now, that would be lovely.'

Mr Brookes took the main foyer stairs down to the auditorium two at a time, and as he crossed the still-dark carpet his mind was working as fast as his feet. He wasn't sure he could afford the old girl in Forest Hill for the frocks this time – what was the name of that piece on Mare Street who'd said to be in touch if he ever needed any second-hand rigs? She was about Pam's size, wasn't she? – and he was sure he could get the outfits on tick if he treated her to a quick reunion. Then there was the apparatus, of course – and which music to use for his entrance. Something smart, he fancied – upbeat, but smart. Jo Stafford's 'You Belong to Me' – just a first idea, obviously, but not bad, not bad at all when he thought about it . . .

He paused for a moment to compose himself. Straight after picking up the wages this evening would probably be the best time to try to confirm with Clements that they could use the stage to rehearse again – the Grand must have pulled down well into three figures with that last house on Saturday, so there was a fair chance that the weekly accounts would have put him in a good mood. And he'd have to have a careful think about how he was going to talk Pam round into working on a new routine when she'd only just got on top of the current one – though he was confident that he'd already successfully laid the groundwork in that department, thank you very much. *Ready when you are, Mr Brookes*, would be his professional assessment of that particular situation.

Smiling, Mr Brookes decided that some sort of celebration might be in order. He visualised the relevant page of his notebook, and landed on the fourth name on his current list. He just felt like somebody else buying the drinks for a change. He wiped his hands, and pulled open the heavy metal of the pass door. It sighed – as always – and slid softly shut behind him.

13

Thursday was matinee day of course, and there's something about doing the bloody thing three times in a row that always gives the company an extra determination to get that final house applauding properly. Even Mr Brookes was not immune to this general impulse, it seems, because when Pam came up from her second dip in their final calls that night he did something that he never did and threw in an impromptu. Turning to her with an extra, unscheduled bow, he kissed the back of her white-gloved hand – right in front of everybody – provoking an extra cheer from the boys upstairs and a ringing shout of *Good luck, mate!* from one of them in particular. Milking it, Mr Brookes winked ostentatiously out at the house as the tabs came down, and patted the trouser pocket where he'd stowed his ropes, getting yet another laugh – making Reg, who was still curled up inside his hot little metal prison in the base of the apparatus, wonder what all the extra noise was for. Once the tabs were down, Mr Brookes surprised Pam by brightly suggesting that they might keep the new piece of business in, if she didn't mind, and if the house seemed to warrant it. Pam said, yes, of course – the move made sense – and wondered what had got into him. As she watched him pull off his gloves and nod a quick *Good evening* to the tall redhead leading Madame Valentine's girls onstage, it occurred to her that Mr Brookes had the definite air of man who was planning a date after work. There'd been an extra spring in his step all the way through the act tonight – an extra lightness. Yes, that was it – look at the way he was pulling his gloves off, grinning already as he headed upstairs to get changed. *God help the lucky lady who's on the receiving end of that one*, she thought to herself as she watched him go.

When Pam got upstairs and peeled one of her own gloves off – the inside of the satin had now taken on the exact colour of her own skin, she noticed – she discovered that Mr Brookes's gallantry had left a carmine stain. She turned the glove right-side out again and laid it flat on her dressing table ready for Reggie to collect for the wash, thinking nothing more about it.

Reggie, when he arrived to help her undress, noticed the lipstick straight away. His lips tightened when he saw it, and he carried on with his usual routine of unzipping her dress and offering his steadying hand in conspicuous silence. All he did say, finally, was that maybe they should get her a second pair of gloves so that she could have one in the wash and one on the go. Pam could tell he was upset about something more than just an extra bit of hand-washing – there was a definite edge to his voice – and when Reg's silence continued she decided that the air definitely needed clearing. She lifted off her wig, and started pulling out the first pins.

'Look, Reg, if you're worried about Mr Brookes getting fresh with me, don't be.'

Reggie kept up his business with the dress. The hands lifted, and patted, and pulled.

'Reg? It's not as if I'm going to let him –'

'What?'

The word had come out harder than he'd meant it to. Their eyes met in the mirror, and Pam was about to reply, but before she had time to do it she was cut off by a sharp rapping on the dressing-room door.

'Are you decent in there? Hello?'

Of course, they knew who it was even before he called out; he'd used his knuckles in exactly the same pattern as he used on the cabinet with his cane – too hard, and a touch too smartly. Pam was the one who broke the contact of their eyes in the mirror.

'Just a minute!'

She gestured, and Reg threw her her dressing gown. She caught it, wrapped it on over her bra and licked her lips.

'Come in!'

'Sorry to bother you, Pamela,' said Mr Brookes, leaning in through the door with his hand still on the door handle, and still in his full make-up, as if the idea of visiting Pam upstairs had struck him all of a sudden. 'But I was just wondering if you fancied going out for a drink after the show tomorrow night. Nothing too posh, just the Queen's Hotel for last orders.'

He leaned forward.

'Well?'

'Well, I –'

The smile flicked on like an illuminated sign.

'Lovely! I've got a little proposition I want to put to you. Sorry about the lipstick on that glove, Reg –' his eyes flicked towards the offending article – 'but you know what I'm like when I'm in the presence of a lady, eh? Just can't help myself.'

The painted smile broadened a little for Reggie's benefit, and, of course, an eyebrow rose.

'If you say so, Mr Brookes,' said Reg, picking up pins off her dressing table. If the boss had suddenly decided to present himself as a cheeky chappie straight out of a front-cloth sketch, Reg was keeping well out of it. He wasn't paid to do dialogue.

'I'm sure you can't,' said Pam, finally coming back on Mr Brookes's last line. 'And in that case I'm sure you won't want to intrude while this particular lady finishes getting dressed.

And by the way, the answer's yes. I'd love to go out for a Friday-night drink.'

'Good. No need to dress right up . . .' He flicked his eyes from Pam to Reg, and then back to Pam.

'See you tomorrow!'

The door clicked smartly shut behind him – right on the button, as they say.

'Well, blow me down with a feather,' said Pam, more or less to herself, and after a suitable pause. 'Anyone would think he'd rehearsed that.'

She looked at Reg in the mirror; he'd turned his back, and one hand was reaching for the burgundy satin again.

'The Queen's Hotel. I'm not sure if that counts as pushing the boat out or not. What d'you reckon? Reg?'

Reggie was making a proper meal of rearranging the dress. For some reason, he couldn't get it to drape straight on the hanger.

'Oh come on Reg . . .'

Pam started attacking her hair again, tugging the pins out of the matted curls rather harder than she needed to. She was getting angry with the boy now. Did he think she couldn't look after herself?

'Look,' she said, 'I've said this before, but I'll say it again so there's no mistake. You don't have to worry about me tomorrow night, you really don't. With any luck, he just wants to buy me a drink and tell me he's got us a ten-week tour at double the money. You do want us to keep on working together, don't you? Reg?'

Her hands stopped. A hairpin fell on the floor.

'Reg?'

His voice was thicker than usual – choked. As if he had a stone in his throat.

'I just think you ought to remember –'

It was her turn to snap.

'What?'

Reggie's hands stopped whatever it was they were doing. One of them clenched and unclenched under the satin, an organ beating under skin, and there was a very full beat of silence.

'That he probably did rehearse it. He rehearses every bloody thing he does.'

Pam's hands seemed undecided about their next action too, but then they made up their mind. She wasn't taking lessons in how to deal with a man in a dinner jacket from a kid of Reggie's age, that was for sure, and certainly not from one of his persuasion. The plucking fingers flew back into action, slamming pins down onto the dressing table.

'Oh, for Christ's sake, Reg! Do you think I can't spot a fibber when I see one? Trust me, I've heard them all before.'

Pam tugged and slammed until the pins were all out; Reg said nothing. Then she took a deep breath, and stared at her hands, and laid them flat on the dressing table. Deciding that it was time to change the subject before somebody said something they shouldn't, she looked up at her clippings, thrust her hands up into her now-released hair and turned her head first to the left and then to the right, inspecting the lines of her neck and jaw, chin up and imaginary diamond-chandelier earrings swinging in the lights. She was damned if she was going to let this nonsense come between them.

'Right,' she said, all determination. 'On to more important matters. Do you think I should get it chopped? Nothing drastic, just a couple of inches. Reg? Come on.'

Reggie felt the same as she did – the last thing he wanted was to have to row, or to have to explain why he'd snapped at her so hard – but it was still an effort to wipe his feelings out of his face before he turned and looked into the mirror over her shoulder.

'How d'you mean?' he said.

'Oh, I don't know,' Pam said, adjusting the angle of her neck again, satisfied that she was getting things back under control between the two of them. 'I just feel like going for something a bit different for a change. Something a bit more . . . you know; royal. What d'you reckon?'

14

He'd got wet, and the sky was threatening more, and it was a Friday morning, not a Sunday like it was supposed to be – but he didn't bloody care. This needed sorting out straight away.

'He always has to get them just where he wants them, doesn't he?'

He wiped his mouth with the back of his hand.

'Doesn't he? – the dressed-up, greased-up, made-up bastard . . . Every time. *Every* time. The hand in the small of her back first, then the word in her ear, then the kiss on the glove, then the *Fancy a quick drink after work?* – it's a bloody routine. She may think she's seen and heard it all before, but I actually bloody have, remember. And the time before that . . .'

Now that he was alone, he badly wanted to thump someone. His fist was clenching again, but all there was to hit up here was stones.

'And she deserves . . .'

His foot stabbed down into the turf. It wasn't the lump in his throat that was stopping him this time; this time, it was blood, rising to his face.

'She deserves a good one, this one, not someone who'll just . . .'

The boot kicked; the mouth twisted; the throat swallowed.

'She deserves . . .'

He stopped, reaching out to touch the gravestone, but then pulled his hand away. He kicked for one last time, forcing the word out between his teeth.

'. . . a lover.'

He wiped his hand across his face again, and tried to make his peace.

'Sorry. No – no, you're right,' he said after a bit, sniffing and straightening up and sticking his hands back in his pockets. 'I shouldn't say a thing. I should trust her to look after her bloody self. No, thank you, that's right. Might put her off her stride for the act, if I did. And who am I, eh? Who am I to be giving her advice? Who am I . . .?'

The question seemed to exhaust him. He wiped some rain away from the stone with his handkerchief, dabbing at it apologetically.

'Sorry to be bothering you on a Friday morning,' he said, 'and this early. I just needed to . . . I needed . . . I needed to talk.'

The handkerchief went back into the pocket, cold and wet.

'See you Sunday, I expect. Thank you for listening.'

He hovered, then gave up.

'Sleep well then.'

The whole thing had taken less than five minutes – less time than it had taken the clouds to gather and get ready to soak him properly this time.

Where had Reggie got that word from? I wonder – the one it had cost him so much effort to throw out at Doreen's stone. *Lover* – it isn't a word that crops much up in casual conversation, is it, in shops or queues or on buses and suchlike? Possibly somebody had used it in the film he'd watched with Pam last Sunday at the Essoldo, or perhaps someone had sung it on the radio that stood on the shelf behind the till in his cafe. Connie Francis, maybe – dropping it into his mind like a coin in the slot of a jukebox. Like a copper in a collecting box. The way it made him blush makes me wonder if Reggie had ever used it before.

He stuck to the advice his mother had given him, and didn't say a word. In fact the only sort of conversation that he and Pam had before or after work that Friday night was when Pam kissed him a quick thank-you for her present – a spare pair of white satin gloves which Reg had stopped off and bought on his way back to work from the cemetery, detouring specially. When she tried them on, he told her that they were to make sure she stayed snow white, kisses or not. She'd laughed when he said that, and wiped the lipstick off his cheek with a handkerchief from her bag.

Those gloves had cost Reggie the best part of two guineas, which was a great deal more than he could really afford. Normally he was expert at ferreting out the cheapest of everything, but not today; as he'd reached the middle of town that afternoon he kept on going through the rain until he reached Hanningtons, which was the priciest department store in the town, all mock-Tudor panelling and staff with ideas above their station. As she took his money, the lady behind the counter kept her eyes averted from his water-stained jacket, and made a point of telling sir how fortunate it was that he'd come in when he had; they'd had quite a run on the white satin line lately, what with people wanting to look their very best for the forthcoming celebrations, as she was sure sir appreciated. Reggie bit back his smile, and said that sir certainly did.

15

Now that it was time to actually get dressed for her date, Pam was feeling slightly peculiar. It had been a while, after all, and although the Queen's certainly wasn't the Dorchester, it wasn't too shabby either – she'd taken the precaution of popping down to the seafront at lunchtime to have a quick look. In the end she'd decided to keep things simple and smart, and instead of getting her hair done had splashed out on a new pair of 12-denier stockings. They'd been pricey, but they were going to look lovely, and they were going to make her feel *right*. Make her feel herself.

Now she just had to get her mouth to work – and it was giving her trouble. She'd already had to wipe it off and start again twice. She flicked her eyes back up to the most recent picture in the collection on her mirror, added one more stroke of red, and decided that that would have to do. She blotted, wiped her fingers and then carefully opened the flat white cardboard box that was lying on her dressing table. They'd never really been her best feature, her legs, she thought, but still . . .

The 12-denier nylon did its expert job at once, turning her calves and thighs into well-turned ivory. She stopped to assess herself full-length; a suspender needed adjusting. She'd decided against all-over black for the date – too like work, she thought – and now she reached up under the ball gown on the back of the door and got the yellow-checked tweed skirt from her best suit off its hanger. Professional as always, she

146

rolled on her sweater, high-stepped into the skirt, reached round for the zipper, cinched her belt as tight as it would go, clasped on her pearls and ran her fingers through her hair for one last time, only then letting herself smile. *Not bad; not bad, for the grand old age of twenty-seven*, she mouthed to herself quietly. Clipping on the soft jangle of her charm bracelet, she crossed herself with the four cold pennies of Elizabeth Arden's Blue Grass that were always her finishing touch – wrists first, then the sides of her neck just below her ears. Sugar, talc, that big bunch of roses . . . Making her final check, she tilted her head, widened her eyes and then – taking herself by surprise with the gesture, and almost making herself laugh – misted herself across both black lambswool-and-cashmere-mix breasts with an impromptu sweep of the little gilt-and-glass bottle and its sage-green atomiser. She put the bottle down and cupped her breasts in her hands, pushing them up and out under the soft black fabric, showing them to the mirror.

'And tonight at the London Palladium, ladies and gentlemen . . .'

She dipped the suggestion of a royal-box curtsy to a newspaper clipping, and matched her smile to Margaret's.

'. . . your Royal Highness – tonight, a very special treat; will you put your hands together please for the very lovely Miss Pamela Rose and her pair of performing beauties . . .'

You had to laugh – and she did, right out loud this time. As her head went back, the double rap on the door came right on cue.

Timing – remember?

'Just a minute!'

She didn't rush. Cigarettes, lipstick, compact, precautions, front-door key – it never hurt to settle yourself and check your bag before they got their first good look . . . She gave herself one last spray behind each ear, and then slipped on her shoes – not brand new, but the black suede had come up nicely under the nail brush – and ran her hands up her stockings for one last time, feeling the slight friction of their grip. Right. Last but not least, she checked the catch on her charm bracelet – it sometimes didn't quite close, but tonight her fingers seemed to have got it in one.

'Nearly there!' she called through the door, her voice going up the scale a notch, and flicking her hair in the mirror one last time. Then she took a deep breath, picked up her coat and opened the door.

Mr Brookes had clearly gone to quite a bit of trouble himself. He'd got on a beautifully cut dark blue suit that Pam hadn't seen before, his coat draped over his arm and a dark grey homburg in his right hand. The hair was impeccable, and the shirt dazzling.

'Good evening,' he said, in a voice almost as scrubbed-up as hers. 'Are we ready for the off then?'

Clattering down the concrete stairs two steps ahead of him, Pamela could feel her feet slipping slightly inside her shoes; the sensation of her thighs just brushing together under her skirt was also heightened by the gloss of the brand-new nylon. It always made you feel better when you'd got something good on underneath, didn't it? She promised herself she wouldn't let them get laddered, not on their very first outing.

As they got to the end of the alley, she stopped to turn up her collar. The rain was over, thank God, but it was still chilly.

'Well then,' she said. 'What's this proposition you've got to make to me, Mr Brookes? Or do you want to get a drink inside you before we get down to business?'

For some reason, Mr English forgot to turn off one of the light fittings up on his top-floor corridor on that particular Friday; in consequence, a thin strip of light was able to seep in under Pam's locked dressing-room door all night long. Undisturbed, it worked patiently to rearrange the shadows which she'd left behind. It edged her now-dark mirror with a bevelled silver frame, and caught at her gilt-and-glass perfume bottle. Gently, it picked out the white cardboard and ghostly tissue paper whose job it had recently been to keep her new stockings a secret, and stroked the expensive sheen of her present from Reg. Up above the mirror, it made sure that the newsprint images taped along its frame stayed subtly and suggestively legible all through the long hours. The Princess's trademarks all still gleamed, even in the dark – the elbow-length gloves, the shining hair, that famous, bold and still-unmarried smile.

On the back of the highest-up of these photographs, the one that Pam had clipped out of that *Argus* centre spread on her first day here by the sea, there was a story that she'd never turned the photograph over to read. Because the columns of print on the back of the clipping weren't exactly aligned with the edges of the picture on the front, Pam's nail scissors had cut some of the sentences in half, but the relevant details were all quite clear. A twenty-four-year-old down on a day trip from London had met a man on the pier, and only later discovered that he was not all that he claimed to be. *I cannot believe how foolish I was*, she told the court, in some distress. *When I think of how my mother warned me, I feel such a –*

But apparently that twenty-four-year-old down from Mitcham didn't think, and neither, when it came down to it, did Pamela. Later that Friday night, after two drinks at the Queen's Hotel and one at the Bedford, she let herself be taken on to a members' club just off the seafront, a place where Mr

149

Brookes's name had been left on the door. It was fun, and noisy, but actually quite tatty; it gave more of an impression of a crowded front room than of a club, with fishing nets around the walls and a record player tucked away in the corner. Over the sound of somebody playing 'September in the Rain' on a trumpet, she leaned forward while Mr Brookes told her all the details of this new act he was planning, the quick changes it would involve and the new prospects it could open up for her if she would only agree to join him in this exciting adventure. She nodded quite a bit, and smiled where appropriate. Then, having said she'd be delighted, she let Mr Brookes escort her back to his room in Hove in a taxi, and there she let him undress her and take her to bed.

Are you surprised? She was, slightly, even as she was letting it happen. She didn't feel the scene was quite in character – not after all the promises she'd made to herself in this bracing seaside air. But then again, as she told herself while his well-practised hands were searching for the zipper at the back of her skirt – that nugget of metal which she'd been aware of all evening, digging into her under the slightly-too-tight grip of her belt – the whole of life is a quick-change act really, isn't it? And never mind, because it's always the same woman inside the outfit, whatever she's wearing. It doesn't *change* anything, what you're wearing, does it? I mean, you're still *you*, no matter what.

16

After he'd finished his Friday-night tidy-up, Reg didn't quite know what to do with the rest of that evening. In particular, he didn't know what to do with the time that he would normally have spent walking Pam back up the Queen's Road to Mrs Brennan's. He murdered some of it by going back upstairs and laying out all of Mr Brookes's handkerchiefs for Saturday's matinee – the boss liked to have a clean one laid out for him to put his watch and signet ring on as soon as he got into work – but he was still back down at the stage door signing himself out at twenty past ten. A pub had never much been his idea of fun, and he didn't fancy a bag of chips, so that really just left walking.

Just as well you're good at it, he told himself. He wished Mr English goodnight, hugged his jacket tight around him as he went up the alley and then struck out left up North Road, turning immediately sharp left again at the very first corner he came to.

Most people who get the train down to Brighton choose to get lost in the Lanes at some point – there's something about a tangle of disreputable alleys being hidden away right in the middle of the town that makes them seem to epitomise the place. Tonight, their maze of squalid corners just suited Reggie's mood.

He headed into them with no particular destination in mind, and then just followed his feet, switching direction if he heard people up ahead coming out of a pub, dodging left and right whenever he needed to. He wasn't, as you or I would have been if we had had that much on our minds, loitering; head down, he kept up his pace, relying on the jarring rhythm of his feet on the wet brick pavements to distract him from the pictures that he was trying to keep out of his head. He passed an alleyway of shops which had their black-painted shutters pulled down and padlocked; noticing that one of the locks looked broken, he stooped down and tugged. The lock held, but the shutter rattled. The sound made him think about all the packing and loading there would be to get done after the last show tomorrow, and of the train back to London. He tapped his pocket, twice.

The twists of the Lanes are disorientating even to locals, and when his feet finally brought him out onto an open street Reg had to stop and look around in order to work out properly where he was. The Clock Tower was just to his right, which meant that the front was away down West Street to his left. Twenty-five to eleven . . . For a few minutes he stood and stared at one of the damaged stone women decorating the base of the tower; she was lifting up the stumps of her handless arms as if she was trying to make some kind of a point, and he wondered if it was him she was trying to talk to. The sea was beginning to make itself felt in a dark and angry wind gusting up West Street from the front, and he definitely didn't want to head right up towards the station and Mrs Brennan's, so after a moment's more calculation he crossed straight over – there was a dark westwards-heading side street that looked promising. As he was crossing the road the cold made him remember that he hadn't eaten, and he stopped at the kerb to rummage in his pockets. A leftover shard of toffee was the best they could do, but he popped it into his mouth anyway, and set to work on smoothing its edges with his tongue.

First things first; maybe she was right. Maybe Mr Brookes did just want to talk to her about work. And if not, and if he did make a play for her, well, surely she'd be able to make a joke of it. She was good at that. Brookes would be in foul mood tomorrow for the matinee, but rather that than the other.

And as for work, well, after tomorrow something was bound to turn up, because it always did. Always.

The iron-railed side street he'd chosen for his route eventually led him out into a square lined with boarding houses and hotels. He watched the signs swinging in the wind – there was even a bloody *Sea View* again, reminding him that eventually he'd have to reverse his direction and head back to Mrs Steed's before the front door got locked. But he was nowhere near tired enough for that yet, so he let the square lead his feet into its neighbour. This one was big, full of a lawn of black grass and tall, staring windows. He didn't want anyone pulling back a curtain and watching him while he was trying to think things through like this, so when a dark lane-mouth invited him to duck out of the building wind he accepted its offer. *Story of my flippin' life*, he thought, wrapping up his jacket again as tight as it would go.

By ten to eleven Reggie had stitched his route through the back alleys of the town as far west as the cluster of mews behind the Metropole Hotel. They were dark, and confusing, and he had to watch his step on the wet cobbles as the wind came knocking round the unlit corners. One rude buffet of air made him stop and steady himself, and he found himself staring up at a cliff of blackness.

The back of the Metropole is eight storeys high – eight storeys of brick and iron – and it reared up over him, sealing off the street and blocking out the clouds tearing across the moon with its fantastic pinnacled roof. *Bedtime*, thought Reg, as he stared up at the blank panes of all the windows. *And there must be hundreds of the buggers in there.* Right up under the crested roof, an eye winked open; through a small panel of frosted glass, one yellow light came on, barred by the steps of an iron fire escape. *Must be for the staff, right up there under the roof,* Reg thought. That was it; some young doorman, taking a late-night piss – or a young barman, unbuttoning his collar to get at the back of his neck before he turned in. Reggie stared up at the window and waited for the moment when the young man would go – when the light would click off again and restore the cliff to darkness. It did. He prised his eyes away, swallowed his last mouthful of toffee'd saliva, and turned, feeling the wind again. He didn't know where he was heading now at all.

He'd been avoiding it all night, but now he could hear it roaring, and decided to get it over with. Ducking his head down straight into the wind, he grabbed the cold metal of the promenade railing with both hands and steadied himself. Squinting away to his left he could just make out a late-night taxi pulling up outside the Metropole, releasing four figures who formed themselves into couples and hurried inside, but everything else was deserted. The piers were dark, and the festoons of naked bulbs strung between the lamp posts along the prom were being rocked and tugged by the wind as they stretched away into the town – pearls, on a black sweater. He swore, wondering who the fuck they kept the lights on for on a night like this anyway. Then he made himself look out straight ahead, at the sea.

The water seemed to be boiling. As he watched, the foam on the breaking waves turned the same filthy white as the broken arms of that woman on the tower. They gestured, and grabbed, rushing towards him, their black hands seeming to want something more than the wet stones they were plucking and dragging and throwing angrily aside. A great shaggy head of water drew back, then crashed up the beach, unleashed. Reggie let go of the rail and stepped back – he'd forgotten it could be this close. This angry, and this black.

Christ, but he was cold.

Suddenly furious with himself, he grabbed his jacket and spun round, ducking his head back down. He turned east, stabbing his boot into the asphalt so hard that it almost made him tilt over – and talking to himself all the way, shouting, telling himself in no uncertain terms to stop thinking and get off home and upstairs before he froze to bloody death. Above him, the ropes of pearls swayed in the wind, looping from lamp post to lamp post all the way along his journey home.

When he got to Fitzroy Place he crawled into bed with all his clothes on, and tried for nearly an hour to imagine the warmth of somebody else's body in there with him, but the chill of all that foaming, tearing darkness seemed to have got right inside him, and he couldn't do it.

17

'Well, come on in if you're going to, Reg! Don't stand in the bloody corridor.'

He winced; he forgot that on these concrete floors his feet sounded different to other people's. He should have knocked straight away like he'd planned to, instead of standing there wondering how he was going to start the conversation. What had happened with Mr Brookes? He shifted himself from boot to boot, opened the door, and decided to get it over with. He made the word a question.

'Morning?'

It was only half past eleven, but Pamela was already sitting in front of her mirror, stripped to her bra and knickers and half made up. She was wearing a pair of clip-on pearl earrings which Reggie had never seen before, and brandishing a handful of shell-pink swansdown that was turning the room hazy with talc.

'So has he told you?'

She narrowed her eyes in her mirror as she said it, assessing the effect of the powder as it settled in a fine shawl across her naked shoulder. What did she mean?

'Told me what?'

The talc was new as well, he realised – stronger-smelling than usual; hyacinths instead of her usual roses-and-sugar.

'Come on – I haven't seen him yet this morning. Told me what?'

The darting powder puff stopped, and her eyes locked onto his. They were shining, but red – had she been crying, or was it just the powder?

'He's only bloody got us another bloody booking, Reg. And by the bloody seaside.'

Reggie thought she was going to turn round and kiss him; her eyes were wide now, and their brightness was flooding straight into her powder-blotched mouth. *Thank Christ for that* was his immediate, private thought – Mr Brookes really had taken her on the date to talk about work.

'What? Where? Not Morecombe bloody Bay – and please don't tell me I'm going back to Weston-super-Mare, I hate fucking sand.'

'Here!'

She changed her mind about the kiss, and the swansdown swooped back to its work. Reg stared, thinking fast. They'd been lucky to get three weeks out of the Grand as it was – did she mean they were coming back for a summer season? What about between now and then? Or did she mean that Clements was giving them an extension? That wouldn't make any sense . . .

'But everybody in this town's already bloody seen the act. We'll get the bird –'

'No, silly.' She said it as if it ought to be obvious, smiling as you would at a child; her hands dumped the swansdown in a cloud of powder, and stretched an imaginary placard across her mirror. '*Coming soon, our very own Grand Coronation Special.* Mr Clements is already getting them printed.'

Still not getting the response she wanted, she spelt it out.

'Third billing in a brand-new show, Reg; single spot, second half, same money – and four new costumes. Opening on the big night itself.'

Now it was Reggie's turn to look wide-eyed; the second of June was three weeks on Tuesday.

'Is this a joke? Because if Mr Brookes –'

157

'No! He's signed. Signed the contract and everything. He told me last night.'

'Blimey . . .'

The smile fell.

'Well, you might look bloody pleased, Reg. A new act. With *me*.'

'No, I am – it's just that we've only just got on top of this one. And he only decided to tell you all of this last night?'

The swansdown hovered over the powder pot again, dipped, and then was left forgotten in the hazy mid-air as the words came tumbling out. She must have been saving this up all night to tell him – no wonder her voice sounded shaky with excitement.

'Well, you know how he is, Reg. Never speaks his mind unless he fancies it. And it's not all bad – starting work this late, I mean – because Clements is going to keep the Grand dark on the Monday, because no one will be going out the night before the ceremony itself, obviously, so at least we get one extra day onstage that week – and a proper run-through with Mr Clifford that evening, most likely – *and –*'

Reggie realised that this must all be a paraphrase. He could just see Teddy's mouth at work in the bar at the Queen's, making it all make smiling sense.

'– and because he's going to let us work on the stage again there'll be no schlepping everything back to London on the train! Teddy says we'll have to get properly cracking to be ready in time, of course, because he's going to make a few changes to the apparatus, and there'll be some bits and pieces to get from London for me, but listen, if we could get me disappearing in one week then I'm sure we can pull something new off in three and a bit. Fit for a queen, he thinks I am –'

It was almost as if she was talking to herself, the words were falling so fast and furious out of her mouth. So there was going to be work on the apparatus as well – and Brookes seriously expected them to get a new routine worked from scratch in sixteen days, did he? – sixteen, because today was Saturday, and the second was a Tuesday – and that was assuming they could start on Monday, which he doubted if there was gear to be fetched down from London. Bloody hell –

'Reg?'

The powder puff was suspended in mid-air again, and she was searching for his eyes in the mirror.

'Are you with me?'

'Sorry. He's not going to actually call it that, is he?'

'What?'

'The new act. "Fit for a Queen".'

'Think I'm too common to be presented, do you, young man?'

His face fell.

'Oh, come on, Reg.'

He had thought she was being serious for a moment, but then she released him from the reprimand with a high peal of laughter, her now-white face cracking right open. He laughed too, and it was with punctuations of loud and relieved laughter on both their parts that the conversation continued.

Pam kept up the work on her face as Reg quizzed her, answering his questions as best she could, telling him everything she could remember from the night before and all the time wiping and repainting like a giddy-brained showgirl. Seeing how happy she was, and wanting to get as much information out of her about the new act as he could without worrying her, Reg completely forgot to ask her where the expensive-looking new powder and earrings had come from.

Or why, indeed, she was so excitedly and clumsily making herself up for a two thirty matinee when it was still only half past eleven in the morning.

Waking to light that was coming in through a strange pair of curtains, Pam had known immediately whose bed she was in. She didn't look back to the head on the pillow, but picked up her shoes, balled her still-unladdered stockings into her handbag and crept from the house like a thief. As the front door clicked shut behind her she found herself standing on a street of suburban front gardens, each corralled behind a closed front gate. It was barely seven o'clock, and in the slanting light of the rising sun the letter boxes and rose bushes seemed to be pursing their lips and quietly averting their eyes. Pamela had grown up on a street like this, and recognised their expressions. She slipped on her shoes and looked around, and then – for want of a better direction – walked towards the sun, thinking that the seafront would probably be as good a way of finding her way back home as any.

It was a beautiful morning out on the promenade, calm and clear. After passing the first pier she sat down on a bench to wait for something to be open. She needed something – or someone – to tell her what to think. There was a small black dog running unaccompanied on the asphalt, and a girl in a very short skirt drawing circles behind the wire fencing of a roller rink, but neither of these details helped her to clear her head. She sat there for a while, watching the water flatten and shimmer, but then as the air began to warm and the first cars pass behind her on the seafront road she became very conscious of her bare legs. There was nowhere to slip on her stockings that she could see, so she got up and walked again. A bit further down the prom she spotted a cafe that was open, so she went in and got herself a cup of tea and a packet of

Player's from the machine. Then she sat in the window in the sun and tried to talk some sense into herself. She got her compact out to check her face at one point, but snapped it shut immediately and laid it on the table by her teacup. She knew she ought to go home and wash, but for some reason couldn't face the thought of walking all the way back up to Mrs Brennan's just to be stared at again, this time by the counterpane of her own, undisturbed bed.

When she'd paid for her tea she walked on again, and when the shops opened found herself buying earrings and a small round box of the new Coty face powder, things she knew that she couldn't afford. Then she remembered her dressing room at the Grand, and the Dettol, and the hot water, and almost ran.

The first thing she noticed as she signed herself in was his key, hanging on the board. It made her stomach turn over. Promising Mr English that she was all right – noticing the sudden closure of her face, he'd frowned and asked whether she was – she headed straight upstairs.

As she closed her dressing-room door behind her she had to control herself so that she didn't slam it. So, this was what it was going to be like from now on – every bloody time she came into work. Checking to see if his key was on the board or not, wondering if he was in already, every *bloody* time . . . *Just get your bloody face on*, she told herself in her mirror. *Have a wash, get your bloody face on and get on with it. You'll think of something. You always do.*

Mr Brookes had said all the right things, of course. How he'd been thinking about this ever since they'd met; how different she was to his last girl; what *fun* she was; how he hoped she knew from the way the punters reacted to her what a class act she was, and how he couldn't believe no one had ever asked her to take a solo spot before. That was all fine; she'd heard versions of all that plenty of times. He'd even said some of it in the taxi, with the man listening, which she'd actually rather enjoyed. But then, later, when they'd got back to his place, he'd said something else, something which had really upset her. When the light had woken her up the next morning it was the first thing she'd remembered, and she remembered it again now after Reggie had gone back downstairs to get himself ready and she was alone again with just the mirror. When Mr Brookes had got all of her clothes off, he'd asked her to go and stand at the foot of the bed so that he could get a proper look at her. She didn't mind doing that; she knew that men liked it like that sometimes, and she knew how good she looked with just a bedside lamp on. The problem was that when he'd seen her stripped, with the soft light of the lamp under its pleated silk shade turning her black and white into black and rose, Mr Brookes had leaned back on the pillow, lit himself a fag and breathed out the one word which always undid her.

Special.

Just the one word – releasing it from his mouth as easily as the smoke from his cigarette. And just like that, she'd felt it strike her right inside.

He smiled, as if he knew what he'd done – as if he somehow knew that that was exactly the right word to use on her. After all these years.

She'd wanted to turn away, but didn't – his face didn't look particularly hard or handsome at all now, but plain and frank, as if the make-up really had come off for once – and then before she could move he'd said it again:

Yes; you really are very special, Miss Rose.

Then they'd settled down to the business – which once she'd got over that moment she'd enjoyed, a lot – but just when she was letting herself go and starting to make the noises, he'd pulled himself up so that he could watch her face and encourage her, and then he'd said the word over and over again, mouthing the word in time with his body, looking her right in the eye, deliberately keeping himself from going too fast.

Special. Special. Special . . .

Pam swiped at her face with her powder puff. Was she? The sound he'd made when he finished, and the look on his face, she'd believed him. She knew it was a mistake – knew it was only the drink talking, and downstairs, and that soft pink light – but there it was; that very ordinary bedroom with its lampshade and bed and carpet and wallpaper and discarded shoes had suddenly seemed very quiet and safe and, well, *special*, despite the noise they were making.

She'd believed him.

So what was she going to bloody do now? She scrabbled on her dressing table for her already-half-empty cigarette pack and lit up the next one, licking the powder off her lips. Wasn't that exactly what she'd told herself she was going to hold out for next, someone who could tell her that and make her believe it?

Lilac and roses, waiting for her when she got home . . .

She stubbed the cigarette out angrily. Now she'd made herself cry. She'd have to wipe her whole bloody face off and start again.

Not surprisingly, the matinee was a bit ropy later that after-noon – Pam almost forgot the glass of champagne on her return – but apart from that the last three Brighton perfor-mances of Teddy Brookes's 'Missing Lady' were clean and solid. After the show, Pam told Reggie that she felt like an early night, but made a provisional arrangement to meet him at the pictures again on Tuesday afternoon – Mr Brookes reckoned he'd be in London until at least that evening, getting all the bits and pieces they'd need together and seeing somebody about her new costumes. Brookes himself seemed to be heading out on a celebratory end-of-run Saturday-night date with somebody, because when Reggie went to collect the laundry after the third house he was vigorously brushing his teeth, and there was what looked like a small red jewellery box laid out next to his cigarette case and watch and signet ring on the dressing table. The Metropole Hotel was mentioned, which made Reg wonder who it could be, and also made him think for a moment about himself staring up at that one small lit window only the night before, imagining young men unbuttoning. After that momentary catch, he went home happy – relieved about Pam, as I said, relieved about work, and looking forward to telling his mum all his news in the morning.

18

He started before he even got to her stone this time, calling out to her as he came limping up the path.

'Bet you're warm enough today then.'

Somewhere high up over his shoulder, an invisible bird was singing – a tap of music, left running in the wind. Sky-blue butterflies were scribbling their erratic messages over the turf, and somewhere in the breezy sunlight he was sure he could smell lilacs, even up here where there were none. He was glad he'd got up early.

'So,' he continued, collecting up the dead irises from two weeks before and cheerfully slinging them away across the path, 'looks like we're going to be seeing quite a bit more of each other after all. Three weeks' rehearsal, then this new act – except that knowing Teddy Brookes Esquire I'm sure it'll be mostly just the old one with a few new bells on.'

The invisible bird stopped, and then restarted. The sun didn't waver, however – this was definitely May now, not April. There was hawthorn somewhere in the air too.

'She's been doing very well, our Pamela. She told me she almost forgot his glass of French's Ginger yesterday afternoon, but then she had had a bit of a night the night before, what with hearing all of Mr B's plans. The good news, I suppose, is that he likes her enough to persevere, which makes a change. Not a good *liker*, in general, our Mr Brookes, is he . . .? And it's going to be for the Coronation, did I say? That's all getting going down in the town here now, flags and stories and special windows popping up all over the place . . . Seems like a lot of fuss to me but everyone else seems to be happy so who am I, eh? No news of a title for the new act yet, but he always plays his cards close where that's concerned. Something corny again probably.'

It all seemed easier today, and the stone was warm when he stroked it. He unshaded his eyes, squinting at it in the light. He was enjoying himself.

'I think you'd like Pam. She's not everyone's cup of tea, what with the way she speaks her mind and doesn't always do her hair in the morning, but she scrubs up lovely. Last night she was tired and didn't want me to walk her home, but you could tell she was in a better mood because she'd got her face on properly just to walk home. Mr English on the stage door is mad about her, the silly old iron. Says she's the real thing, whatever that means.'

The squint turned into an almost-smile. It was funny, the things he thought of up here.

'I've never asked you what you used to look like, have I?'

The bird was still lavishing its praise on the empty sky, and Reggie let it sing for a bit to fill in the gap in the conversation. Then he rummaged in a pocket.

'Oh, I got something for you. I don't know why, really, but it made me think of you. There.'

He held up his trophy to show her.

'Looks like a nice place, don't you think? I asked the man in the newsagent's, and he said it's only about twenty minutes on the bus. Lots of people go out there on a Sunday, apparently. Tea shops on the green, and a walk round the pond to let the kiddies feed the ducks, like in the picture. I thought the three of us could get ourselves done up all smart and get the bus over together. Pam and you and me, I mean. She'd like that – Pam. I'm sure she'd like to meet you. The two of you could talk about me.'

He bent down and propped up the brightly coloured post-card on a tuft of grass at the foot of the stone, and then coughed to clear his throat.

'Oh, and another thing . . .'

Reg has never talked about this – not ever, not about any of it. Not about the boys in the street, not about the Rigolettos, not about the man in the Bradford boarding house. This was 1953, remember; talking was hard. But now that the proper occasion had finally arisen, it seemed easy, as easy – and as odd – as pouring his mother a cup of tea. Perhaps it was the clearing of the air with Pam that had done it, or the news about the booking, or the weather, or even just the beautiful sound of that out-of-sight companion of his, descanting around Reggie's half-laughing stumbles with its heartless, silver and unstoppable love song – or perhaps, like I said before, it was just time.

'. . . The thing is, since we're going to be here for another few weeks, I could do with a spot of advice. You know . . . about this somebody special I'm supposed to be looking for.'

He's a bit embarrassed to be doing this, but he perseveres. As does the bird.

'I mean, I can hardly go and stand on street corners just on the off-chance, can I? So I wondered if you could just drop me a hint. A hint of some likely spots to stand in. Or maybe you could give me a dream about him or something, so if he does just pass me on the street one lunchtime, I'll recognise him. You never know, do you? Only not a pub, please, you know I can't do that.'

Reggie knows this is all a game, and smiles again, properly this time – he knows there can be no reply, especially not out here in all this sunshine – but like I said, he's enjoying himself. He waits a moment, giving his mum a chance to answer should she care to, and then carries on.

'No suggestions? Oh well, I'll just have to rely on him to hunt me down and introduce himself, won't I?'

He pauses again, and his features slowly soften, in the way they sometimes do when nobody's watching him, and his voice loses its edges.

'No, he doesn't have to be anything too lovely. Quite an ordinary one will do me. But nice eyes, and not too tall, if you can manage it. Not that beggars can be choosers, can they?'

His fingers tap gently on the stone, and the boot shifts.

'No; no, you're right. Best not to answer that one.'

He says it again, patting the stone absent-mindedly while he does it:

'Best not.'

Apparently deciding that he's had enough, or at least that he needs to think about something else for a moment, Reggie looks up for the first time to see if he can spot that bird. The sun is quite high, and he can see nothing but dazzle, so he wipes the back of his hand across his nose and stoops down to settle the postcard into its tussock of grass. He does it using exactly the same gesture that you or I would use to prop a note up against a vase of flowers on a bedside cabinet, something to be read after we've quietly left the ward. Satisfied that it's firmly enough in place for the wind not to be able to steal it after he's gone, he stands up and steps away from the stone, dusting off his hands.

'Well . . .' he says, 'see you next week.'

The bird is silent for a moment.

'Wish me luck.'

They can be full of false promises, those first warm days in May. The newly strong sun can make you sweat if you catch it full on your back – especially if you're in a heavy tweed jacket, like Reggie always was – but the air can still chill you if it gets in under your shirt. That's what it tried to do now, as Reggie limped off towards the gate, but he didn't notice; as he hobbledehoyed his way down through the gate he stuck to his routine as always, and patted the penknife in his breast pocket twice undercover of its metallic shriek. As he emerged back out into the sun from under the bay trees, he stuck his hands in his pockets and started to whistle. It's an odd sound for a cemetery, a cheerfully out-of-tune rendition of the slave's chorus from *Aida* – but Reggie didn't care about that any more than he did about catching a chill in May, and made it ring out as loud and brassy as he could.

Whenever that tune was running through his head, you could be sure that Reg was thinking about standing in the wings back in Wimbledon, and about the smell of coal tar soap and sweat on still-damp wool. They were bloody beautiful, those two brothers, especially the little wiry one, the one who always jumped second but flew highest. He could just see him now, in the lights, with the diamonds . . .

So maybe Reggie didn't really want to meet someone ordinary after all, despite what he'd said to his mum.

19

A spot of good luck for the new act, Mr Brookes had said, pushing the little red jeweller's box across the table at the Metropole. Then he'd flipped it open and showed her the little gold cat for her charm bracelet curled asleep inside it, and that had been lovely – really lovely, actually. She'd enjoyed the drinks, too, and she'd enjoyed the sex again, even when he grabbed her wrists and slammed into her a little harder than she usually liked; seeing him take the precautions out of his wallet and put them on the bedside table this time had been a nice touch as well, making her feel properly taken care of – but despite all of this she still hadn't been able to spend the whole night with him. Something about the thought of taking that early-morning walk home again with all its sunlight and staring front doors and windows was dreadful, and it had made her suddenly swing her legs off the bed and start reaching underneath it for her shoes. He'd looked a bit surprised when she'd asked him where was the best place to find a taxi in Hove at this time of night, but as she'd said, no hard feelings; she just didn't feel quite ready to start waking up with somebody regularly.

She hadn't enjoyed not telling Reggie. She'd felt bad about not saying anything before the matinee on Saturday, and even worse after the third house when Brookes had popped in to ask her out for that second drink and then Reggie had turned up for the laundry two minutes later when she was getting her face on. She hated lying to him, white lies or not, and knew she was going to have to tell him sooner or later. Once that was done, she thought, she was probably going to feel better about the whole business.

On Monday afternoon, she'd dropped in on Mr English at the stage door – just for some company, really. Mr Brookes's plans had all sounded so urgent that the hiatus while he was away up in London caught her rather by surprise. They'd had a nice chat through the stage-door window about whose radio was going to be brought into the building on the big day so that they could follow the ceremony backstage, and she duly admired the rather yellowing newsprint wedding-day picture of the happy couple which he'd dug out from somewhere and pinned up in pride of place over his keyboard. Elizabeth looked very young in all her wedding satin and lace, and Philip very Greek and handsome with his gold stripes and high chin – and hair just like Mr Brookes, she noticed. November 1947 . . . that would have been about the time she did her first stint at Murray's, and that man with the flat in Bayswater had bought her her very first charm for her brace-let. The little gold Eiffel Tower, it had been – but then he'd never taken her to Paris after all.

Looking up at the royal couple, her arm on his, she couldn't work out if all that was a long time ago, or last week. And she still couldn't work out why she'd said yes to that second drink, the one at the Metropole. Her mouth had been so close to shaping a *no*, but the sound just hadn't come out for some reason.

On Tuesday, she met up with Reg at the pictures. The afternoon newsreel was all about the royal coaches doing their rehearsal for the procession down the Mall – honestly, the big day was all over everywhere now, like a rash – and the sight of schoolchildren wagging paper pennants at a big empty gilded box as it trundled past ought to have made her laugh, but instead it left her feeling uneasy. Who'd told them all to grin like that at the plate-glass windows as they slid past? It made her think about the cabinet, and Mr Brookes; he'd left a message saying that he'd be back down on the six o'clock, and now, as the empty coaches swayed round a corner and off down the Mall, her mind kept straying to his face. The message had ended *See you at 8, Teddy*, and knowing the piece of paper was in her bag was giving her that underwater feeling again, the feeling she always had when the doors clicked shut, of things doing themselves, instead of her doing them. What did it mean, if you said yes three times in a row?

After the film, which was all sailors and the war, and which she hadn't much enjoyed at all, they had a cup of tea and a fag, and then when they were leaving the tea shop Reggie mentioned how odd it was knowing they wouldn't ever be doing the old act again. Pam asked him how long it would take her to forget the moves, and Reg laughed and told her that your body never forgets something that gives it bruises. That remark almost made her blurt everything out, but standing together on a sunny street corner didn't seem either the time or the place, and she decided to leave it. After all, there'd be no point in upsetting the apple cart if this was all just a flash in the pan. So to speak.

Before they parted, Reg asked her again if Mr Brookes had dropped any hints about the new routine beyond the quick changes he'd mentioned. He'd been thinking about it, he said, and wished he knew a bit more about what they were going to be up against. Quickly remembering that she wasn't supposed to have seen Teddy since leaving the theatre on Saturday night, she said that he hadn't – which was true, more or less. She'd ribbed him briefly about it when they were in the taxi back to his place, she recalled, asking him whether he was going to at least tell her the title, but he'd just tapped his nose and said that that was for him to know and her to find out. At the time, she'd laughed, the way you do after a couple of proper drinks, but now, she didn't see why he couldn't just have come out and told her.

Reggie, meanwhile, had rather enjoyed his two spare days. The Monday had been fresher, but just as warm. Breakfast had been good, the breeze had been slicing the tops off the waves all along the front on his way into town, and the rest of the day seemed to get nicely filled up with a visit to the library and then a hunt to see if any of the corner shops or Woolworths had anything worth totting up the last few sugar points in his ration book for. Tuesday morning had been enlivened by five minutes spent watching a very respectably built young man brushing up a poster for the new show at the Aquarium in just his vest, and then there'd been the sailors at the Essoldo with Pam in the afternoon. After their tea in the cafe – featuring a not at all bad buttered teacake, he must say – he'd found himself wandering up to the Clock Tower by way of the windows at Hanningtons, all red and white and blue and special offers. Ignoring the woman with the gesturing stumps – she looked ridiculous, he thought, now that the sun was out – he'd loitered in a shop doorway on the corner of the Queen's Road and scanned the crowds just for the hell of it. He felt as if that last conversation with his mother had given him a secret to keep in his pocket alongside his penknife, and a good one; now, whenever he spotted a suitable candidate for scrutiny, he smiled to himself straight away instead of waiting until they'd walked past to stab a quick stare at their retreating backs. If you'd have seen him on one of those two days – suddenly diverting himself down past the steps of the Liberty Ballroom, for instance, or ducking down a side street to get a better look at someone when his errand really should have taken him straight on – then I think you would have noticed a new spring in that distinctive fall-and-catch stride of his. It wasn't so much that Reg wasn't still keeping his head down and dodging – he was – but rather that his gait didn't look anywhere near as angry, either with himself or the pavement. When he was mounting a kerb, for instance, the lurch sometimes threatened to become a positive leap. He even let himself be caught grinning at the occasional delivery boy, and once – even – at a uniformed policeman.

On Wednesday, having looked in early with Mr English and found out that they would be starting work with Mr Brookes onstage at twelve noon sharp, Reggie checked his sewing box and discovered that he was low on both dress pins and tailoring chalk. He wanted to be able to get to work on the new rigs as soon as they arrived, so off he set. Cutting left, left and left again from the stage door brought him quickly round to the main entrance of Hanningtons, and he went up the step and plunged straight in.

There were two sets of stairs that Hanningtons' customers had to negotiate on their way up to Haberdashery on the second floor; the first was the main staircase just inside the entrance, all would-be grand oak panelling and redundant bits of carving, and the second was a smaller and steeper set which you reached by turning left, cutting through Ladies' Wear and making a sharp right at the entrance to the Tea Room. This second set wasn't really steep enough to present Reg with any major problems (no more than the stares of the assistants in Ladies' Wear had been as he scuttled past them), but he had been hurrying and whistling not particularly gently through his teeth as he went, and so when he got to the first landing he needed to pause for a moment to get his breath back. The view from the banister was down into the Tea Room, and while he rested he enjoyed how smart the chequerboard of white tablecloths looked, all starched and ready for custom. It was early in the day, and apart from the palms in their big brass pots the place looked more or less empty.

But it wasn't. She was sitting quietly by herself, right over on the far side of the room, with her back half turned and one hand resting on the cool white cloth in front of her. Pamela. Pamela, but different. Pamela, transformed.

20

No gentleman required; that would have been the caption if she'd been a picture in a magazine. Very straight-backed and solitary she looked – it was one of those ones where the photographer has gone for simple black and white and told the model to think about nothing. Although the bevelled and frosted glass of the window next to her table was opaque, Pam was holding it in her turned-away gaze exactly as if she could see through it to whatever was on the other side. A spray of white carnations and maidenhair fern gave a touch of class to the still life set in front of her, and as Reg watched she lifted her elegantly brace-leted hand off the cloth and reached for her bag. She turned out of her pensive three-quarters profile, and Reg saw with a slight shock that she was wearing not just her usual powder-and-slash but a full pale daytime make-up, vividly and carefully drawn. She lit a cigarette, waved her match out in three deft strokes and picked a fragment of tobacco from her bottom lip. There was just the one china cup in front of her.

'Excuse me, sir, might I *help?*'

The waitress had materialised as soon as Reg had got down to the sign saying *Please wait here to be seated.* She was polite, of course, but the edge to the voice in which she made her enquiry made more than clear what she thought of the suit-ability of this particular customer to her establishment. Luckily for her, Reg was too busy staring at Pam to answer with any of the lines he usually kept in reserve for that particu-lar question.

'Oh, yes, I –'

That was when Pam looked round. For moment, she looked confused, as if she couldn't quite believe who had arrived to interrupt her thoughts, and here of all places – but then she lifted a hand, and waggled three fingers in an approximate welcome.

'I think I'll just go and join my lady friend – if you don't mind,' said Reg, sidestepping deftly.

By the time he reached her table she'd stubbed her cigarette out in the cut-glass ashtray and quietly put her hands back in her lap.

'Blimey, this is a bit posher than the Essoldo, isn't it?' He was half whispering, enjoying the conspiracy. Grinning. 'Just as well I put on a clean shirt this morning. If I'd –'

'Madam?'

'Yes. A cup for my friend, please –' Pam was editing her voice to go with the room, making Reg smile even more – 'and some more hot water. Do you have teacakes this morning?'

'Certainly, madam.'

'One, with butter, if you have it.'

See, Reg thought. *That's put you in your place.*

The waitress retreated.

'Well, go on then,' Pam said. 'What's your excuse?'

'Haberdashery,' said Reg, grinning again, and indicating the staircase. 'Pins and chalk, so that I can get stuck straight in to the alterations this evening after work. They're not the cheapest, but it is just round the corner . . . And what's yours?'

'Oh . . . A cigarette and a spot of quiet before we start work on the new routine. You know. This was the only place I could think of where I wouldn't bump into anyone I knew.'

'Sorry. I can always —'

'No. No, honestly. I've ordered your teacake now.'

She still had her hands in her lap.

'I do know, though,' he offered, sure that he knew what she was being so pensive about. 'It's always a bit daunting starting on a new act, especially when you're new to the game. Still, nothing ventured, and all that. Brookes does know his business.'

She looked at him oddly, and seemed to think before she spoke.

'Took the words right out of my mouth again, Reg. I'll be Mother, shall I?'

She took the hot water from the proffered tray, and helped Reg to milk.

'One lump, or two?'

'Two please.'

The days of help-yourself sugar bowls were still a couple of years off even at Hanningtons, and the sugar had come as four small lumps on a plate. Pam dropped three of the four into Reggie's tea with a pair of silver-plated tongs, and passed him his cup across the table.

'Where d'you get that then?' he asked, with a nod that indicated her wrist.

Pam was concentrating on topping up her own tea, but when she saw where Reggie was looking she put the pot down abruptly. A spot of tea slopped out onto the white cloth, and spread.

'What d'you mean?'

'That's a new one, isn't it? Let's have a look at him.'

'Oh, that . . . Yes.'

Pam looked down at her bracelet as if she had forgotten she was wearing it, and held out her wrist to shake it down to the end of her black wool sleeve. The charms rang together softly, and the little gold cat with his ruby-chip eyes ended up on top, resting his head against the miniature Eiffel Tower.

'Very nice,' said Reg, sipping his tea. 'Where d'you find it?' He flipped his head towards the window. 'In one of the little shops round the back there? I like the eyes. He looks like he's smiling.'

The spot of tea had spread to the size of a half-crown. Pam laid her hand down next to it, and looked from the bracelet to the stain as if they were somehow connected.

'I didn't find it anywhere, Reg,' she said, spreading her ringless fingers flat across the cloth, and bringing her eyes to rest on the little gold cat. 'Mr Brookes gave it to me.'

Reg laughed.

'Blimey, did he? . . . There's not many people get a present out of that one.'

'Yes he did, Reg.' Her voice pressed down firmly on the words, just as the palm of her hand was pressing down firmly on the tablecloth. 'He gave it to me when I went out with him for a drink again, after the third house on Saturday night.'

She'd been expecting him to be angry, but she hadn't expected the hurt. Seeing it, she flinched, lifting her hand off the table-cloth and laying it at her throat; as she did that, the charm bracelet slipped down over the sleeve of her sweater, exposing what she had hitherto been trying to conceal. The bruise was new – an emerging watermark, just beneath the skin – but you could see the impress of fingers printed quite clearly around her wrist.

Reg's eyes flicked, then flicked away. He knew the waitress on the other side of the room was watching them, and could have shouted – wanted to, in fact, loud enough to make the woman come running in dismay – but he did the opposite, for Pam's sake, lowering his voice with his eyes.

'So he's hurting you already, is he? That didn't take long.'

Now it was her turn to collect herself. She rearranged the softly spoken bracelet, and made every effort to keep her voice firm and low.

'No, not at all. He's just a bit rough sometimes.'

There was no reply.

'Would you believe he thinks I'm special, Reg?'

Reg's hands had started to misbehave. One was plucking at the corduroy of his trouser leg under the table, and now the other reached inside his jacket pocket for the reassuring nugget of his penknife. He was determined not to shout – not at her, anyway – but it was hard. His face worked itself into and out of a frown, and when he finally spoke the words barely emerged. He knew what he wanted to say, but that familiar enemy in his throat was getting a very firm grip.

'Since when?'

She couldn't see any point in denying it.

'Since Friday. Friday night, after the Queen's Hotel. Listen, Reg –'

Reg had moved his fidgeting right hand up onto the table-cloth, and Pam reached across to take hold of it as she spoke; he snatched it away as quickly as you would from something that might scald you. She looked at him for a moment, biting her scarlet lip, and then turned and beckoned brusquely to the staring waitress.

'Is everything all right here, madam?'

'Yes it is. The bill, please, and straight away. I'm afraid my colleague and I are due at work almost immediately.'

She was gathering up her bag as if she took her refreshment in superior places like Hanningtons' Tea Room all the time. The moves were as clipped as the words, and went well with the painted face and its swinging pearls.

'Certainly, madam.'

'I can see you're upset, Reg,' said Pam, not caring if the woman heard this time or not, 'but we can't talk here.'

She was standing already, opening her purse for a sixpence.

'Finish that tea, and we'll go and find somewhere a little more private, shall we? We've got nearly an hour.'

'Reg!'

The shout was raw with exasperation; the edge in her voice was caught and echoed in the cry of a gull as it wheeled away above her head into the blindingly bright sky.

'I know what I'm bloody doing!'

When they'd left the tea room all Pam could think about was how she was going to tell him about the bruises without sounding impossibly vulgar. She was pretty sure bracing your hands back against the headboard while a man pinned your wrists to the mattress wasn't something young Reggie was going to know anything about – and it certainly wasn't the sort of thing she wanted the job of explaining. Now that they were out here on the prom, however, in all this light and air, she just wanted to get the words out of her mouth and have done with them. There was no point in beating about the bloody bush, was there? At least the wind would mean they'd be hurled away at once, rubbish to the gulls.

She tried again, coat flapping and hair flying.

'Reg! Stop!'

This time, he did, and turned, shouting back at her through the wind.

'Well I'm glad to hear it. And I'm sure he does too.'

The face was a mask of fury, and his fists were clenching so hard that the nails must be cutting the palms of his hands. He walked back towards her stiffly – was he going to actually hit her? she wondered. There was no mistaking his voice for a boy's now; it was hard, and dark.

'He'll leave you. You do know that? He'll pick you up and throw you away just like he did Sandra, and the one before her, and the one before. He'll –'

His mouth twisted and swallowed, as if somebody had just stung his face with the back of their hand. A couple in buttoned-up overcoats walked past them quickly, staring; as they passed, Pam dragged a handful of hair back out of her eyes. Fighting the lump that was trying to close his throat, Reg kicked the asphalt, staring at her painted face just like he stared at Doreen's stone sometimes: desperately. The blunt edges of his voice had been sharpened, and he turned them on himself; it was suddenly the sound of somebody bleeding inside, miserable and weary with pain.

'He'll leave you just like my dad left my mum, Pam. Just like. Just like my dad left my mum –' He strangled, then swallowed again. 'It's what they bloody do.'

She'd never seen his eyes so black – knapped flints, in a sad, angry face – and now that it had been said, she understood. *So that's why he minds so much*, she thought. *That's why he minds so much about what happens to me. Why did I never think of that before?* She stared at him, blinking, feeling the wind wreck her hair.

'Oh, Reg –'

It was almost a moan. She stepped forward to take hold of his arm.

'Don't.'

The arm was pulled away brusquely, and the eyes went dead. There was a woman stalking past them, this one pushing a great boat of a pram. She glared at them, judging their messy public intimacy with her mouth and sharply lifted chin, but Pam didn't care. She reached for Reggie's other arm; the wind was making a mess of his hair too, and it was all she could do to stop herself from reaching out and stroking it. She grabbed his jacket, pulling him close, getting her face as close to his as if she meant to kiss him.

'I know, Reg. I know that's what they do. But it doesn't mean you can stop trying.'

His eyes were closed and his face averted, but she wasn't taking no for answer.

'Does it? . . . Does it, darling? . . . And sometimes . . . I don't know about you, but sometimes . . .'

Now it was Pam's turn to feel a hand trying to squeeze her throat shut.

'Sometimes what?'

She tried to laugh it away, but it was too late for that.

'Sometimes I'm as much of a fool as the next girl. You of all people must be able to understand that.'

'Why?'

'Oh come on Reg, you know. Being alone. You think you're fine with it one night, but the next night you're not. It's nothing to be ashamed of –'

He pulled back, but Pamela refused to let him get away.

'Oh for Christ's sake I don't mean your foot, Reg. Look at me. I said look at me.'

She lowered her voice to an urgent, steady stream, and spoke straight into his face, releasing his arms now and holding his head between her hands as if she really was going to kiss him.

'And I don't mean because you're bloody queer either. I mean your mum. You've been alone all your bloody life – well I've been alone too, Reg, just in a rather more crowded way. So trust me, I know. I know.'

The crisis seemed to have passed; she breathed, and released his face. She was still fighting the urge to tame his hair – like a mother would – and so she stepped back as if she wanted to be able see him better, and shoved her hands into her pockets.

'You can talk about her, you know. If you miss somebody, then it's good to talk about them.'

Reggie still wasn't looking at her, but at least his eyes were open now. She fought to stop herself holding him, because she knew that wouldn't help.

'How do you miss somebody you never had?'

'Oh . . . all the time.'

'Really? You've never even bloody mentioned a mother. You –'

'No, Reg, but I've been one.'

It came out of her so directly, so without hesitation, that Reg thought he'd misheard. A gull screamed and flashed overhead, asking for something, and Pam bit her lip. She stared, then laughed, then cut herself off. She turned quickly half away, as if she'd suddenly remembered she ought to look out at the sea. It dazzled her, and she threw up her hand to shade her eyes.

'I don't understand . . .'

'I'm sure you don't. Forget I mentioned it.'

She sniffed hard, and started rooting in her handbag, and almost laughed.

'Christ! What a time to discover you've left your fags in a bloody tea room.'

'Pam –'

Something uncontrolled about her face as she rummaged in her bag made Reggie realise how very wrong a turning had just been taken. He mirrored her earlier gesture, and reached out to put his hand on the sleeve of her coat.

'Pam? What is it?'

'You know I was sure I put them in here somewhere. Shit!'

The handkerchief she was trying to use on her nose bowled away down the promenade, and now it was Reggie's turn to understand. The nanny who had passed them earlier was now walking back towards them, and as she approached the whirling accent of the lost handkerchief led Pam's eyes back to the great black pram the woman was pushing. Reggie saw them widen, and her teeth clench – he'd seen a man break his arm onstage once, and that man had done almost exactly the same thing with his mouth as Pam was doing now, clamping the sides down to try to keep himself silent. The woman passed them, tutting at the spectacle, and wheeled her charge safely away towards the Hove Lawns. Pam's eyes followed it.

Reggie stared too, but at Pam.

He waited for her outside the newsagent's, and then followed her as she hurried up a narrow side street to get out of the wind. Neither of them had spoken. When they spotted the sign announcing *Home Made Cake Available Today* they both knew that a backstreet cafe was a ridiculous place in which to try to understand what had just happened to them, but what options did they have? Neither of them could face Mr English, and it was too far to walk to either of their rooms before they were due at work.

At least the place was empty.

The woman who appeared when the bell rang on the opening door had the same kind of face as that woman in the cemetery with the daffodils, Reg thought. Two rows of pale green china cups and plates of cakes under a smeared glass dome were laid out on the counter in front of her, waiting.

'Two teas, please.'

'No bun, dear? Those rocks are fresh this morning.'

185

Pam didn't think she could trust her stomach to keep anything down, and really only wanted a cigarette and to fix her face – but it seemed easier to say yes.

'Oh, all right. Reg?'

He didn't say anything, but punctuated his silence with a nod. Why had she never said anything before?

'Make that two then, please.'

The urn hissed, and a plate caught the side of the cake dome.

'There we are then, dear. Sugar's in the spoons.'

'Thank you.'

Pam knew the tea would turn her stomach, but felt she ought to show willing. At least it was hot.

'Well,' she said, placing her cup carefully back down on its saucer after the second sip, 'I know you probably don't want to hear this story, Reg, but here goes anyway.'

When Reg played it back in his head that night, staring himself to sleep in the silent company of Mrs Steed's roses, the story Pamela told him in the cafe seemed both as familiar and as strange as a fairy tale. Even the half-seen tea lady and her hissing urn seemed to be a natural part of it. The place was so small, and so empty – they were her only customers – that she must have heard every word they'd said, but somehow, it didn't seem to matter; in the years it must have taken her to wear out that faded apron, she'd surely heard it all before.

Although it was long, the actual details of the story seemed to be unimportant. There were no names or dates to anchor it to any particular place, and those facts that were left seemed to have been rubbed smooth by the years Pam had been carrying them around in her bag. She had been very young, she said; fifteen and a half if she was a day. The man was married, and had a car, and that was what they had used for their meetings. Once what had happened had happened –

Pamela said the phrase twice, with enough space between its first and second versions for the bracelet on her wrist to be twisted through two full circles. Reg waited, and knew better than to interrupt.

Once what had happened had happened, she had never felt that she had any choice about what happened next, she said, and the man with the car had certainly never offered her one. It had all been horrible, very horrible, but after it was all over she'd promised herself that she would never once let herself get caught like that again. Not once. This concluding moral of the story came out with its edges still sharp; she repeated it with her voice drained of all colour, vehemently stubbing out the last inch of her cigarette into the pressed tin ashtray on the table between them as she did it.

'. . . honestly. I never have been, and I never will be, I promise you that, Reg. Promise you. Never.'

Her recitation over, she picked up the spoon and stirred her sugar into her now-cold tea. A sudden spurt of steam from the tea urn seemed to bring her back into the room, and she looked abruptly up at the door as if she'd had a premonition that somebody was about to walk in and break the silence by ringing its bell – as if she *wanted* them to, whoever they were. No one did. Reg left it for a moment, then cleared his throat.

'Did you give him away?'

The voice was as blunt as the question.

'I didn't give him away, Reg . . . I lost him.'

Reg paused, and seemed to be thinking. She wondered if he was imagining a face – people did that, when you told them that you'd lost a child.

'How old was he? Little?'

Pamela's right hand had been lying naked on the table, still holding her teaspoon – they'd both forgotten that it was the bruises on her wrists that had started all of this – but now she laid the spoon gently down in the saucer, punctuating the quiet of the cafe with a single conductor's tap of metal on china. It didn't matter how many times she'd formulated this particular sentence of the story, either to herself or to a girlfriend – she knew she had to compose herself before she said it. As she always did, she laid the words down quietly and firmly, like cutlery for a Sunday dinnertime, steadying herself so that the job could be done without a trace of harshness.

'Let's just say he never really got started, shall we?'

Reggie couldn't help but glance up at her then – he hadn't been able to, before. She was looking down at her tea, with a very faint smile just smudging the corners of her mouth. As it happened, Reg understood exactly what she'd just told him, and eventually he said the only thing anyone can say under the circumstances.

'I'm really sorry.'

'Are you? Thanks.' She was grateful to him for not asking any more questions. 'If I'd have kept him, I hope he'd have been like you.'

'How d'you mean?'

'Oh, you know. Kind.'

She looked up at him.

'And that's what we're all looking for really, isn't it? Somebody kind.'

The smile wavered, weak as water, but stayed.

'That's what I'd like, anyway,' she said. 'One day. Somebody kind.'

Their eyes met. Met properly.

They walked up to the Grand via the bottom end of the Queen's Road, and when Pam caught sight of the Clock Tower she stopped in mid-stride. Her first thought was that the clockface must be wrong. Then she checked her watch, and realised it wasn't.

'Christ, Reg,' she said, treading out her fag, 'he'll bloody kill us.'

Together, they ran.

They made it to the stage door of the Grand just in time. They were both badly out of breath, but after a quick, panting stop in the concrete-floored corridor for Pam to check her face they made a reasonable job of walking out onto the stage as if there was nothing on their minds except finally hearing all about the new act. For his part, Mr Brookes didn't ask them where or why they had been together that morning, and if, when he saw them arriving so conspicuously à *deux*, the thought occurred to him of finding a private moment to ask Pam if she'd said anything to the boy yet about the two of them, then it certainly didn't show in his face; his mind, you might say, was almost entirely on his work.

Pam and Reggie didn't seem to feel the need to talk either – or at least not straight away. The things they had said to each other that morning never exactly went away – wherever the seafront wind and the urn- and bell-punctuated quiet of that backstreet cafe had put their sentences for temporary safe-keeping, they had certainly not erased them – but they both seemed to find things easier if the strange closeness into which they now found themselves thrown wasn't referred to directly. On the Friday, for instance, the two of them bowled into Mr English's alleyway from different directions at exactly the same time, both of them as late as the other and neither of them looking where they were going; narrowly avoiding a serious collision, they ended up back in each other's shocked, clutching arms. They instinctively inspected each other's faces for harm, but neither of them asked or thought of asking *Are you all right?*

Instead, they laughed. Pam linked her arm through Reggie's as she always did, and strode him briskly up to the stage door – exactly as if she was Debbie Reynolds turning up for work at the studio in *Singin' in the Rain*, and he was her limping, leather-booted Donald O'Connor, and everything would be just fine, so long as they kept their brave little chins up.

But I'm getting ahead of myself. That was on the Friday – Friday the fifteenth of May, eighteen days before the Coronation. For now, it was still only twelve o'clock on the Wednesday, and they had a whole new act to rehearse.

Four

North Road With Flags

To state the bleedin' obvious, a magic act only works when the audience fills up its rudimentary pantomime with their own thoughts and feelings. That was Mr Brookes's real skill as an illusionist, I think; as he vanished, produced, roped and revealed, his suggestively blank-faced performance invited the audience to scribble their own dirty secrets all over its simple script. As he casually looped that scarlet silk out of his trouser pocket, every man in the audience knew that he was in fact unspooling their own unspoken desires to bind and disable that infuriating maid; as that same maid swung on from the wings transformed and smiling, every married woman in the stalls and shopgirl in the gods smiled along with her, recognising from their own experience the exact ways in which the lines of her now ball-gowned body promised her lord and master everything he thought he wanted, while in fact always keeping a bit of herself back in reserve.

His hands may have been working fast, but his public's minds were working even faster. Well, this morning it was time for those thin blue pages of Mr Brookes's notebook to bear fruit in the form of a brand-new story for them to keep up with.

Respectable at Last, you will remember, was the title. He'd set two chairs for Pam and Reggie out on the stage, and asked Mr English to turn on the white working lights overhead. Once the two of them had settled, he flexed and wiped his hands, and explained the whole thing. He didn't use any of the props or costumes; his hands did everything, swooping through the lights to sketch, indicate, pluck and hover like two assistants doing their eager and well-trained best. They were clear, but tactful, imparting only as much information as was necessary.

He started with his back to them.

'The curtain rises —'

Mr Brookes coughed, unnecessarily, and started again, altering the angle of his hand so that the gesture became even more exact.

'The curtain rises, to reveal . . .'

Two light fingers indicated his chest as he turned.

'. . . a gentleman. A gentleman, who is . . . waiting. We can be sure that he is a gentleman because of his top hat, tails and grey kid gloves.'

The fingers fanned for a moment, were inspected, and then sank back to rest at his sides.

'And we can be sure he's waiting because the first thing he does is look at his wristwatch.'

An imaginary watch was inspected; a cuff slid back to cover the exposed skin.

'In the course of this simple action the gentleman inevitably catches sight of his public, and he seems reasonably pleased to see them. Sauntering across to a small table downstage left, he removes his hat, and then his gloves, finger by finger – the hat, please note, is shown to be empty. He checks his watch again; clearly there are a few minutes to spare. He produces a cigarette . . .'

His right hand twisted, hovered and rose to his lips. The lips pursed, then opened into a soft exhalation as the fingers moved away.

'. . . a cigarette . . . which is already lit.'

He paused, presumably for the house to enjoy the sight of the rising cigarette smoke. Pam shifted in her seat, but Mr Brookes didn't look at her.

'The gentleman checks his watch again, but discovers that it is no longer there. Dismay – hesitation . . . he discovers it on his *other* wrist. He still has a minute or two. He produces a white carnation . . .'

The hand curled, plucked – and mimed an insertion.

'. . . and fixes it in his buttonhole. He produces a comb and combs his hair. He wipes his hands; the comb and handkerchief both vanish. Are the house still with him? He checks; they are. Good. He checks his watch again – which wrist is it on now, boys and girls? – ah yes, the *right* one again. He has time for one last preparation, it seems. He produces a small yet promising jewellery box. He displays it. He does *not* open it. He replaces it in the appropriate pocket. He pats the pocket. He waits. All he needs now is . . . The Girl!'

A slight cough; a slight hesitation – even in this simple pantomime, Mr Brookes can't resist giving himself a bit of a build-up. He indicated the pit behind him.

'Music, "To Each His Own". Last drag on the cigarette; visible vanish; prompt cross to downstage left. Are you with me so far, boys and girls?'

The question wasn't in need of an answer, and didn't get one. Mr Brookes pressed on. He pointed upstage right, and widened his eyes.

'A *Lady* enters.'

His eyes stayed on their imaginary target, but a turned finger scanned Pam on her chair; up, and down.

'Fitted bodice, elbow-length gloves, full supported skirt at mid-calf, black and red all over. Red shoes. Sheer stockings.'

Pam crossed her legs. Reggie wondered how much work there'd be to do on this first gown. And would the shoes fit, if they were second-hand?

'She parades the frock. Admiration on both sides; she parades the frock again. A kiss on the back of the hand. Corsage produced – a red silk rose to match her gloves. He steps neatly in behind her to pin it on; business; with his other hand, he produces the jewellery box. Jewellery box flipped open. She sees the diamond ring. He extracts it, polishes it, displays it. Delight, on the Lady's part. He suggests a deal.'

At this point in the story Mr Brookes paused again. He interlaced his fingers and gave them a brisk crack and massage, shaking them in preparation. Reg had been relieved to see that so far the new act was all solo handwork, stuff he'd seen Mr Brookes do before, but clearly this next sequence was going to involve something more demanding. Probably involving Pam, he reckoned.

Pam, meanwhile, flicked her eyes across to Reggie then back to Mr Brookes. He hadn't looked at her once, not in the whole sequence. Why did he always make it a point of pride to make you feel that you had no idea what was actually going on? Weren't they supposed to be working together?

Reggie was right on both counts.

A hand slid into a pocket, emerged, cradled and displayed. Mr Brookes picked up his pace.

'Our old friend the coil of scarlet rope makes a welcome reappearance. Clearly, if the Lady cooperates, then she gets the ring. Hesitation business; encouragement business . . . The Lady makes her choice, stepping away and offering up her wrists. The ring goes back into the ring box – the box is closed – the box is placed on the table. Please note: *on the table*. Meanwhile . . . to work! Finger-spread, rope around her wrists – no ankles, Pam, this time, you'll be pleased to hear –'

Still he didn't look at her – though he did smile.

'– but the gentleman is not quite satisfied. He doesn't quite *trust* her, perhaps. He has an idea. He produces a pair of handcuffs. Dismay on the part of the Lady. He looks at the box on the table; she looks at the box on the table; they both look at the handcuffs . . . *Consent*, on the part of the Lady. Clearly she's a game girl –'

Still, he didn't look at her. She tapped a foot.

'– and the handcuffs are applied. A blindfold is applied. Whistle! The apparatus is wheeled on, undraped – we'd best get straight down to business this time, I thought.'

Now Mr Brookes stepped aside, and let his voice fall into a more natural register, taking the opportunity to relax and wipe his hands again.

'We'll be using two stagehands for the entrance, Reg, like before – the lads here seem pretty up to the mark – and you and I have quite a substantial look-it's-empty routine to work on at this point. I'm having the apparatus modified so that there's a full door in each of the two sides as well as a fully opening one in front, and it's going to involve quite a bit of back-of-door work on your conceals. So I hope your fingers are feeling good and strong.'

'Yes, Mr Brookes.'

'Good. Good . . .'

He flexed his hands again, pocketed his handkerchief and dropped back into showman mode.

'Full rotation with Reg stowed inside as before; Reg slips out onto the back, I open the front door to prove its empty, Reg moves round to behind the door *left*; quarter-rotation clockwise, I open the second door *right*, continue round, full rotation anticlockwise to the house to show it's still empty, Reg holding both doors to achieve the conceal and clinging on like mad.'

Brookes was rattling through this as if Reggie already knew how to do all of this – as indeed he did.

'Yes, Mr Brookes.'

'I call for the treads; treads affixed; I run up and pop inside to flip open the ceiling – look, no tricks – ceiling closed – sides closed – front-door left open; Reg is now concealed on the back. I turn my attention back to the Lady . . .'

He slowed down now, and looked at Pamela – or, at least, at the spot where he had indicated that her blindfolded figure would still be patiently standing.

'The Lady is escorted up into her new home by our two charmingly unskilled assistants. I, please note, keep well clear. At my command, they shut her in. I produce a padlock and chain and throw it; they promptly padlock the doors shut, throw the key cross-stage to me and lift the treads and exit, taking the treads with them as they do so. I am, please note, still nowhere near.'

Pam frowned; surely the steps had gone too quickly for her to be able to get into them in time in a big frock? And where was Reg at this point? Still clinging to the back?

'At this point, a change . . .' said Mr Brookes – as if he'd anticipated or even overheard her thoughts. 'A change of *tack*.'

He waited.

Pam shifted in her chair again, but Mr Brookes's eyes refused to be drawn. He slowed down again, making his gestures larger and clearer now. A cuff shot, and a hand arced suddenly up and out.

'I produce a wand. A spot of tradition never goes amiss, does it? And then . . . then, I turn my attention back to the table.'

The eyes swung; the hand pressed slowly down.

'With a little assistance from Mr Clifford in the pit, I dim the lights. Drum roll; a pass with the wand, then a tap on the ring box. A spurt of flame. The ring box is now empty. I display the box to the house. I replace it on the table. I turn my attention to the apparatus. Drum roll number two; pass with the wand, and, *while I am on the other side of the stage*, please note . . . the padlock and chain fall off the box. Lights up, music change, I cross smartly over and reach up to throw open the apparatus, revealing . . . revealing . . .'

His hands hung in the air as the sentence trailed away, joining his raised eyebrows in sketching out the question.

'Any suggestions?'

Pam bit her lip. Cigarette smoke, sheer stockings, a jewellery box – she of all bloody people ought to know where the story went next. Where the bruises were going to land.

'Well, there's no way you can get both Reggie and me in the bottom of that box,' she snapped. 'And the treads have gone too early for me to get in on my own in a big formal frock. And anyway, just getting rid of me, they've seen you do that before.'

'Quite. Reg?'

'Full rig change into a speciality, Mr Brookes, me down below with the previous?'

'Quite right too. Full rig change into a speciality it is. Now –'

Before Pam had time to ask what the bloody hell the two of them were talking about, Mr Brookes was off. He walked briskly across the stage, and knelt down next to the largest and most battered of the three suitcases which he had previously lined up in a row against the corner of the proscenium arch. Laying the case down on its side, he snapped it open.

'*Voilà!*'

'You are bloody joking,' said Pamela, staring.

Released from its confinement, the fabric of the dress was slowly levering itself out of the suitcase in a confectioner's-cream sprawl of machine lace and white nylon tulle. Pamela looked at it as if it was something it would only be safe to poke with a stick.

'Trust me,' said Mr Brookes, 'one previous owner, and after a few nips and tucks from our Reg it'll come up a treat.'

'I'm sure it will, but who's going to believe me being walked up the aisle in white? Especially after they've seen me come on looking like I'm touting for business in the front bar of the Dorchester.'

'Ah . . . but if the punters could see what was coming next, that would rather defeat the purpose of our work, don't you think? And surely you're not saying that we won't make a handsome couple? Or that playing Lady in White isn't every girl's dream?'

The question was clearly rhetorical; one quick finger-flex, and he launched into his finale.

'The band cuts to "Here Comes the Bride" – of course – and the Lady poses for a moment. She demonstrates that the lost diamond ring is now – hey presto, you might say – on the third finger of her right hand; I swing her down to join me. We pose for a quick snap – magnesium flash from down on the footlights, operated by stage management – veil, tiara, spray of carnations, the works. Trust me, the whole effect will be very classy. Very . . .'

The hands hovered again.

Having set it up so well with those little private reminders – the stockings, the box, the cigarette – Mr Brookes delivered his *coup de grâce* as elegantly as ever. Underlining the word as neatly as if he were signing away a bill, he looked at Pam directly for the very first time, flicking the word's accompanying dart of a glance straight into her caught-off-guard eyes.

'. . . very *special*.'

Close-up work, it's called in the trade – using the intimacy of a set-up to heighten the mark's bafflement. When his black glass eyes hooked into hers, Pam didn't so much shift in her chair as flinch. Everything from their first time together came back – the bedspread, the lamplight, the expression on his face, the heat in hers – everything.

Then she controlled herself, and breathed out – just as she'd learnt to do when the trap opened under her feet and the black water was waiting. Because of that conversation with Reg in the tea shop – because her feelings about her body and who owned it were very close to the surface that afternoon – she knew straight away that she now had only two options. She could either stand up and blush and shout and tell him exactly where he could stick his tulle and bruises and bouquets and reminders, or she could stay sitting in her chair and trust herself. She hesitated, twisting her bracelet – a Lady's prerogative, surely – and in that hesitation heard again the words she'd said to Reg out on the prom, the ones the sea wind had stolen so swiftly – not the dirty ones, but the ones about never letting what you knew become a reason to give up. And then she made her choice.

'All right,' she said, meeting Mr Brookes's eyes full on. 'So some girls will do anything for a piece of jewellery. And once you've got me trussed up to the nines and looking like something out of a Bridal Department window display, how does the story end?'

With a simple adjustment of his smile, and without even blinking, Mr Brookes turned from showman back into salesman; from lover, to stranger.

'Madam,' he said, 'I'd be more than happy to show you exactly that. The rest of the routine is actually pretty straightforward.'

It was – so straightforward, he might as well have written it out on a postcard and stuck it up in a newsagent's window: *Gentleman seeks Lady, preferably compliant, for mutually satisfactory conclusion.*

I'm sure you know the kind of thing.

After the flash of the wedding photo, the groom would spin his lady love into his arms for a kiss. The kissing done, he'd spin her out again, and the rigged wedding dress would split and fly off, leaving her displayed in the traditional white basque-and-suspenders with matching garter. Then came the finesse – the twist designed to make the house feel that the illusion was made to measure for this particular night. The groom would toss her dress stage right, the bride her bouquet stage left; she would then cross her arms demurely across her chest. He'd collect his hat – previously proven empty, you will remember – and with a bravado flourish release a shower of confetti over her head; she'd release two rigged elastics, and by the time the confetti settled around her ankles her basque would have been translated in the twinkling of a moist Coronation-day eye from bridal white into a fetching patchwork of miniature Union Jacks, and – a nice touch, this – even her *garter* would be decorated with a red, white and blue cockade. The band would shift from Mendelssohn to 'God Save the Queen', the groom would wave his last white silk handkerchief into a handily sized Union Jack and they'd skip into their bows as the tabs came down – looking forward, the pair of them, to celebrating a well-earned night of patriotic conjugal bliss. *Happy and glorious*, as the anthem says.

His precis complete, Mr Brookes looked to Pam again for her response.

She smiled.

Reg, watching her do it, was already thinking about all the stitching involved in the four new rigs, and wondering why the hell Mr Brookes hadn't released the rest of them out of the cases yet – they'd be creasing to buggery cramped up in there. And how the hell was Pam supposed to pull off that final confetti-drop change with only two and half weeks' rehearsal?

2

Reggie's fingers were already sore by Friday. The final Union Jack basque was built over a nipping frame of metal stays, and taking it apart and restitching the covering so that it fitted Pam exactly enough for her to get three more figure-hugging layers over the top required a lot of work. Pins can run themselves surprisingly deep into a finger when you're working too fast; thimbles cramp, and elastic snaps. The hot iron required to press the jigsaw of red, white and blue linen back into its newly adjusted shape caught him twice, blistering him badly. And these weren't the only discomforts; now that he'd had time to get used to the idea, Reggie couldn't help but be interrupted by thoughts of Mr Brookes's fingers performing their own nightly variations on the same tasks as he repeatedly adjusted fastenings and lifted skirts and smoothed down seams. He didn't know – and deliberately didn't ask – if she was going home with him every night now, but the pictures got in his way nonetheless. He tried to compensate for them by taking even more care of her than usual – working till his eyes ached, pressing and repressing the bodice of the black-and-red frock so that it would mould to her breasts and nobody else's, even taking her first pair of shoes home and forcing his own naked feet into them so that they would slip more easily on and off hers at the next day's rehearsal – but still, the pictures wouldn't go away.

By Saturday lunchtime, all three of them were getting a little ratty – Pam's first attempts at quick-releasing herself from the trick handcuffs were desperately clumsy – and Mr Brookes was glad to stop work. Needing a break, Reg left the two of them alone and took his sandwich down past the Pavilion to the seafront to get some air.

There is often a day around the middle of May when something seems to shift in the atmosphere of a seaside town – a point where something in the air or light seems to license people to venture off the prom and down onto the beach for the first time that year – and without any warning, this particular Friday seemed to be the one when it happened. Hazy figures were dotted all over the stones, and there was one group of five or six lads and their girls larking about right down at the edge of the silver-edged water. The girls had their shoes in their hands, and were shrieking at the sea as it glittered round their kicking legs; the boys were laughing and jostling each other with their jackets off, shirts flashing in the sun. Their words were inaudible, but the hoots and shrieks came across the stones like the cries of birds. One of the boys fell – heavily – the distant laughter rose – and watching the blurred figure stagger back up to its feet made Reggie realise that he himself hadn't ventured out onto the beach the whole time he'd been here. He knew why, though; he knew all he needed to know about the bruises involved in falling on stones, thank you very much. The heat from the sun was just starting to make the air above the beach shimmer, and turn the grey flints black. He went cautiously down a flight of concrete steps which led from the promenade to the shingle, stooped with his hand on the rail on the bottom step, and picked up one of his old familiar enemies. It was warm. He remembered that, now – how they'd sometimes been warm while the water was still icy. Cutting.

Testing the stone's weight in his hand, he stared again at the distant figures. Something about the fractured silver of the sea behind them was making him picture the cabinet back at work — its mirrors — and Pam's wedding dress. It was still too tight, too constricting for her — and he couldn't for the life of him get the release fastenings to snap when she needed them to. The thing just wouldn't *fit* . . . Then he heard Pam's voice saying the question which she'd asked Mr Brookes at the end of his explanation, the one about *how does it all end*. He frowned, turning away from the sea, and stuck the stone in his pocket.

Sunday tomorrow. What the hell was he going to say?

3

'Well,' he said quietly, digging at the turf with his toe.

After a week out in the open the postcard had blistered and spotted, so he picked it up and tore it into pieces. The paper left his hands wet, and he wiped them on his trousers. It was better to just come straight out and say it, he supposed.

'I suppose you knew about it all along – about him and her, I mean. And about her . . . her story, I mean.'

There was no need to explain.

'And I suppose you're sure she's taking good care of herself with him now, aren't you, else you would have said something?'

He looked up briefly to see if he could spot that bird, the one that had been there before, but there was nothing.

'Just have to trust you on that one, won't I?'

The quiet was as thick as it had been in the cafe; then a sudden, thrown-knife screaming over his head brought back the sound of those lunchtime girls and their boys down on the beach, shrieking and pretending that they minded being chased. It was a flight of swifts, scything through the space where the missing lark had been. He straightened up.

'Can't say that I'm finding it easy, seeing them together all the time, but I'm managing. More or less. Friday afternoon's session with the wedding dress was a disaster, like I expected – I'm going to have to replace those fastenings – and getting the change worked out in the apparatus is going to take for ever, I can see that – but the important thing . . . the important thing –'

The hand settled its familiar grip on his windpipe, squeezing, but he coughed it away. He needed her to hear this.

'The important thing is that she stays all right. Even when he gets short with her over those handcuffs. Even when he takes her home. Even when she makes her smile look brighter than it is, thinking I won't notice. It would really help me if you could promise me that she's safe. But you can't. Can you? Funny how things can change in just a week.'

He talked for another whole hour, stopping and starting, leaving long silences in which everything he *had* said seemed to unravel, and always coming back to the same point: was Pam going to be all right? When he was done, he walked back down the hill in head-down silence, forgetting even to pat his knife as he squeezed through the gate. A couple of young men in their shirtsleeves passed him as he turned out through the cemetery gates and headed back into town, but Reg didn't even look up to see what they were like. He was too busy revisiting his week, trying to make it fit – the dress, the shoes, the stuck fastenings, those figures on the beach, the stone, the handcuffs, the screaming. He'd even forgotten to tell his mother that he'd see her next week.

4

Mr Brookes had sent the apparatus to a workshop just round the back of the Metropole, right close to where Reggie had stood and stared up at that high window during his long nocturnal ramble. According to the head flyman at the Grand this was the cheapest of the several workshops which the theatres in town and the seafront attractions used, and the cabinet had been there for a whole week now, locked away each night and patiently enduring having its secrets exposed and modified each day. There were now six new hinges on the doors, a removable hand grip for Pamela in the ceiling, a set of spring-bolts to achieve that dropping of the chain and padlock, and two new cunningly mirrored compartments to hide the veil and collapsable silk bouquet required for the reveal. Nothing about the work had proved too challenging, though the spring-bolts had taken some setting – when it came to metal, the man who ran the workshop knew exactly what he was doing. Mr Brookes was surprised by his skill, but he shouldn't have been. After all, every seaside pleasure has it mechanics, its points of friction and purchase. Out on the piers every chained rifle, every sparking strip on a dodgem car, every one of the clicking locks that kept the Chair-o-plane passengers from spinning out of their seats into neck-snapping flight, even the gilded horses of the carousels – each with a precisely calibrated ring sliding round the pole that steadied its implacable, imperious, endless up-and-down – they all needed maintaining. As far as the man in the workshop was concerned, Mr Brookes's adjustments to his engine of deception was just one more little job among many.

The work had been done on credit, and without anything being drawn or written down. When they'd shaken hands on the price, the man had grinned and said, *Honestly, anyone would think you were engaged in some sort of a bloody crime, the way you lot carry on about your secrets.*

Once the apparatus was back the rehearsals got harder. Reg had kept up a good front all through the previous week, laughing with Pam when he could, looking away when he had to – but now the presence of the cabinet was bringing the difficulty of the new routine home to them both.

The two trickiest passages were Reggie's steel-fingered invisibility on the back and sides, and then the suffocating twenty-four seconds in which he and Pam had to achieve her translation from Lady to Bride. Releasing the black-and-red cocktail dress once the ropes and handcuffs were off and dropping the underdressed skirt of the bridal outfit were relatively easy in themselves, but became near impossible once they moved inside the cabinet. The surging fabric seemed to want to get itself into their eyes and mouths; hooks and eyes refused to respond; the heels of the red shoes developed a malicious habit of going for Reggie's face as he worked to cram himself under the trap with the dress. He pulled and pushed as if he had a body to conceal, but it fought back, determined to betray its hiding place. Reaching ruthlessly round, through and over each other, they felt like a pair of second-counting lovers, matching every lift, pull and last-minute tug – and all the time that they were at work inside their locked room the jealous figure of Mr Brookes would be pacing up and down outside, calling out and counting impatiently, and then, breaking all the rules of the usual story, angrily telling them to do it again, and again, and again.

Reg had particular trouble with the diamond ring. The double to the one that Mr Brookes vanished out on the stage lived in his pocket, and it was his job to remember to pass it to Pam last thing before she hoisted herself on the handles and he dropped under the trap. However, the first three times they made the change, he completely forgot to do it. Mr Brookes shouted at him, but to no avail; twice more, when the bride finally appeared – panting, dishevelled, but otherwise complete – she was still ringless. The problem, of course, wasn't in the timing, but in Reggie's head. This time there was no lever for him to reach for and pull on the reveal, and his only function once he was under the trap was to wait; wait, listen – and think. Every time they ran the sequence, he lay curled in the dark, panting and counting and spitting as Pam's heels ground and clicked over his head, trying not to breathe in her smell as the hot fabric pressed into his face and wishing – for the first time in his life – that he did anything at all in the world for a living except this; this hateful crouching in the dark; this twisting and hiding; this hateful, stupid, relentless trickery of his being invisible while she got served up to the world on a plate.

No wonder he forgot the bloody ring.

The week passed, as it must, and after ten days of rehearsals the act finally began to take shape – once, they even got as far as the final tableau, bride and groom united at last in a crash-bang-wallop parody of a church-step photograph. While they worked in the darkened theatre, gradually getting the hang of their new routine, the Brighton spring took gradual possession of the air outside and the light on the sea got brighter. The water seemed to rise in a glittering wall at the end of every single street Reg chose to turn down, and against that strange backdrop the swelling life of the town seemed determined to taunt and harry him. Everywhere he looked there were couples, arm in arm, hand in hand, mouth to mouth. On the streets, out on the stones, in the newsagents, under the lamp posts, even on the bloody postcards. Hate it as he might, they all seemed to be agreeing on one thing: this wedding was definitely going ahead.

Mr Brookes knew that getting people down from town was going to be tricky given the date of the opening, but at least one booker had been back in touch to say that he'd try. Nothing definite – but it was a start. And if the act went over well on the big night, who knew, things might soon be looking up. He was squiring Miss Rose just about every other night while they were rehearsing, just to keep things ticking over – always asking her if she fancied it discreetly, not in front of people, and certainly not in front of the limping wonder, and so far she'd always said yes. On the Saturday he'd even suggested that they might all go out together for an end-of-the-week drink, the three of them – *a proper family outing*, he'd joked – and she seemed to have liked that. Reggie had fussed about with that bloody boot of his, trying to keep it tucked under the table and almost taking the drinks over at one point, but the evening hadn't been too much hard work. A slightly sharp conversation about Princess Margaret and her latest appearance out on the town had been a bit of a rocky moment – he'd wanted to know why the woman couldn't just get married like her sister instead of parading herself around town with every Tom, Dick and Right Honourable Harry, and Pam had taken umbrage. But all in all, like the rest of his labours, the evening had definitely been worth it.

Pam?

Pam was working as hard as she'd ever worked in her life.

Editing herself into each of the four successive women in the act, she kept on waiting to recognise herself. Sometimes, when they did finally get her down to the last basque, she wanted to rip that off too, just to take a look in the pier glass and remind herself of what she looked like when she wasn't wearing anything except her name. It seemed that Reggie had been right when he'd explained how hard rehearsing a new routine was, because you never knew whether what you were rehearsing was going to finally make any sense. You were always too stuck in the middle of it all to ever really be able to see anything clearly, he'd said, and she'd thought (but hadn't said) *well, yes, but that goes for everything.*

The only thing she was sure of was that she couldn't really blame anyone but herself, this time.

On the nights when she did go home alone, the bed felt strange, and she found herself having that stupid old dream of what it would be like to come home to find flowers waiting for her; lilac and roses, just for her.

5

Now that he was out of the pub and in the air, Reggie felt as restless as a cat. It wasn't just the relief of getting away from Mr Brookes and his arm round Pam's shoulder, or out of the brightness and din of a Saturday-night saloon; Reggie's body was a creature of habit, and its muscles wanted to know why they weren't just coming offstage. He shook himself, and looked left and right. The pub Pam had chosen for their family outing was well down in the Lanes, and the alleyways were dark, and beginning to empty. A trio of young men in drape-collared overcoats who looked like they might be looking for trouble passed him, and Reg discreetly patted his penknife as they walked by. If he ever found out that Mr Brookes was hurting her . . . He shrugged off the thought. It was no use worrying. No bloody use at all.

Laughter came out through the etched-glass door – high laughter, and a song.

Not knowing what else to do, he walked. His one-twoing feet led him up past the Meeting House, round some corners, and eventually down the same damp alleyway of black-shuttered shops that he'd been down the previous Friday night. Then it was round the top end of Hanningtons, round the back of the Theatre Royal and then eventually out halfway up North Road itself, one corner away from the Grand. Here he stopped, and rolled himself a fag. The raft of red, white and blue bunting which had been going up outside the theatre all through the week was now complete, criss-crossing between the lamp posts all the way down the street from the Queen's Road to the bottom. The night air was haloing the street lamps, and as he looked down the sloping street the hundreds of little triangular teeth of fabric coalesced in the light to make a sort of ghostly, bleached ceiling; a pale, hovering canopy of wire and cloth. It was as if all his painstaking work on Pam's basque had been silently scissored up, multiplied and hung out to dry in a still, eloquent mockery.

Chilled, Reg sucked his teeth. He definitely wasn't going to go straight home tonight. He hadn't enjoyed that pub full of starers and laughers, and he wasn't looking forward to Mrs Steed's roses, but that didn't mean there weren't any other options.

Despite what people say now – and despite what most of them assumed, back then – it is very far from the truth that everything was hidden away behind locked doors in the spring of 1953. It wasn't – not in this town. Already, the laughter coming out through certain doors was getting less than discreet, and quite a few of those doors' addresses were common knowledge to the town's policemen and landladies and stage-door keepers. Even Reggie, for instance, who very much kept himself to himself, would have been perfectly well aware from the backstage gossip at the Grand that if his feet had led him right instead of left that evening, and then left and left again, they would have eventually brought him round to Middle Street, and there, halfway down on the left-hand side, he'd have found himself standing outside the saloon-door entrance of a pub called The Spotted Dog. This was just beginning to be known as the most notorious of those addresses, the one that even some sniggering local schoolboys had heard of – the place whose 'colourful' customers the girl from Madame Valentine's troupe had warned Pam about. He could have been there in ten minutes. But if the Dog (as its customers always loyally called it) felt too obvious, if he'd asked around – if he'd asked, for instance, his cravat-wearing colleague Mr English – he could have easily found other places to which he might have headed that night; places where the customers might well have stared at him for his foot, but not because they wondered why he was there or what he was looking for. Heads might have turned when he walked in just before last orders on a Saturday night – they always do when a new face arrives at that time of night, whatever the decade – but trust me, he would have been welcomed.

Two breakfasts ago, he'd heard a workman on the table next to him deliver a warning to his mates to steer clear of the saloon bar at the Dog – *Not unless you're bloody desperate, mate* had been the crowing punchline of the story. The other men at the table had laughed, throwing back their heads and showing their teeth. Reggie had kept himself busy with his tea and slice, head down. One of the man's overalled friends had chipped in with a story of his own, one about an offer he'd been made – *a spot of bother*, he called it – on the stones under the Palace Pier. He'd only gone down onto the stones for a quick piss, he said, and the men all laughed again. That laughter and the men's careless, white-teethed faces were the pieces of information that Reggie's restless body now retrieved. Looking up at the flags turning pale around the lamps on North Road, he picked at the memory like a twist of sugar he'd been saving for later – like a short cut; an alleyway on a map, one that the day-trippers never noticed.

It wasn't what he wanted, but it would bloody do. The air was starting to thicken with sea mist, and he hunched himself up against the cold. He pictured the flight of concrete steps down on the seafront where he'd picked up that pebble last week – they had a handrail, so far as he remembered, and that would probably be the best way of getting down onto the shingle at this time of night.

That thickening of the air had been a warning.

Everything on the seafront was gone – lost, in a thick wall of sea fret. He'd only been able to find the steps by following the promenade railings and waiting for a gap to appear, and now that he'd found it all he could see when he looked down was blackness. The lamps up above him on the front had been reduced to suspended globes, glowing, but shedding no light. *Ah well*, he told himself, *all the better to hide you with*. Throwing away his fag, he did something he hadn't done in years: holding tight to the metal rail to make sure he didn't slip, he headed down the stairs backwards, counting them under his breath like a child. When his boot hit the first stones they chuckled and shifted, slick with damp. So long as he took care where the beach suddenly tipped into that steep bank at the high-water mark, he told himself, he'd be fine.

At some exceptionally low spring tides the flints of Brighton beach give way to sand, and that night there was a hard level of it stretching a hundred yards before it met the water, right to the far end of the Palace Pier. Sliding down the stones, Reggie didn't see the sand coming, and because his feet were expecting more shingle, and because he was in a hurry, he fell. He righted himself, scraped his hands clean on his trousers, and realised what he was walking on. The lights behind him on the prom had disappeared entirely into the fret now, but floating above him and to his right his destination was still visible as a raft of hazy colour, pink, green and yellow. One whole long connecting section of lights suddenly went out as he looked, casting the raft adrift into the surrounding darkness. *Good*, he muttered. *Closing Time*.

He hurried on across the bare sand. The fret was absorbing the sound as well as the light now – the sea was nowhere, and the last late traffic and shouting of the town had been entirely swallowed. All that was left was his own stabbing feet, and breath. The remaining lights of the pier loomed up above him, and he began to smell seaweed – harsh, iodine, rank. Then, suddenly, with no warning, a stinking pillar of metal walked up out of the darkness and blocked his path. He stopped, and went forward carefully.

The pillars and cross-struts of the thick-trunked forest that supported the pier were all around him. He reached forward to guide himself, and his hand was met by a cutting cluster of mussel shells; he shivered, feeling the cold of the water that would be pressing round this drowned world in just a few hours' time. He stopped to look up; somewhere above his head there must be a cathedral ceiling of boards, but his eyes couldn't find it. This was it, then. This was where the man in the cafe had meant. He steadied himself, quietened his breathing, and let his eyes adjust to the darkness.

First there was a cough, some distance away. Then, after about a minute, something in the darkness in front of him shifted and made itself distinct. What he had taken for another pillar resolved itself into the fog-softened outline of a body, and when its owner turned, the scene acquired its first faint punctuation mark of light. The pulsing tip of a cigarette came, and went. The man seemed to be wearing an overcoat. As Reggie watched, the red ember glowed, died, shifted, glowed brighter – then arced and hissed itself out as the man tossed the butt end away. Reggie stayed quite still, and listened, scanning the dark. He knew there'd be others.

As if in reply to the cigarette, the flare of a lighter defined a charcoal figure away to his right. This man still had his hat on. Reggie would have moved to investigate, but before he could do it the silence right behind him was interrupted. He stilled himself. There it was again; a sharp, repeated, inter-rogative scratch. Someone was trying to strike a light. Reggie turned slowly, not giving himself away. Another short, enquiring cough came through the dark away to his right, and Reggie held his breath, waiting to see if his newer and closer companion would stay and reveal himself. The match rasped again, and took; the blue flash of phosphorous was followed by the pink of a cupping hand. The man was so close that Reg could see each finger. No rings. Reg stiffened, and shifted. The owner of the match lifted it to his face to catch the tip of his fag, and the flame sketched his features in a quick, softly stroked-in grisaille. Reggie flinched, not sure if the light was catching his own face; the match guttered, and was flicked away, but it was enough. The smudged proof of wet hair, searching eyes and a damp macintosh collar had already been inked and pulled. Reggie felt a warm, decisive kick in the pit of his stomach.

It was his twisted left foot that moved first. It did it without permission, and just as well – places like this aren't meant for conversation, and it is your body that has to speak your mind. As clumsily as he had lurched across the stones of the beach, Reggie took three sudden steps through the dark, waited for the cigarette to come out from between the young man's lips, and then kissed him before he had time to refuse the offer.

Reggie was a good kisser – a fierce one, when roused – and soon got the man's mouth open. Emboldened by the lack of refusal, he reached up and round and filled his free hand with the man's hair, pulling him closer. Then, as whoever he was got over his surprise and began to kiss Reggie back, the dynamic of their embrace shifted. Now it was Reggie who was having his mouth explored. Full as it was, he whimpered as hands began to graze first his back, and then his chest. He pulled away, momentarily breathless, and his partner wiped his mouth for him with the back of his hand. This may seem too intimate and animal a gesture for so early in the proceedings, but trust me; it happens. For just a moment they simply stood there, their breaths fogging and mixing between them, entirely unconcerned now as to whether they were alone in the dark or not. Then Reggie licked his top lip, and moved in.

I wish I could tell you it was romantic, what happened next, or at least tender, but it wasn't. Reggie fell on this other man's face as if he'd heard the bell ring for a second round, or as if he hadn't eaten for weeks, taking hold of it with both hands the better to take his opponent's breath away, or to finish his meal before someone snatched the plate away . . . There was a collar and tie underneath the macintosh, and Reg began trying to find a way in past the buttons to the man's skin. The sound of something tearing produced the first urgent whisper of the scene, but Reggie was in no mood to stop. His mouth and hands became insistent, his frustrated fingers dug in hard, and somewhere inside their lips enamel caught on enamel. The young man pushed him away with a snort.

'Christ, you – oh dear –'

At first Reggie had no idea what the taste inside his mouth could be, but when he saw the flash of a white handkerchief coming up to the other man's face, he realised. One of them had bitten down on something – a tongue or lip-lining – and his mouth was suddenly full of his own or somebody else's blood.

'Are you all right?'

The question was whispered. Reggie stepped back, almost falling over, spitting. Looked-for stranger or not, this wasn't what he wanted. This wasn't how he wanted it to be at all. Not in the dark, and certainly not with bleeding.

'Are you all right? Look, borrow this –'

The voice was shocked, but gentle, and accompanied by the reach of the other man's hand. Reggie knocked it away. Whatever its proper name was, the awful scrambling together of fear and need had now left him as suddenly as it had descended, and now he needed to leave too – to get away, and get back to the lights. The dark was suddenly very, very cold.

'Sorry. Sorry.'

That was all he managed. Avoiding the outstretched hand, he turned, and ducked. Which way? Pillars with arms loomed on both sides; his eyes were dark-adapted now, but the metal seemed to be everywhere. He ducked, dodged, spat, dodged another cross-piece as it dashed its stinking festoon into his face, spun on the spot – narrowly missing another figure, human this time – and then, in desperation, unable to see a way out, did what he did in the cabinet: closed his eyes, and just lunged. Throwing his arms in front of his face to protect it, he lurched recklessly into what he could only hope was space.

It worked. When his feet realised that they were out on the unimpeded sand of the beach, Reggie broke into a limping run, his jacket flapping, sobs tearing at his side. Something tripped him, but he clawed his way back up to his feet again and stumbled on, swearing; an angry, frightened, foul-mouthed child. The darkness of the fog swallowed him, and soon he was nowhere.

Later that night – towards dawn, in fact, at about half past four – the fret tore and dispersed as quickly as it had thickened, and the Brighton promenade was graced by the year's first clear sighting of the Pleiades, rising low over the eastern horizon in all their pale beauty.

If you had been standing at the top of Mrs Steed's stairs at that time, watching the skylight over the stairs turn from black serge to grey silk, you would have heard a curious sound coming from the other side of Reggie's bedroom door. Even if you had placed your ear right against the door, you would probably have found it hard to tell if what was being whispered on his bed was a curse or an endearment. It was in fact the sound of Reggie repeatedly drawing the blade of his mother-of-pearl-handled penknife down and across the surface of a black flint pebble, the one he'd carried back from those steps the week before and had placed on his washstand as some kind of souvenir. He was turning the blade with each stroke, honing it sharper with each grating whisper, completely intent on his task. The sound carried on until it was nearly light.

Flint makes a good whetstone.

Blood isn't always a bad taste.

6

Reggie didn't say good morning or ask if she was cold, didn't even wait till he'd properly reached the stone, but started shouting straight away. He didn't see why she should have a fucking lie-in when he hadn't slept all night. He asked her in no uncertain terms what she thought she was playing at with that laughing bastard of a workman and his directions to the pier; told her exactly how foul his mouth still tasted, how broken and caked his fingernails were from where he'd fallen. He said that if she wanted to see him tearing the clothes off some stranger in the dark then she should be bloody ashamed of herself. He told her that if that was all there was, then she could fucking stick it for a game of soldiers. He told her to stop telling him that everything would be all right on the night, to just stop it, stop telling him everything would be fine once rehearsals were over, shouting at her that that was just a fucking lie, and that he was never coming here again, not ever.

He waited, and shouted the word again. The cemetery wind did its duty of hurrying it away as quietly as it decently could, and Reggie wiped his handkerchief across his face. A witness, had there been one, would have assumed that he'd been crying out there in that clear May sunshine, but in fact it was sweat and spittle and blood that streaked the cloth. Around him, the gravestones were as mute as they were pale, a patient, voiceless congregation.

He balled up his handkerchief and threw it away. You could tell from the way he was lurching towards the gate that he'd meant what he'd said. His mother didn't call him back, or use his name – and the gate swung closed behind him, sealing off her silence with its metallic, heron-harsh creak.

7

Reggie got through the rest of that dreadful Sunday without really knowing how he was doing it. He had a vague memory of standing outside the Essoldo looking up at the titles in their black-and-white letters, and wondering what they actually meant. *I'll Cry Tomorrow*, one said.

Later he'd sat on the bed looking at the roses, and at the stone and the knife on the top of his washstand. He closed the blade on the knife, and thought about tossing the stone out of the window or carrying it back to the beach and throwing it to join its friends. But he didn't; he was exhausted, and knew it – the light-headed, heavy-bodied exhaustion that comes after you've thrown up all your feelings.

When the darkness finally came, he hardly slept at all. A gull woke him with a start at about eight, and he splashed his face and tramped to his cafe in bright sunshine. This was habit, pure and simple; it was only when his hand was actually on the door handle that he remembered that this was where that workman and his tableful of laughing mates had been, and that they might be there again, joshing and showing their teeth. Even if they weren't, likely as not the young Italian chef with the curled black hair would be serving again this morning, and he'd have to decide all over again whether to stare at him or not. Exhaustion hit him – again – making him feel slightly sick. Willing his mind to stay empty, he pushed his way in and ordered a tea with two sugars. He kept his eyes down, seeing no more of the Italian than his hands; when he'd finished, he went up to the counter and dropped a three-penny bit in the saucer set out for tips. Outside, he told himself that tomorrow he'd go somewhere else. Then he re-wrapped his jacket, and set out to tramp along the front. That, however, meant seeing the pier – you couldn't avoid it, walking into town. The sight of it made him duck his head and wince, but he forced himself to get his chin back up and stare at it, white in the morning sunshine on its stilts.

At least the tide was in.

He imagined the black water pressing through the submerged metal forest, lifting the beards of weed; scouring away all traces of the night before. The idea gave him an angry satisfaction – he liked the idea of all that *stupidity* being drowned under a weight of darkness and cold that nothing could survive. He watched the skin of the water break and glitter around the tops of the black metal branches for a bit, then walked on. Feeling the need to finally clean his mouth out once and for all, he lurched along the promenade railing until he reached the top of the stairs that had led him down to the stones two nights ago, stared down the steps, and spat.

He held on to the rail for a bit, then let go. The hot tea had settled his stomach, and the sugar was doing its job now – *Monday bloody morning is right*, he muttered. *People who want to get paid need to get themselves to work on bloody time.*

Mr Brookes had called them in for half nine, and he had all the costumes to check before then. He swung straight across the roundabout by the Royal Albion, ignoring the pavements, and headed on past the Pavilion, past the library and up North Road.

Mr English seemed a bit preoccupied about something, but Reg was in no mood to ask how anyone was this morning. He could see from the keyboard that Pam and Mr Brookes were both in already, but that was only to be expected, and he told himself again to stop worrying and to just get on with his job. He scrawled his name in the book, and was already heading off down the corridor when Mr English called him back in that funny high-pitched voice of his. *What now, you old fusspot?* thought Reg. Mr English explained that he was a bit worried about Miss Rose. One of the Devere girls who had come in to collect a parcel had mentioned that she'd popped downstairs to the Ladies, and heard the sound of crying. It wasn't his place to pry, of course, but might Reggie just pop down and make sure Miss Rose was all right?

There'd been no sound when he'd knocked, so he'd just pushed the door open. She was leaning with her hands on one of the basins, staring into the mirror, and his first thought was that she must have been being sick. When she eventually turned and looked at him, however, he knew straight away that that wasn't it. Her skin was powderless, and the marks under her eyes were so dark that he was shocked. Her lips were dry, and cracked, and the bottom one was trembling.

8

'Has he hit you?'

She looked down, then up in the mirror again, and pushed her hair back. He waited.

'No, Reg. Nothing like that.'

The voice was barely there.

'Well, what then? Mr English said you've –'

'I've clicked.'

One of the taps in front of her was dripping into the hand-basin, and she twisted it shut. He hadn't understood what she was saying. Was she –

'Well, come on then, Reg, say something. Tell me off.'

She twisted the tap again, and squeezed her voice into an ugly whisper.

''Cause it's my fault, that's for sure. People say the cap doesn't work if you put it in in a hurry, and I was certainly that –' she spat the words out – 'I was certainly that, three Friday nights ago, in the Ladies toilet of the Bedford Hotel.'

Then she let out a laugh so bitter it strangled itself – Reg wanted to step into the room and stop her, but a lifted hand made him stop.

'God! – the rigmarole they make you go through to get that bloody thing, Reg . . . The girl I shared with at Murray's was married, and at least four of us must have borrowed her certificate for that all-important little *interview* at the clinic.'

The bitter laugh came back, and she turned her voice into a whining parody of gentility.

'Oh yes, Doctor, I certainly *do* have my husband's permission. He says if we just wait another year or two for Baby to arrive, he feels he'll be better able to provide properly for all three of us . . .'

The voice dropped, and the hand slammed down onto the tiled shelf in front of the mirror. Reg took five steps towards her, then another.

'. . . Christ!'

'But how long?' Reg was trying his best to keep up with what she was telling him, but most of it was over his head. He really hoped that that was the right question.

'Eighteen fucking days –' she inspected a nail, uselessly, – 'and yes, I have done the sums. Ticked the days off on my sodding calendar, counted them, told myself it's too soon to be sure till I'm blue in the face –'

'Are you not sure then? I thought –'

'Tell it to these,' said Pam, cupping her breasts with both hands and offering them up as if she were offering two pieces of fruit from a stall. 'Sore as if they've been punched, Reg. Ripe. Sweaty. And I'm clogged up inside. True, I've only missed once, and they say it has to be twice, but trust me, I'm sure. Remember that time when you told me your body never makes mistakes about things that hurt it? Well, you were right.'

'That is a spot of bad luck.'

The voice dropped into the windowless room like a stone, and they turned their heads together to identify its source. Mr Brookes was standing just where Reggie had been, framed in the doorway with one hand up and resting against the woodwork.

'Still, I'm sure we can sort you out.'

His face was as calm as it was in the act when he was palming something. The voice, too – measured, like a doctor's. He took his hand away from the door frame, and wiped it.

'Well, first things first. *Are* you sure?'

For the first time, Pam sounded more frightened than angry. Like Reg, she didn't how long Mr Brookes had been standing there, and didn't know how much he'd heard.

'Too soon to tell until the sixth week, they say. I'm probably just fussing, Ted, honestly. I –'

'I lie for a living, remember,' said Mr Brookes. 'Now, let's see . . .'

He reached into his jacket, produced his wallet, and counted nine banknotes out onto the tiled shelf in front of her; nine, one after the other. Each note snapped slightly as it was lifted from the pigskin.

'You can't troupe with a kid, that's for sure,' he said as he worked, 'and personally I'm hoping that you and I will be touring together for quite some time, Pam –' the voice was almost purring now – 'quite some time – and I'm sure you feel the same way, after all our . . . after all the hard work the two of us have put into our new act together. You just concentrate on that for a few days, and then when the time is right we'll pop you off to somebody I know here in town who'll be able to take care of you. Or rather, to somebody who knows somebody who will. There.'

He'd aligned the notes into a neat pile, exactly as if he'd been laying out cards for the start of a trick. He thought for a moment, and then, as if he had just recalculated the acceptable amount for a tip in a club or restaurant he was visiting for the first time, added two more notes for luck, and dug into a trouser pocket for two half-crowns, which he laid on top of the last note as his finishing touch.

'Now,' he said, the dirty work done, 'why don't you tuck that little lot away in your handbag, my darling – or ask Reggie to look after it for you if that would be easier – then splash your face, pop upstairs and get yourself changed for today's rehearsal. Reggie'll make you a nice hot cup of tea – two sugars today please, Reg, nice and strong – and we'll start work in five minutes. Take your mind off things. Always the best policy in a crisis.'

As if he'd just completed a routine, he checked both their faces for a smile to match his own. His eyebrows rose.

'No time like the present, boys and girls . . .'

The silence after he left them was long. Neither of them moved, and when Pam finally spoke it was in a voice Reggie hadn't ever heard from her before. She sounded as though something very big was being compressed into a space that was much too small. She wasn't staring after Mr Brookes, but at the money on the tiles – four blue fivers, five singles, two brick-red ten-bob notes and the two silver half-crowns, each note creased just the once from Mr Brookes's wallet.

'Put that somewhere where I can't see it, would you, Reg?' she said carefully, twisting her bracelet. 'Otherwise I think I might do something silly.'

Reg picked up the money and stowed it away. He knew that Mr English kept a quarter-bottle of brandy at the stage door somewhere, and was wondering what would be the best way to get some of it down her before they started work – she was looking as white as a bloody sheet now. They could talk about what she was planning to do later.

'Shall we go and –'

'Notice he didn't ask if it was his or not,' Pam interrupted, her voice sharpening. 'Which is a bit rich – don't you think? Perhaps he'll get Mr Clements to slip the programmes for the show with a title change – but then I shouldn't think "Not So Bloody Respectable After All" would go down that well, even here at the Grand. And I doubt if Her Majesty would care for it, especially not on her big day, when everything's going to be so . . . so very fucking *nice*.'

The control tightened, and almost slipped. She made a desperate attempt to keep her temper leashed, raking her fingers through her hair.

'And did you see the way he put the notes down? Like he was counting them out on a tart's mantelpiece. Like he was paying a flippin' Frith Street *tart*.'

Reg was about to answer, but she didn't give him time. She started to pace up and down the tiny room as if it were a cage, her voice getting louder and sharper with each turn.

'He's done that before, wouldn't you say? In fact, he's done that whole bloody scene before if you ask me. Notice he already knows exactly who to send me to – gives a whole new meaning to the phrase *one in every town*, doesn't it? Still, as the gentleman said, no time like the present; I may as well go and get myself done and dusted as soon as he gives us a morning off. After all, there's no point in pretending I can keep the wretched little –'

It was only when she saw the words strike Reg across the face that she realised what she'd done.

'Oh Christ, Reg,' she whispered, stricken, and reaching for him straight away. 'I'm so sorry. I'm so sorry. But you know I have to, don't you?'

She stroked his face, trying to get him to open his eyes.

'Believe me I don't want to, but I have to. Come on, Reg, say something, please. Please. Don't be angry.'

'I'm not,' he said, his eyes still closed. 'Honestly. Not with you. It's just that . . .'

'What?'

Reg jerked his chin up, trying to get his face away from her hand, and swallowed hard.

'Later,' he said. 'Later, all right?'

He was already past her and out through the door when he spoke again, his voice thrown abruptly over his shoulder down the white-tiled corridor.

'For now let's just do what he says and get back to work. That spin out of the wedding dress is still nowhere near quick enough, and your garter needs tightening . . . Come on, I'll make us that tea.'

Pam watched him go, but didn't follow. Her feet wouldn't move.

Reggie wasn't lying when he said that about not being angry with her. Horrified, yes – but not angry. When he'd seen Pam's mouth twist as she spat out those words about getting rid of her child he'd realised – as immediately as if he was feeling bile or vomit rising to his mouth – that he was watching his own mother. His mother, on the day she'd found out she was carrying him; watching her pace and rail and swear against her body's trap as she felt it closing shut around her.

And Mr Brookes, standing there in the doorway with his face all stone as he reached for his wallet – well, now he knew. Now he knew what his father had looked like.

9

I need to explain about the money. In particular, I need to explain why Mr Brookes was able to count out the price of an abortion from his wallet as if that was the easiest thing in the world, because twenty-five guineas – which was what he counted out onto that shelf – was more than four times the weekly wage of almost everyone in this story.

Being seen as the kind of man who always had the price of a drink or taxi about his person was an important detail of Mr Brookes's act, and apart from when he was onstage – in which case it was locked in his dressing room and the key handed over to Reggie for safe keeping – that pigskin wallet never left his jacket pocket. Even so, it was fortuitous that Pam's expensive little bit of news arrived on his doorstep on that particular Monday morning, because, as luck would have it (so to speak), that particular Monday morning was one when Mr Brookes was positively flush.

Over the years, Mr Brookes had accumulated a small collection of gold or gold-plated jewellery. A few of the pieces had been gifts, but mostly they were stolen – little morning-after trophies, rings taken from a bedside handbag and suchlike, trinkets like Pamela's gold cat, the kind of thing it would be too much trouble for a married woman to report missing – and knowing that once the new act was open he'd have to pay off some of the bills incurred in getting it up and running, he'd kept a previously made appointment that morning to turn some of this stolen jewellery into cash. The meeting was in a small and not particularly reputable premises at the back end of the Lanes – one of the shuttered-up second-hand places I've shown you Reggie lurching past a couple of times, in fact. There had been some toing and froing on the price, but in the end Mr Brookes had come away with thirty-five quid and no questions asked. Obviously, he hadn't been planning on giving this money away, but as he told himself as he headed back upstairs from the Ladies towards the stage to start his morning warm-up, the unexpected outlay was more of an inconvenience than a disaster. In fact, it was an invest-ment – he could hardly tell Pam to sling her hook a week before their opening night, could he? Having seen other girls through this little difficulty before, he was pretty sure he could rely on her not to bolt. Once they'd quietened down a bit and were feeling more sensible, pointing out the advan-tages of keeping their jobs usually did the trick. Not to mention the convenience of his knowing somebody safe he could send her to. As for his bills, the ones for the apparatus and rigs and so on . . . well, there were a couple of outstand-ing bar loans to acquaintances at the Arts that could be called in if he got short towards the end of the week, and he could easily talk his landlady into another week or so's credit on his rent – and even then he would still have his cigarette case, his lighter, his watch and his signet ring in reserve, any of which he was sure his friend in the Lanes would be happy to bargain for if push came to shove. Come the opening night, he was sure his pigskin would be well lined again. If he could just keep Pam working hard, he didn't see any reason why they couldn't all get over this together.

He'd organise the rest of the day's rehearsal so that it didn't require him to touch her too much, he decided, and then get Reg to walk her home early. Things were temporarily strained, he'd admit that, but very far from impossible. Yes, they only had one more week to get the act finished, and sending her home early would lose them a couple of hours, but no point in spoiling the ship for a ha'porth, and so on.

At four'clock, Pam and Reg walked up the Queen's Road in silence. They both knew that there was nothing much useful that could be said out loud – not today, not while they were both still so raw – and simply concentrated on getting them-selves home. They said their goodbyes on the usual corner. Reggie asked her if she wanted to take the money, but she said that she didn't want it in the same room as her, and would he please keep it for a day or two; she didn't think she'd be able to sleep, she said, knowing it was in her bag. As she let go of his arm, she offered him a conciliatory squeeze just above the elbow, and a thin smile, but that was all.

10

Reg stood and watched her walk all the way to her front gate, keeping his eyes on her until she was hidden by the laburnum tree. Jamming his hands into his pockets, he discovered a packet of sandwiches wrapped in greaseproof paper that he'd bought himself at lunchtime, and realising how hungry he now was, he set off to find somewhere to sit and eat them.

He found a park, found a bench, opened the greaseproof packet – but then, deciding that a cigarette would be more like it, folded the sandwich back into its wrapping and stuffed it into a bin. Two speckled birds came and tried to get at it while he smoked, and he watched them, but didn't chase them away.

He stayed on the bench for hours – until his tobacco tin was empty, in fact.

When the park bell came for sunset, he walked for a bit, not really looking or caring where he was going, and only stopping occasionally to watch the street lamps coming on across the town. At one point he crossed a railway bridge, and passed an odd-looking white-and-green-tiled factory which smelt of soap. Knowing that he was exhausting himself, he eventually decided to turn around, and limped up a long elm-lined avenue that he hoped would lead him back to a main road into town. Through the black lace of the branches, a bright spring moon was now rising.

Still, he couldn't think straight.

A passing bus pulled in in front of him, but Reggie decided to save his fourpence, and let the bus ring itself away from the stop without him. He was sure he remembered from the map in the back of his guidebook that somewhere up ahead would be the station – then he could head straight down the Queen's Road and cut through North Road to the front and his bed.

However, when he got to the next junction, Reg faltered, and paused for thought; and then, instead of choosing to head left towards the great curving glass roof of the railway station and thence to the top of the Queen's Road, he turned right. Two more turns and ten minutes later – he was limping slowly now – his route brought him back into the very same street of dilapidated white-faced villas where he had left Pam some five hours earlier.

The lamps were all lit now, and he went and stood under their usual lamp post, staring at the house and imagining her lying alone and sleepless in her bed in the room at the back. There was a second street lamp right across from Mrs Brennan's front door, and it was close enough to the laburnum tree to be fusing its heavy load of blossoms into a single, shimmering blaze. Even from his vantage point on the corner, Reggie was drenched in its perfume. He breathed it in. Rank, heady; foxlike. Warm . . .

I think he was intending to stand sentinel and watch all night, as if that might help prevent some harm that he couldn't even put a name to, but then, as he stood there, letting the perfume and the night and his tiredness take hold of him, he realised that next to Pam's bed wasn't where he needed to be tonight at all. He knew the cemetery gates would be locked by now, and he knew how high the surrounding wall was. He knew he'd sworn he was never going to talk to his mother again, and knew how much his left foot was hurting, but none of that seemed to matter. He had to.

11

The leap up the cemetery wall from the top of the stolen dustbin took all of Reggie's skill, but on the third try, his fingers found their grip. He'd swung his jacket up ahead to try to protect himself from the worst of the broken glass, but even so he felt something come through the tweed and tear at the palm of his right hand. He gasped, swore, gritted his teeth, gasped again with the pain, and hauled. A second blade burnt his right leg as he swung it up and over, stinging the meat on the back of his calf. He took a deep breath, and let himself fall. After he'd dropped, he picked himself and inspected the damage. His trousers were ruined, with a neat wet slice where the glass had caught him, and the palm of his right hand had been opened. In the moonlight, the blood was black. After flexing his fingers to make sure they were still working, he shook the blood off as best he could, and bound the already-throbbing hand up with his handkerchief.

Everything looked different in the dark, and it took him a while to get his bearings in the thickly wooded lower part of the cemetery. Using the slope of the hill to guide him, he picked his way through the leaning black graves and columns until he found a path he recognised. Then it was up, along the wall, under the bay trees and out onto the open grass.

He'd never seen the stones by moonlight before. They stretched away from him in pale, orderly rows, each one attended by its own bright shadow – as if they were hospital beds, Reg thought, with each sheet turned down by a black, attendant nurse. But if it was a hospital, it was a very peaceful one; no voices called out as he passed, and he deliberately stepped off the path and onto the grass so that his feet wouldn't wake anyone up. Everything was edged with silver, and the names on the stones had been freshly inked. When he arrived at Doreen's, he instinctively spoke in a whisper.

'Hello my darling.'

All around him, the moonlight was smoothing the turf into a blanket, and for once he knew he needn't worry about her being cold. He gently ran the back of his damaged hand across her name, tracing its letters with his aching knuckles. Then, without thinking about it, he knelt down, reached his arms around the stone, and kissed it.

In January, of course, a stone can take the skin off your lips – but not in May. After a day of sunshine, it gives you back the warmth of your own mouth even after dark. The effect is always strange, and it was now for Reggie. He shifted his position so that he could get both of his arms around the stone more comfortably, and rested his cheek against its hard edge – to him, it felt like a pillow. He closed his eyes. Hugging the stone closer, he pulled his knees up almost to his chin.

That's right; if the stone *had* been a bed, he would have climbed right in and held her, all night.

People who think they have never had it – or who fear they have no right to it – often ask themselves what possible proof of love there can be. Of course, for the rest of us there are kind actions, shared moments, histories of glance and touch – but this is Reggie, remember, and he has had none of that in his life. For him, love hasn't ever been a verb, but only ever the most abstract of nouns, and out here in the moonlit silence of this cemetery especially his imagination has no use for the cruel nonsense of rings or white dresses or red silk roses. He's touched on some of the things men will do to shy away from or scrabble towards love, but he has never felt it course incontrovertibly though his body.

But now – trust me – with his eyes closed and his arms full of warm stone, lit only by the moon, he does.

Trust me.

Only flesh can speak to flesh. Without any warning except the slightest prickling at the back of his neck, Reggie feels something which is as close as a voice in his ear, and as tangible as a change from hot to cold. Indeed, a change of temperature is exactly the first thing that he is aware of. A hand, warmer than the stone he's holding, places itself gently on his shoulder.

He's not sure at first if he's got that right. He doesn't open his eyes, but closes them tighter – and holds his breath. The pressure of the hand, fugitive at first, becomes definite. Gasping out loud, Reggie feels a second hand join it on his other shoulder. They press, warming him. Whirling, staggering, he stands – his eyes still closed – and now he wants to cry, because there are suddenly two arms wrapped close around him and pressing into his back, holding him as firmly as he has just been holding the stone, whether he wants it or not. The sensation isn't elusive, but absolutely real; as his mother holds him, she is pressing herself gently into his chest, resting her face on it, and he can feel the warmth of her body as he now reaches out and folds his arms carefully around her in reciprocation. To his surprise, his mother is slightly shorter than he is; her face dips gently into his breastbone, so that his lips can almost feel her hair. As he cradles her, and she hugs him, her warmth floods him. People say *she went through me*, and they're right; she is inside him, too. Their breaths rise and fall together.

Reggie doesn't want ever to be let go – he can't imagine it. He doesn't want this ever to end, but of course – eventually – gently, and slowly, it must. The warmth doesn't pull away, or vanish, or evaporate; he doesn't feel abandoned, or bereft. Just before she goes, he feels her fingers graze his cheek, and that is enough. He stands still for a very long time, and only then does he slowly open his eyes. The stones – those silent witnesses – are still sleeping as peacefully as they were before, still all laid out in their pale hospital rows. Very far away and over to his right, he can hear a night train picking up speed as it leaves the town.

He stands there for a very long time.

Not wanting to wake them, but needing to thank them all the same, Reggie whispers the stones a quiet, collective *Goodnight*. He gathers himself, but isn't quite ready to leave. He waits until he is, and then gently – gently – turns himself away. This bit is quite hard; after just a few steps on the gravel, he stops and turns round, wondering if he mightn't just go back and curl up against the stone for the rest of the night, sleep with it as his pillow until the dew comes and drenches him – but he knows that that would be to trespass on his mother's rest, and he turns again and continues down the path. It's only when he gets to the metal gate that he realises that his face is wet with tears, but he doesn't mind. The gate clicks shut behind him, its voice quietened for once; he remembers to gently tap his knife with his bloodied hand; and now he taps and drags his mismatched feet in their distinctive rhythm down through the trees. It'll be a few hours before they open the big black gates of the main entrance, he realises, but he'll be happy to just sit quietly on a grave and wait till they do. The cut on the back of his leg is starting to sting, and he knows he should get some of Pam's Dettol on that, and see to his sliced hand with some hot water and plasters, but all of that can wait. As he reaches the gate, he settles down to sit and wait, and soon he hears the first birds just beginning to sing.

Thank you.

Pamela heard him coming up her corridor, and considered saying she just needed a minute – but Reg lurched into her dressing room without even knocking. His up-all-night eyes took in the newspaper cuttings lying crumpled in the spilt powder and then locked onto hers, staring. Did he have a fever or something? And what the hell had happened to his hand?

'You just can't see it, can you?'

'What? What can't I see?' replied Pamela, dabbing at her eyes – and then, trying to make a joke of it, trying to look affronted, as if someone had given her a lovely little piece of new jewellery and she'd somehow mislaid it amid the litter of her disarranged dressing table, silly empty-headed little tart that she was. 'What can't I see, Reggie?'

'The way out.'

12

After that slightly rocky start, the week went as well as could have been expected. Much to her credit, Mr Brookes thought, Pam seemed to have pulled herself together. *The show*, as she put it on the Tuesday morning as she climbed into the apparatus to start drilling her quick change once again with Reg, *does have to bloody go on, after all.* She certainly wasn't looking her best, which was a bit of a worry with regards to the opening, but on the other hand she wasn't making any scenes or asking him to talk things over. In particular, she didn't ask him if they were going to keep on seeing each other, which was a relief; he'd had enough of that bloody carry-on with the last one, thank you very much. He did have to be a bit careful when it came to manhandling her at certain points in rehearsals, obviously, especially when she was blindfolded and tied, but he could manage that. After all, everyone knew they got a bit moody in the early weeks, so it was only to be expected.

To his surprise she'd even been perfectly professional when he gave her the address he'd arranged for her to visit, scribbled down on a page torn from his notebook. Commendably, it seemed to be a point of pride with her that she wanted to get everything over and done with as soon as she could. He'd assumed that she'd want to leave getting herself seen to until after the opening of the new show, but after rehearsal on the Thursday she came and asked him if he could arrange things for Saturday afternoon. That way, she said, she could take advantage of the Sunday off and get back to work on the Monday. It had cost him another two quid for the short notice to get her the appointment – and there'd be her taxi fare there and back on top of that, because the place was right out on the edge of town, and she'd have to go as soon as they'd finished work – but he didn't mind. As she herself pointed out, the sooner this whole thing was off her mind, the better.

There were only a couple of properly tricky moments between them. A few times, he'd pushed her a bit too far, and there'd been tears – once, for instance, when making her repeat her frock-parading on her entrance, and then again with their business when the Gentleman offered his Lady the diamond ring. As he always did at this stage of rehearsals, he was talking the story though out loud while they worked, marking in the punctuation points for the percussion from the band and counting her moves where required. As he worked the produce of the jewellery box he'd stupidly used the phrase *He lets you know he's got something for his very special girl* right in her ear, and obviously – obviously – that had been the wrong thing to say. She'd pulled away, asked him if he minded if they took a break for a moment, and then walked off, rummaging in her bag so that he couldn't see her face. However, it was obvious that she was crying, and next thing he knew he was having to ask Reggie to go and get her out of the downstairs Ladies with a cup of tea before they could continue.

Reggie had been a bit of a godsend all round, in fact, and not just when madam got tearful. He'd more or less taken care of her throughout, leaving Mr Brookes free to concentrate on the work in hand. Admittedly it hadn't been the best bit of timing in the world for the boy to choose this *particular* week to slice his right hand open on a corned beef tin, but at least it didn't seem to be affecting his work. The sequence where he dodged and clung to the sides of the apparatus while Mr Brookes flipped the doors open and shut was coming along very prettily indeed, and once they were up to full speed together, it was going to give a very nice clean edge to the overall presentation.

If he could just make the time to get his own produces and vanishes in the opening sequence as smooth as he wanted them to be, and to iron out the adding of the handcuffs to the rope on her wrists – which was proving trickier than it looked – then he thought they could really be onto a winner.

On the Saturday they stopped rehearsals at lunchtime, as always. Reggie offered to go and get Pam into a taxi up at the station, and Mr Brookes, after asking him to check that Pam had remembered the money, shut himself into his dressing room to work in his mirror. He was still working on the sequence with the comb and watch and carnation when Reggie knocked at the door at seven o'clock that evening – the sequence was proving a bastard, and his fingers were properly hurting. Reg didn't actually come in, seeing straight away that Mr Brookes wasn't in a mood to be interrupted, but just stuck his head round the door and said rather nervously that he thought Mr Brookes would like to know he'd just dropped by at Mrs Brennan's to see if Pam was doing all right after her appointment, and that she was, and that he'd drop in again tomorrow to double-check she was OK for work on Monday if that was all right with him. Mr Brookes assured him that it was, and once he'd shut the door went back to checking the action of his right wrist on the produce with his comb. *First impressions count*, he reminded himself. For the umpteenth time that evening his wrist flicked and circled in the mirror; flicked, and circled. There was a telegram from London lying open on his dressing table, confirming that that booking agent from Poland Street would be there for the second half of the six twenty house on Tuesday. He must remember to speak to Clements about getting the man a good ticket.

Christ, it had better go well.

Just a couple more days.

The wrist flicked, circled.

Pageants, parades, HMS *Eagle* moored off the West Pier, synchronised fireworks, the Hove Girl Guides in their special choral tribute, Dress Uniform balls at the Royal Albion and Metropole, communal midnight singing of the National Anthem all along the seafront, new programmes at the Grand, Royal, Palace Pier and Aquarium theatres – according to the *Argus*, there seemed to be no end to the plans for the big day. Backstage, everyone was talking about food and drink, and who knew who'd bought a television. There was much reno-vating of costumes and accessories as girls worried about whether their outfits would be quite right for the day, and Mr English invested in a new silver, maroon and royal-blue cravat, not wanting to be too obvious with his colour scheme, but feeling obliged to be patriotic nonetheless. Everyone was worried that things wouldn't be ready in time, but they really needn't have been. As I'm sure you know, it's amazing what people can pull together under pressure when they absolutely have to.

13

When people who were there talk about that day, it's often the silence that they mention first. It seems to have lodged in people's minds even more than the shouting or the crowds or the disappointing weather. At ten minutes past eleven, as the great doors of the Abbey up in Westminster finally swung open and the trumpets blared out in greeting, a synchronised quiet fell across Brighton like a slowly spreading cloud-shadow. In people's memories at least, even the traffic stopped. On the Queen's Road and West Street, buses pulled over; people got off and stood clustered around the open windows of pubs and shops to listen in silence to radios which had been placed out on the window ledges. In the crowds gathered round the loudspeakers that had been set up at intervals along the seafront, men doffed their hats in the drizzle. Even in houses like that of Mrs Steed's sister, where half the street seemed to have pushed its way into the darkened front room, the plates of sandwiches and sausage rolls sat untouched, and the children were kept hushed on strangers' laps as everybody stared at the television. The black-and-white figures blurred and fractured as they moved around the carefully polished ten-inch screen, but it was all very beautiful – everyone agreed about that. As the bishops hovered and shifted around the young woman in white who was in the middle of it all, helping her to change her gowns and jewellery, escorting and conducting her, they looked very strange and far away; none-theless, everyone behaved as if they were right there in the room, and could easily be disturbed in their solemn business. When the camera seemed to catch the young woman herself smiling bravely, just the once, people murmured, and cried – but only quietly.

Then, at just past one o'clock, the silence broke like a wave; at the moment when the crown touched the young woman's head – the moment when her transformation was effected, that is (the *reveal*, you might even say), people forgot themselves, and started to clap. Most people's windows were open, and the pattering applause from one house joined up with that emerging from next door, and together they combined with the sound of the next street and then the next, so that the sound spread and dispersed itself as mysteriously as distant rainfall heard at sea, slowly connecting street to street to seafront to suburb until it gathered and then unfurled itself above the town like some great ragged banner of noise, cresting and glittering in rising outbreaks of cheers and shouts. Then, to underwrite this majesty, the distant boom of the twenty-one guns being fired from the Tower of London came thudding through the loudspeakers on the prom, and people threw their hats, and the gulls huddled out on the sand of the low-tide beach lifted and wheeled in alarm, adding their wild obbligato to the strange, involuntary tumult. Out at sea, the sky broke into light behind the great ship moored off the West Pier; the drizzle eased, and stopped, and everyone agreed that this was a good sign, and waved their flags and hugged each other tight. No one really knew why they were crying, but now lots of people were.

Pamela missed all of that.

She'd done fine on the Monday; the run-through onstage in rehearsal clothes and with the band had been subdued, obviously, but had passed without any major mishaps. The two stagehands who were going to bring on the apparatus and strike the steps were introduced, and she'd even managed to have a laugh with one of them over the business with the blindfold. But then she'd told Mr Brookes that she felt sore, and needed to lie down; if he wouldn't mind, she'd said, she'd like to spend the Tuesday morning in bed, and then just meet up with Reggie in the afternoon to check through a couple of things with her costumes before the show and then go straight on. Mr Brookes had reluctantly agreed, not wanting to push his luck or risk upsetting her at this late stage of the game, and that was more or less what had happened; Reggie had gone up to her place to meet her, and then they'd walked down into town together.

It had taken them a while. The pavements on the Queen's Road were getting crowded already, especially outside a couple of the small hotels, and people were striding around in groups, linking their arms and singing and waving their flags. Someone had even set up a barrel organ. The curtain was going up on the first house at twenty past six, and even at four o'clock North Road was packed; they could see throngs of people crowded under the bunting outside the theatre, laughing and cheering as they moved from street party to street party. Even when they got up the alley and safely inside, the noise continued; Mr English had set up his radio in the bottom of the backstage stairwell for everybody to hear, and when the man from the BBC described the happy couple stepping out onto their balcony there was cheering and clapping from the dressing rooms all the way up and down the corridors, making the tiled walls ring.

It was clearly going to be quite a night.

Pamela frowned, and took a swig from the small bottle of brandy that she'd talked out of Mr English on her way in. Apparently Margaret had worn embroidered white satin at the Abbey, and had been officially described by the radio as looking 'stately' at the ceremony; well, Pam wasn't having any of that *she's a good girl really* nonsense tonight, thank you very much, not after what she'd just been through. She'd got a bit of a surprise planned. She had retrieved one of her clippings from the waste-paper basket in her dressing room, and using it as his guide – it was a recent one of the Princess laughing and waving as she stepped out of yet another taxi – Reg had given her hair a snip and set up at Mrs Brennan's, putting a right-hand side parting into the curls, whereas Pam's was usually on the left. Reggie wasn't what you would call a professional, but once the new style was fixed into place with a quick once-over from a borrowed can of Spray Net they'd both agreed it looked pretty much exactly right. Now all Pam had to do was to get her version of Margaret's full lips and velvet eyebrows as spot on as her shaking hands would allow, and the illusion would be complete. She'd show that Teddy Brookes a thing or two on his opening night. A thing or two about Ladies, about what they would and wouldn't put up with for the sake of a bit of jewellery.

She blotted her lips, stood up straight, and smoothed the wrinkled satin of her gloves. She smiled, keeping her lips soft and promising just like her heroine always did, glad that the scarlet of her first costume looked so emphatically bloody. Bringing off a character was all to do with how you considered yourself, she thought. How you felt inside when you looked in the mirror.

She just wished she could stop this bloody shaking.

There's always a slight edge to the atmosphere backstage on the first house of a brand-new bill – nobody knows how the running order is going to go down, not least the acts themselves, so nerves are quite a bit sharper than usual. And this, obviously, was going to be no ordinary first house. People had been celebrating since eleven o'clock already, and were bound to be rowdy; word had also gone round that the *House Full* sign was up at the box office – which would be the first time in a very long time that *that* had been dusted off at the Grand – and that always raised the temperature. Mr Clements had been spotted greedily rubbing his hands. The corridors were crowded as people ran to get themselves ready; the stage manager was shouting the calls, and the radio was still booming up the stairwell. As Pam made her way down to the stage the Devere Girls' dressing room was as loud with laughter as an aviary, and two of the Queens of England – already in costume for their first parade, and having a quick final fag out in the corridor – shrieked in recognition and then dropped into a full court curtsy as she passed them. Pam waved in character, rotating one upraised, satin-gloved wrist, and reduced them to helpless giggling. Only her slightly startled eyes and a slight tightness at the corners of her mouth betrayed her nerves, and when she reached the top of the last flight of stairs, the ones that led down to the back of the stage, she took a deep breath to steady herself. Then she broadened her royal smile, and swept down in one go.

Mr Brookes laughed. The look was most convincing, he said. More to the point, he was relieved to see that his assistant had finally decided to rally and do a proper job with her face and hair. She was looking very presentable – very presentable indeed – despite the obvious first-night nerves, and once again he congratulated himself on having acquired such a first-class asset.

Pam wasn't the only one who was feeling their nerves, however.

As the last but two of the Devere Girls swept on from the wings to join their tableau – she was meant to be Henrietta

Maria, apparently, in not *quite* enough lace to cover her chest – Mr Brookes reached into his inside breast pocket and discovered that Reggie had made a stupid and uncharacteristic mistake. Mr Brookes always set his own hand props, loading the concealed compartments and pochettes of his tailcoat himself in the privacy of his dressing room before the half, but then it was always Reggie's job to set the clean handkerchief that went in this particular pocket, the one Brookes used to wipe his hands if they got sweaty during the act. Tonight of all nights, he was going to need it to be there – and it wasn't. Reg realised what he'd done as soon as he saw Mr Brookes's hand reach inside his jacket; he grimaced with dismay, and bolted, calculating that he just had time to make it before Mr Clifford started up with their music. He took the stairs back up to Mr Brookes's dressing room two at a time, almost twisting his ankle on the last turn of the handrail, and only just got back down in time.

'Sorry,' he panted, hobbling on his hurt foot as he held out the offending article. 'Really sorry, Mr Brookes – I know the last thing you bloody need tonight is for me to be –'

'Steady the buffs,' said Mr Brookes, taking the handkerchief and firmly wiping each finger in turn as the applause greeted Good Queen Bess – in a particularly revealing ruff – taking the crowning place in the onstage tableau. 'No particular harm done.'

'No, Mr Brookes.' Reg was still breathless, and hopping.

'Right.'

Brookes tucked the handkerchief away, checked his bow tie for one last time in the pier glass, and shot a final glance at Pam. She was staring straight ahead. Out onstage, the pyramid of girls was being slowly sliced by the shadow of the descending curtain; the applause built to cheers, and then was muffled as the heavy fabric kissed the stage. Mr Brookes patted the rope coiled in his right-hand pocket, and walked straight on. Reggie patted his penknife, licked his lips and mouthed a quick hard *All right?* across the wing to Pam – but she was staring at Mr Brookes, and didn't seem to have eyes for anything else. Reg shook himself like a dog, cursing the pain in his ankle, and set off for his wing.

From then on, of course, it all happened very quickly. The Devere Girls giggled themselves offstage for their change, the silver drapes dropped halfway up the stage to hide the descending backdrop for the finale, and the lights shifted colour; out in the pit, the music rallied, ended and then struck up again with Mr Brookes's play-in. In the auditorium, people looked in their programmes to remind themselves which act was coming up next, and quite a few of the more well-oiled members of the crowd smiled at the title. In the centre of the stage, Mr Brookes turned his back, flexed his hands and assumed his opening position. Only when she'd seen him do that did Pam swing her bloody, stiffened skirt round to the upstage wing to await her cue. And then, at just gone half past seven on the evening of June the second 1953 – that long-awaited day – the curtain finally rose on Teddy Brookes's Coronation tribute.

The trick of starting with your back to the house is always a good one – provided, of course, that you've got the looks to bring it off when you finally turn. Mr Brookes had, and from the first moment he glanced round at the audience he seemed to have them on his side. The top hat and tails helped, of course. He'd got the mix of distinguished, delayed and debonair just right; the long and exciting day that his audience had just shared had been all about waiting for a very special lady to arrive, and now his nicely judged combination of anticipation and suavity as he shot his first cuff and checked his watch meant that they all knew straight away what this particular gentleman was doing. The single boys who'd brought their dates with them knew just how he felt as he checked his hair and watch one more time, and laughed; the girls by their sides smiled because they were glad to see a man getting himself in a bit of a state for a change. The unaccompanied men mentally wished him luck – but after the beers and laughter of the day they were as sure he'd get his prize as they were that they themselves would get lucky before the night was over. The booking agent down from London, sitting in a house seat next to Mr Clements, was impressed by the neatness of the presentation. A married woman sitting next to her husband in the sixth row in the stalls shifted from thigh to thigh as Mr Brookes directed one of his subtly interrogative stares right at her, and was glad she'd come.

Pam's entrance went down even better. An amused ripple of comment ran round the house as people clocked her daring resemblance to a certain glamorous and still conspicuously unmarried royal lady, and the way she paraded her costume – swinging the stiffly supported skirt from her hips with each turn – earned her a good-hearted chorus of whistles from the boys up in the gods. Milking the moment, she dropped a curtsy, and then lifted one glove in a cool approximation of a Buckingham Palace wave. At that, the laughter turned into applause. The business with producing and pinning on the red rose corsage went down well – except with Mr Clements, who couldn't help but take note of the difference between the grateful response to her floral tribute of the distinguished-looking lovely up on stage and that of his wife, whose own opening-night corsage, far from being magicked from under a silk handkerchief, had cost him seven and six, and not even earned him a kiss. When the engagement ring appeared, the audience seemed momentarily confused – surely such a glamorous creature as this had no particular reason to fall for that old trick? However, the saucy rise of Pamela's eyebrows persuaded them that the lady knew exactly what she was after this evening. It was quite a ring, after all — and from the look of her, she was enjoying herself. The ropes, handcuffs and blindfold were all swiftly and elegantly applied — Mr Brookes was careful with her hair — and when the apparatus appeared, gliding between its two attendant stagehands, the audience accepted Mr Brookes's elaborate demonstration of its emptiness in good faith, recognising this as the necessary prelude to the revelation of its true function: to confine and test the young lady and her well-dressed nerve. It was all looking very promising.

Once Pamela was safely padlocked away inside, the anticipatory tension began to rise. The audience scented — as they always do — a challenge. The ring was on the table, shut away in its box, and she was shut away in hers; how was she — and he — going to get out of this one? Mr Brookes paused for a moment, and swiftly wiped his hands — and just when he did that, the more eagle-eyed members of the audience spotted a mistake. As the two stagehands wheeled away the set of treads behind him, one of them stumbled — it looked as if one of the castors might have been loose, or had jammed — and almost tipped the stairs over. The incident was so slight and sudden that Mr Brookes, working downstage, didn't even see it, and the treads were quickly back on course, but the sudden reminder that all of this smoothly rehearsed nonsense could at any moment go badly and entertainingly wrong brought people forward in their seats. Mr Brookes produced his wand, dimmed the lights, and flexed his fingers as he prepared to magic the ring from its spotlight box on the table into the cabinet. The drum rolled, the wand waved, the flame from his fingers flashed — and now that the ring box was empty, people were genuinely wondering what he had up his sleeve. Mr Brookes directed their attention across the stage to the padlock and chain around the cabinet, and prepared himself. The drum rolled again – and he seemed to hesitate.

For the audience, of course, this just seemed like showmanship. As far as they were concerned, everything was part of the act – even the sweat. Their eyes made no distinction between the silk handkerchiefs Mr Brookes used to produce and vanish his props and the linen one which Reggie had forgotten to set in his breast pocket and which Mr Brookes now quickly but expressively patted across his brow; they had no idea that he was genuinely trying to buy some time. This very last moment before he made the final pass with the wand – the build-up to the reveal that the ring was now firmly fixed on the lady's finger, and she was his – was the one bit of the act that still made him feel helpless. If for any reason Pam hadn't completed her change into the wedding dress in time then her hands wouldn't be ready on the quick-release bolts for the chain and padlock. If the chain didn't fall on cue from the cabinet handles, the whole illusion of his control would be blown, and there was nothing he could do about it. He flicked a warning glance to the percussionist in the pit, and trusted to opening-night luck.

The wand thrust; a cymbal crashed in the pit, and the padlock and chain fell – right on cue.

Bloody good girl . . .

Mr Brookes wasn't sure if he muttered it, or if he just thought it. Vanishing the wand, he took one brief moment to tease his lady friends in the stalls with a raised eyebrow, wiped his hands for the last time, and crossed to the apparatus. Now he broadened his attention to take in the whole house, cheap seats included. Did they know what was coming, or didn't they? Any suggestions? Flicking Mr Clifford his standby for the downbeat on 'Here Comes the Bride', he reached up to the handle on the cabinet's front door. He paused, grinned, and proudly threw the door open, presenting its contents to the packed and expectant house.

The woman in the sixth row was disappointed. A lot of empty mirrors, and no music. What sense did that make?

Mr Clements scented disaster, and stiffened. That couldn't possibly be right, could it?

Mr Clifford's baton stayed in the air.

Mr Brookes saw Mr Clifford's upraised hand, but not, at first, his frozen face. Then, as silence came crashing down exactly where there should have been music, he turned away from the house to see what his colleague was staring at.

Mirrors.

Not Pam, in a wedding dress; mirrors. Empty ones.

His skin started to crawl. He turned to face the house, his mind a blank, and felt his smile stretch into a rictus. Then a cold sweat began to break in the pit of his back.

Walking straight down to the footlights, Mr Brookes jerked the last of his seven trick silks out of his pocket, scrunched it into a ball with both hands and unfolded it into a Union Jack. No one responded, but he could think of nothing else. His face began to burn with shame. Still grinning, he waved the flag stiffly over his head, and gestured towards the empty cabinet as if it deserved a hearty round. A few desultory claps started in the stalls, followed by murmurs of confusion. Mr Clifford – who knew a proper first night fuck-up when he saw one – hissed a quick instruction to the band, and they duly cut into a ragged rendition of the last eight bars of the national anthem. That produced a slight thickening in the applause – the audience wasn't at all sure why the woman had just vanished after all that palaver with the ring, but was too well-oiled not to respond automatically to the red, white and blue – and Mr Brookes doubled himself up into a deep, face-saving bow. The stage manager gave the cue to bring in the curtain, Mr Brookes straightened and doubled one more time and then stepped back – still idiotically brandishing his flag, and still grinning. Finally the tabs hit the deck, and everyone started talking about what the hell had just gone wrong.

As soon as he could, Mr Brookes spun round. The now-dark mirrors of the cabinet returned his stare, and he stepped towards it. Around him, of course, a muffled, half-lit chaos was breaking loose – girls were running onstage clutching at unsteady headdresses, the stage manager was shouting, and the upstage drapes were already rising. He reached forward to touch one of the empty zinc panels as if touching might be believing – and only then did he notice that the interior of the cabinet wasn't actually empty at all. Lying in the exact centre of its mirrored floor was a small tangle of red silk rope – but not the single, familiar rope that would have dropped from Pam's wrists as the first step in her change. This was a handful of short, neatly chopped-up pieces of scarlet. How had she done that? He reached in and picked up one of the mutilated fragments.

'Bloody hell, you might have told us, mate.'

It was the older of the two stagehands, trying to close the cabinet door so that it could be dragged offstage. Two others came running up to join him.

'What?'

'The bloody treads. I almost went arse over elbow. Move!'

The door clicked shut, the next piece of music was already starting out front, and the stage manager was desperately

ɔle more
go up a
Christ's
. One of
his grip.
ging the
worked,
ng them

est to be
Brookes
ut being
ɔarticular
sed, and
way was
bout the

ver inter-
Now you
ɔn fire, in
one and

ping the
ion, and
ly, as did

girls tried to get into position but
the still-unshifted cabinet.

t Mr Brookes's chest.
e somebody bloody inside them,
I have rehearsed. Now get out of
t this bastard off before the tabs go

r to get the apparatus moving, and
ɔlace inside Mr Brookes's head as
as the closing of a handcuff around
wrist. He spun – so violently that
-naked girls almost to the floor –
ral more out of his way. The stag-
elf back into position, swearing,
crown. Much to their professional
t about got themselves appropri-
as the curtain rose, plastering their
for the lights to hit their already-

why Pam had done this to him –
to his lovely scarlet rope – but he
e'd have gone to hide herself.

; even before he started kicking
ɹick glance under the partition of
ɲfirmed that it was her, the silly
ɲk that he wouldn't look for her
ck against the nearest washbasin,
both hands, and kicked out with
ngaged, the lock said – well, they'd
e second slam of his feet, the dark

wood began to splinter, and he began to grin. A cou
thrusts, and he'd be in. He heard the crying nois
key – and he could even bloody *smell* her now, fo
sake, smell that stinking cheap scent she always use
his hands slipped on the porcelain, and he adjustec
For no reason that he could think of, he was sir
music from the opening of the new act while he
spitting the words out through his teeth, punctuat
with kicks.

'*To each, his own –*'

Another panel splintered.

'*To ev'ry boy, a girl –*'

That was the lock going – good – and –

'Mr Brookes!'

The voice was thin and querulous, but doing its
brave; it went with the white hair and the cravat. M
had never liked Mr English at the best of times,
interrupted by an old quean in the midst of this
labour of love was the last fucking straw. He pa
snarled – he could see that the figure in the doo
shaking already, and he was in no mood to beat
bush.

'What?'

'I really don't think you –'

'Don't you? Well you take my advice dear, and ne
rupt a real man when he's on the job – all right?
just run along and leave me be, unless the theatre's
which case I suggest you get on the fucking telep
tell somebody about it.'

The knuckles on the elderly hand that was gri
door frame for support whitened with determina
Mr English held his ground. His chin rose percepti
his pitch.

'Very well, but I thought you might like to know that Mr Clements is in the wings and would like to see you at once,' he said.

Mr Brookes drew back his feet for another kick, laughing.

'And that your guest from London is with him. A booking agent of some kind, I think he said. I got the distinct impression that he'd rather like a word too.'

The feet stopped. Mr English pressed his advantage, throwing caution to the winds.

'At *once*, Mr Clements said. Shall I tell the gentlemen you're coming?'

You might have expected Mr Brookes to find it difficult to compose himself, seeing that his prey was almost within reach, but in fact, true professional that he was, it only took him a minute. Telling Mr English to inform Mr Clements and his London guest that he would be up with them shortly, and that he was sure he'd be able to explain everything to their satisfaction, he took a deep breath, shuddered, and turned round to check his appearance in the mirror over the washbasin against which he had been bracing himself. He was still panting from his exertions, and a little white round the gills – *white with fury* is, I believe, the proper technical term for a man in Mr Brookes's condition, no matter how much make-up he is wearing. Patting his face briefly with his handkerchief, he restored his disarranged hair by repeating the first produce from the act; flicking the comb neatly from his cuff, he smoothed the fallen locks back into place with two smart, decisive sweeps. A brief adjustment of his bow tie, a licked finger across each eyebrow, and he was ready to do business. He shot his cuffs, breathed out into a cupped hand to check his breath, and flicked a speck of something off his right shoulder. *First impressions count.* A quick cough to clear his throat, a quick final wipe of his hands, and Mr Brookes left the Ladies without even looking back over his shoulder. All the time he was checking his appearance in the mirror, he had been able to hear Pam on the other side of the half-splintered cubicle door, trying not to cry, holding her breath, the silly, swollen-ankled, silk-stockinged, scarlet-shod bitch. He'd deal with her later.

The rest of the show went down a storm. The Devere Girls in their Coronation-night regalia and spangles were a triumph – the final blackout as all was revealed brought the house down – and after the headliner had turned the air blue for twenty minutes with some more than usually near-the-knuckle material the National Anthem was sung so raucously that the sound shook flakes of gilt down from the ceiling. The first-house audience spilled out into the crowds on North Road laughing and happy.

The rest of their evening was no disappointment, either. The fireworks were better than expected, the piers were mobbed, the community singing was lusty and the five hundred sailors from HMS *Eagle* wreaked various kinds of handsomely uniformed havoc as they made their way through the crowds – one party involving some of their admirers, out on the western edge of Hove, was still going strong when the police were called to interrupt the music three days later. Some people, however, did not have such a good night. Mr J. Clements Sole Prop, waiting in the wings, was furious. As soon as he saw him, he told Mr 'Teddy' Brookes Esq. – straight to his flaming face, and right out in front of the booking agent from London, would you mind – that as far as he could see it was just the same bloody act as before – his lady wife had been most disappointed – and if Brookes thought any self-respecting management in the country was going to book a piece of second-hand tat like that, never mind the Grand keeping it on as the number-three spot in a bill which looked like topping the box-office records for the entire year, well then he'd got another bloody think coming, because not on Mr Clements's watch it bloody wasn't, contract or no contract. After one or two useless attempts to interrupt, Mr Brookes heard him out in silence, wiping and rewiping his hands, carrying on doing it even after the two men had turned and gone and left him to stand there alone in his dress shirt and tails, clutching his handkerchief and listening to the laughter for the headliner as it rose and fell; rose, and fell, like the waves of a slowly and inexorably retreating tide.

And that was that. Apart from the last Brighton appearance of the legendary Phyllis Dixey, who headlined there six weeks later, the Coronation Special of June 1953 was probably the last really popular show that the Grand ever put on. It was downhill all the way, after Mr Brookes.

So, here's how it was done:

14

The mechanics were simple. It was Reggie who was carried off the stage hidden in the steps; Reggie's feet that Mr Brookes saw wedged into Pam's shoes under the toilet cubicle door with one ankle swollen from that near-disaster on the stairs; Reggie he could smell, and Reggie whose stifled attacks of hysterical laughter he mistook for crying coming through the woodwork. Meanwhile, upstairs, it was Pam who was still curled under the trapdoor of the apparatus when it was wheeled offstage to create space for the Devere Girls; Pam who was then free to uncurl herself when it reached the wings, Pam who grabbed a suitcase and her handbag from their prearranged hiding places and then ran barefoot to alert Mr English to the emergency downstairs. Mr English met the outraged Mr Clements as he and the booking agent were coming backstage through the pass door to see what the hell had happened – and the rest of that chain of events you know.

Substitution; it's one of the oldest and most basic tricks in the book. All it took for Mr Brookes to believe what he was seeing was for Reggie to jam on Pam's shoes – though I must say that the 12-denier stockings (already on under Reggie's trousers from the top of the act) and the spray of perfume from a bottle already hidden in the cubicle were nice additional touches, and certainly made the deception more sure-fire.

What was really clever about the routine was the way Pam and Reg had misdirected Mr Brookes away from what they were up to all through that last week of rehearsals. They controlled his attention, making him congratulate himself on how little he had to worry about from his colleagues at precisely the point when he should have been worrying most about what they were up to. All week, Reggie had done his crafty best to be always on Mr Brookes's side, ever-ready to keep things running smoothly. Most cleverly of all, by crying when her employer expected her to – and then suddenly smiling bravely, just when he didn't – Pam had persuaded Teddy that she was exactly the kind of scared, compliant fool he thought all of the women who slept with him were; the kind of fool, for instance, who'd let him arrange an illegal and dangerous abortion for her before her body gave her the cast-iron proof that she actually needed one. The kind of fool who would then be happy to go back to work less than thirty-six hours after her supposed procedure – and then suddenly change her mind and need a day in bed. Under that cover, she and Reggie had stolen almost the whole of the last weekend to work on their moves, and even some of the Tuesday, and Mr Brookes never once suspected the real reason why they were spending so much time together.

The riskiest – and cleverest – part of the whole deception was the force; the strategy whereby they made Mr Brookes's rattled mind assume it was Pam who had been wheeled offstage in the treads, and not Reggie. They both knew that the minute the curtain came down the obvious thing for Mr Brookes to do would be to lift the trapdoor in the cabinet to see who was under it, but to make sure he didn't, they had carefully coached him to see her – not Reggie – as the bolter. All of those tearful runs down to the Ladies of hers had in fact been carefully staged. On the night, the ruse worked; faced with the sight of those empty mirrors, Mr Brookes's mind dutifully jumped to exactly the wrong conclusion, forgetting completely that the routine allowed no time for Pam to cram herself into the stairs before they were removed. The sight of the pieces of cut rope on the floor of the cabinet momentarily baffled him, creating a space in which the familiar image of her tottering downstairs in tears and high heels could drop unbidden into place behind his misled eyes. His rage did the rest – and that they knew they could rely on.

Of course, they hadn't been able to think through or plan everything. After she'd made it out into the alley, breathless and shoeless, clutching at her bag and case and with the scarlet-and-black dress from the act still hanging half off her, Pamela was on her own.

The Queen's Road was mayhem, full of grabbing hands and leering faces; now that she'd made it into the station, however, the noise retreated, and she found herself marooned in quiet. The announcement board was blank – everything was haywire, tonight – and she looked desperately around for somebody she could ask about the next train to London. One coming in had just disgorged its passengers, and the stragglers brushed past her as she searched, laughing and staring at her scarlet dress and bare feet, but then leaving her once more alone. A firework boomed somewhere over the great glass roof, more cheers went up outside – and then a whistle blew somewhere behind her, making her spin and panic, and decide to run. She had no idea if this was the right train, but she knew she couldn't afford to wait. She ducked through a gate, and swore her way across the platforms – there was broken glass from a beer bottle splintered between her and the train – all the time cursing her too-heavy case for holding her back. Somebody swinging a flag shouted the magic word *London*, and the whistle went again. She wrenched a door open just as the train started to move, and threw her case and herself aboard. The door swung shut like a gunshot, and she instinctively closed her eyes and pressed herself back into a corner, holding her breath, willing the next sound not to be that of a man shouting and running and pulling the door open again, willing the train to jolt and gather speed and take her away.

It did.

As the train began to sway and steady itself for the journey, she let herself begin to breathe, but didn't open her eyes. There was something crumpled between her fingers – some-one on the Queen's Road had pressed a little paper Union Jack on a stick into her hand, and she must have taken it just to get away. She couldn't properly remember. Uncurling her hand, she let the pennant drop to the floor. Something torn was catching at the backs of her calves and tickling her, and when she finally did open her eyes she discovered that one of the quick-change fasteners on her dress had given way; the wrecked nylon underskirts and lace of the wedding gown were foaming out around her thighs and ankles, making her half scarlet woman, half runaway bride. The thought made her want to laugh, but she couldn't quite manage it – not yet. She pushed herself up on the seat. A reflection in a dark window showed her the ruin of her carefully arranged face and hair, and as the lights of the northern edge of Brighton slid away behind that picture she slumped back against the seat again and watched the dark pane of glass, waiting for the full blackness that would tell her that the town was now safely falling away behind her, and that she could begin the work of forgetting it. She tried to smile, but failed. Then she sat up, found her bag, rummaged, lit herself a cigarette, took three deep drags, grabbed her bag again and tipped its contents into her lap.

As you've probably guessed by now, that last-minute dash upstairs by Reggie to get Mr Brookes's missing handkerchief just before the curtain went up was all part of the deception. The handkerchief was in his pocket all the time, next to the key to Mr Brookes's dressing room. Once inside the dressing room, it had taken him only seconds to scoop up everything he needed from the dressing table – the signet ring, the watch, the cigarette case, the lighter and the well-stuffed wallet – and head back downstairs. The near-desperate effort involved in hauling himself up and then throwing himself back down those four flights of concrete stairs at the necessary speed meant that his breathlessness as he limped back into the wings after stuffing his hoard into Pam's hidden handbag was genuine; like the adrenalin in his eyes, and the limp from where he'd nearly come a cropper on the last turn of the stairs, it only served to make the fraud look more convincing.

It's all in the presentation, you see; Mr Brookes had taught him that, if nothing else.

Pam stared at the jumbled mess, and ran her fingers through it. Pearls, bracelet, powder; comb, scent bottle, hairspray. Her Dutch cap in its case, her fags, matches, two dirty lipsticks and three stained handkerchiefs knotted together. Everything a girl needed – and everything Reggie had lifted from Mr Brookes for her too, including his signet ring and watch. Her purse.

His wallet.

She knew exactly how much was in the purse: the money for the abortion, the extra two pounds for the late appointment, the ten-bob note he'd given her for the taxi, and her own savings of eighteen pounds in notes and nine shillings and sixpence in change. Brookes's wallet looked heavy, but she couldn't bring herself to open it just yet. She looked down at it sitting in her lap amidst the rest of her loot, and wondered how much time the heap would buy her. It was just going to have to be enough, wasn't it? She didn't have the strength to actually count or calculate anything just now – she'd do that later, she told herself, when she was feeling a bit calmer. However, looking at the wallet, and seeing its owner's face in her mind – hearing his voice, standing in the toilet doorway – she knew that there was one thing she needed to get done straight away.

Opening her purse, Pam pulled out a small piece of tightly folded blue paper. She stared at this, too. There had been several times in the past week when she'd got it out of her purse and looked at it for other reasons – something, by the way, that she'd never told Reggie – but now she knew exactly how she felt. The time for choosing had already passed. Scooping up everything that was heaped in her lap and carefully placing it on the seat opposite, she pulled down the window, tore the paper into pieces and released them – and the now-fragmented address that had been scrawled across them – into the darkness. Then she sat down again, leaving the window open for some air, and looked again at Mr Brookes's pigskin wallet, now lying nestled against her bracelet. She pulled it out of the pile, making the charms shift and ring, took a nice deep breath and made herself snap it open.

The leather felt like skin, she thought, but old. Unfeeling. There were four more carefully folded fivers inside, and several singles, and they came out and were added to the hoard on the seat beside her – moving, slightly, in the air coming in through the window. As well as the money she could see the protruding edges of some cards and bills, some more bits of blue paper that looked like they would have addresses and telephone numbers on them if she were to open them up and look, and even the chipped edge of one worn, folded photograph. Her fingers hesitated, and then decided; she walked over to the window and flipped the wallet through it before she had time to reconsider, staring after it at the rectangle of rushing darkness that had taken it away. It was gone, and so was he.

As she was staring, the train entered a tunnel, slamming air and noise back into her face. Pam stumbled, but didn't fall. Grabbing the edge of the window frame, she stood there and let the night air batter her. She knew it must be filthy, but it felt as though it was washing her clean.

The Balcombe tunnel under the Downs is the longest one on the Brighton to London line, and it takes a full minute to go through; after that, you're free and into the night for a good long stretch. As the train settled down for its journey, Pam closed the window, contemplated the state of her frock, collected the notes that had been blown onto the compartment floor by that blast of air and decided that she'd better get herself looking halfway decent in case a ticket inspector turned up. She had shoes and clean clothes in her suitcase, and she could change in the toilet. It would be cramped, getting this torn and tangled dress off in there – but she'd had the training for that.

Opening her case to look for her tweed suit, the first thing she saw was the maroon satin ball gown. She pulled it out and shook it. Why not? Let's face it, only a few months from now, it was going to be goodbye to anything with a fitted waist, that was for sure.

She never did get round to digging out a pair of shoes, but doing herself up in the ball gown did inspire Pam to open her handbag again, fish out her compact and lipstick and comb and repair the night's damage to her face and her brand-new hairstyle. She probably didn't know it, but I would say that she had never looked lovelier; wild, but perfect. That was why, less than an hour later, when the train finally delivered her into the teeming chaos of London on Coronation night, two tired porters nudged each other and winked in disbelief as they saw Princess Margaret herself – radiant, and barefoot – stepping out across the concourse of Victoria Station, carrying a handbag and suitcase, and laughing.

15

If I'm honest, I think that little pile of cut rope which Reggie suggested they leave on the floor of the cabinet as the finesse of their routine was about much more than just earning a few crucial seconds of bafflement from Mr Brookes. If he hadn't been able to displace his feelings into razoring one of those hated coils of imprisoning silk into twelve separate six-inch lengths then I really think that at some point Reggie might have actually done what he was starting to dream about doing during that last strange week of play-acting, which was to draw the whispering blade of his penknife right across the features of Mr Brookes's handsome face. As it was, when Mr Brookes was kicking at the cubicle door, Reggie already had the knife open and ready – ready to nip into action if the wood gave way. With such a small blade, what else could he have gone for but the face? Thank God things never went that far; as you know, that blade was sharp.

Getting his trousers back on, finding his own shoes and then finally getting out of the building without being seen wasn't that easy, but the chaos of that particular night helped – and Reggie was a dodger, remember. When he did get outside, he found he was shaking with relief. He needed a drink, and instinct led him to the one place he never thought he'd be driven to choose as a refuge – partly, I suppose, because he thought no one would think to look for him there. The Spotted Dog was, on Coronation night, riotous – *crowded with incident*, as we used to say, and noisy with outrageous laughter. As Pam stepped down from the train to join the revellers around Victoria, that was where Reggie was celebrating – or at least, holding on to the bar and downing several straight Scotches in swift succession. When he was sure he'd stopped shaking, he left them all to it, and headed down Middle Street to the seafront. This was partly I think because he needed to get some of his old friend, the air, but partly I think because he wanted – perhaps for the first time in his life – to join the crowds.

I'm not going to take you there to join him, I'm afraid, because it's time he was left alone – but let me just say that I have looked up the weather for that extraordinary night in the big bound set of volumes of the *Argus* that they still keep upstairs in the library, and although I can report that it was cold, and that there was a little more drizzle around eleven o'clock, there was no sea fret shrouding the piers or promenade that evening. Which means that although you will have to imagine Reggie making his way through those damp but noisy streets for yourself, at least you are free to imagine him doing so unconcealed.

There he goes, threading himself through the cheering crowds, exhilarated by those Scotches and what he's done, knowing and surely not caring that he's lost his job –¸and not caring either whether Mrs Steed will have forgotten to bolt her door tonight, or whether he'll just have to stay out among the crowds until tomorrow. You can imagine him joining in the communal midnight singing of the National Anthem down on the jam-packed prom if you like, becoming just one of a thousand lifted voices – or perhaps you'd prefer to imagine him leaning on a railing, his face catching the blaze as he watches the fireworks from HMS *Eagle* paint the water with all the colours of his name. Perhaps you should imagine him doing it at the very same spot on the promenade where he once leaned on the rail to eat that bag of chips, staring at the sea while he did it and wondering just where the hell he was and who he was in this, the twenty-third year of his life. Imagine him trying to think all of that through all over again, now that everything is different. Imagine him thinking about his dead mother, and about Pam, and about the differences and samenesses between the two of them. Imagine him thinking what tomorrow will be like. Imagine him starting in surprise, as he once again feels the inexplicable warmth of a hand coming to rest on his shoulder.

Imagine that he turns round.

Reggie recognised him at once, even though he wasn't wearing his macintosh, and they'd only ever kissed in the dark.

16

Well, there you are; misdirection, force, vanish, reveal and finesse. All you need to put together a whole routine. Or, as Mr Brookes would have said: *Hook, Skin, Finish.*

Of all the pictures that I could send you away with, I'd like to end by showing you a photograph of *my* mother. It's the kind of shot every bride and groom had taken on their big day back then; a formal six by nine black-and-white double portrait, nicely printed on matt paper and mounted on a heavy cream card. The two of them are standing arm in arm on the steps of the church, and although they're both doing their best to remain solemn for the benefit of the photographer, both of their faces are openly registering the happy shock of what they've just done to their lives. Both of them are smiling. My father, on the right, is a good six inches taller than his wife – as convention dictated a husband should be, at that time – and is, on this particular morning, looking only a bit less handsome than our Mr Brookes. His hair is brilliantined, and he's sporting a six-buttoned wool-mixture doubled-breasted dinner jacket with the double peak of a starched handkerchief peeking from his breast pocket. He's even carrying a pair of gloves with one pearl button at the wrist. My mother is standing with her ring-displaying hand slipped through the crook of his proudly offered arm – they are, in other words, standing in exactly the same pose as the one Pam and Mr Brookes would have struck if they had ever got as far as the magnesium flash that was supposed to bring their act to its triumphant close. The cut of my mother's machine lace dress very closely matches that of Pam's in the act, and she is carrying an almost-identical spray of maidenhair fern and white carnations – though her flowers are real, not silk, and threaded through with three stems of those luxurious pale freesias that she was to love all her life. Her hair isn't as exact a copy of Princess Margaret's as Pamela's was, but the influence is clear. I can even be reasonably sure that my mother is wearing the same *eau de parfum* as Pam did – Elizabeth Arden's Blue Grass was what she always wore on a special occasion.

The thing I always notice the most when I study this picture is how very young they both look – how young she looks especially – and how brave. She has slight bags under her eyes, from not having slept much the night before I suppose, but she is looking the camera right in the eye. She is truly facing the future.

That future, of course, is the same one into which Pamela was walking barefoot across the concourse of Victoria Station – the one into which her illegitimate son will be born in the harsh late January of 1954. It is the future in which my mother gets to share her life with the man she chose, and in which Princess Margaret – after all that waiting, and speculation, and looking up and down – doesn't. It is the future which starts for Reggie as soon as he wakes up the next morning.

The first thing he notices is that the mirror on the washstand has been somehow knocked off its usual axis. Instead of reflecting his face, like it usually does, it is showing him four bare feet sticking out from under a blanket. They look odd, framed by all those surging roses. There are clothes all over the floor, and one of Reggie's boots is stranded up on the chair. He has a vague memory of himself and his companion splitting a pair of pyjamas before they eventually went to sleep last night, and of the unsuccessfully stifled laughter that accompanied that process. He remembers undoing his companion's shirt buttons – successfully, this time – and discovering how unexpectedly white his skin was once the shirt came off completely. He remembers discovering the freckles high up on the man's right-hand shoulder blade, and thinking how they weren't exactly laid out right, but still nonetheless reminded him of those stars up on the ceiling of the Grand.

He remembers wondering, in the middle of all the noise they were making, if his mother was watching him.

The window is open; the curtain stirs in a breeze. Doing it very carefully so as not to wake his companion, Reg prises himself out from under an overdraped arm and swings both naked feet to the floor. He limps over to the window, because it's cold, and he's stiff – Reggie hadn't ever realised quite how uncomfortable it could be sharing a bed, even when the two of you were a good fit, and Mrs Steed's blanket was clearly meant for one. Nonetheless, before he closes the window, he leans out to get some air. After all the noise of last night, it's quiet. Gull-less. Reggie got the top half of the pyjamas, which means that the edge of the wooden windowsill digs into his naked pubis as he leans, but he doesn't mind, because he wants to see the sea. The sky above it is cloudy but clearing, and the sea itself looks grey and quiet, with no waves to speak of, and there is no sound coming from the shingle. In fact, the only sound that Reggie can hear, now that he really listens, is some distant idiot still singing the National Anthem. He thinks briefly about his mother again, and hopes that whoever she was, she had everything that he had on the bed last night, and more than just once. Taking one last lungful of salt air, he levers himself back in through the window and quietly pulls the sash down closed. He restores the mirror on the washstand to its correct angle, and takes a quick look at himself, barelegged as he is. Not too bad, he reckons, considering how little he actually slept last night. Then he turns back into the room, and takes a good look at the sleeping head on his pillow.

He has no idea if this is the man with whom he is going to spend the rest of his life, but he is looking forward to finding out.

He reaches out, and gently tickles the crown of the sleeping head, stroking its hair back into place.

Its owner groans – there was quite a bit of drink involved on the way back home last night, as well as everything else – and stirs. As the young man in question struggles to unglue his eyes, Reggie's mouth twists into a special good-morning version of his thin-lipped, rat-toothed grin, and then, as the young man succeeds in getting his eyes open, and props himself up on one elbow to look at Reggie, the grin opens out into a proper, sunny, full-on smile. The young man smiles back, and then, still smiling, and timing the line just perfectly as the sun comes in through the curtain and the young man in question groans in pain and drops his head back onto the waiting pillow, Reggie asks what it feels like he's been waiting years to ask, which is *What d'you want for your breakfast then, mister?*

The future, eh?

Here's how it's done;

Acknowledgements

This novel is respectfully dedicated to my great-grandmother, my great-aunt and my grandmother, all of whom worked in the Pit Bar of the Wimbledon Theatre before the war, and to my partner's father, who was the stage-door keeper at the Golders Green Hippodrome from 1946 to 1949.

Its writing was skillfully supported by Clare Conville and Michael Fishwick. To them, my thanks.

Neil Bartlett
Brighton and London, 2014

A Note on the Author

Neil Bartlett's first novel, *Ready to Catch Him Should He Fall*, was voted Capital Gay Book of the Year; his second, *Mr Clive and Mr Page*, was nominated for the Whitbread Prize; his third and most recent, *Skin Lane*, was shortlisted for the Costa Novel Award in 2007. In 2000 he was awarded an OBE for his work as a theatre director and playwright. He lives in Brighton and London with his partner of twenty-five years, James Gardiner. You can find out more about Neil and his work at www.neil-bartlett.com.

A Note on the Type

The text of this book is set in Bembo. This type was first used in 1495 by the Venetian printer Aldus Manutius for Cardinal Bembo's *De Aetna*, and was cut for Manutius by Francesco Griffo. It was one of the types used by Claude Garamond (1480–1561) as a model for his Romain de L'Université, and so it was the forerunner of what became standard European type for the following two centuries. Its modern form follows the original types and was designed for Monotype in 1929.